# Shipwrecked Family

# Publications of the North American Jules Verne Society

**The Palik Series** (edited by Brian Taves)

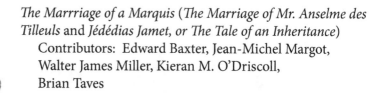

*The Marrriage of a Marquis* (*The Marriage of Mr. Anselme des Tilleuls* and *Jédédias Jamet, or The Tale of an Inheritance*)
Contributors: Edward Baxter, Jean-Michel Margot, Walter James Miller, Kieran M. O'Driscoll, Brian Taves

*Shipwrecked Family: Marooned with Uncle Robinson*
Translated by Sidney Kravitz

*The Count of Chanteleine: A Tale of the French Revolution*
Translated by Edward Baxter; Notes by Garmt de Vries-Uiterweed, Volker Dehs

*Stories by Jules and Michel Verne* (*Fact-Finding Mission, Pierre-Jean*, and *The Fate of Jean Morénas*)
Translated, with notes, by Kieran M. O'Driscoll

Historical Novels: *San Carlos* and *The Siege of Rome*
Translated by Edward Baxter

(Other volumes in preparation)

**The North American Jules Verne Society also copublished (with Prometheus)**

*Journey Through the Impossible*
Translated by Edward Baxter; Notes by Jean-Michel Margot

**Editorial Committee of the
North American Jules Verne Society:**

Henry G. Franke III
Jean-Michel Margot

Dr. Terry Harpold
Dr. Brian Taves

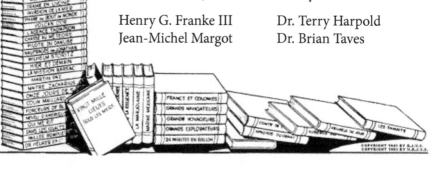

# Shipwrecked Family

## Marooned with Uncle Robinson

## by Jules Verne

Translated by Sidney Kravitz

Edited and with an introduction by Brian Taves
for the
North American Jules Verne Society

## The Palik Series

BearManor Fiction
2011

Shipwrecked Family: Marooned With Uncle Robinson
by Jules Verne

Translation © 2005 Sidney Kravitz and
published by permission of the Kravitz estate

Introduction © 2011 by Brian Taves

For information, address:

BearManor Fiction
P. O. Box 71426
Albany, GA  31708

bearmanormedia.com

North American Jules Verne Society: najvs.org

Cover design by

Typesetting and layout by John Teehan

Published in the USA by BearManor Media

ISBN—1-59393-362-2
978-1-59393-362-3

# Table of Contents

# Introduction

# Jules Verne and the Robinsonade— Adventures In Survival

## by Brian Taves

For many years, Jules Verne was regarded as an author of gee-whiz science fiction, who rhapsodized over the marvels of 19th century technology. An astounding prophet, yes, but a bit hazy in his scientific descriptions and shallow in his characterization. Certainly an author of classics for children, but hardly a writer for adults.

The literary qualities that French critics appreciated in Verne only began to be recognized in the English speaking world since the 1950s. New translations of many of his classic novels revealed that the shortcomings attributed to him were the result of inferior 19th century translators, not the original source. Verne was edited, by up to 25%, diluting not only scientific exactitude, but also the political content on issues from imperialism to evolution. From the 1870s through the 1890s, English-language renderings of Verne were often prepared intially for serialization in the British weekly *The Boy's Own Paper*, and subsequent reprints used what had been molded to fit the bias of this journal and others of similar ilk. For instance, in translating the 1874 novel, *L'Île mystérieuse*, as *The Mysterious Island*, W.H.G. Kingston reversed the motivation Verne gave Captain Nemo, as he explains his early life as the Indian rebel, Prince Dakkar. Verne has Dakkar learn from his western rulers in order to overthrow them and helping lead the Sepoy mutiny of 1857. In Kingston's changed version, Dakkar went to the West in order to better his so-called "primitive" people. Not until 2002 did an accurate, new translation *The Mysterious Island* appear.

Today an ongoing Verne renaissance is at its height, which has also brought publication of many of his books that never appeared in English, and others only recently discovered. Accompanying this activity is the blossoming of Verne's literary reputation, so that he has become an author esteemed by scholars and studied in academia. Verne is now regarded, like Edgar Allan Poe, as an author for all ages, whose thrills can be enjoyed by children, but whose complexities require adult appreciation.

The literary model that most influenced Verne was the Robinsonade, as pioneered in modern literature by Daniel Defoe's *Robinson Crusoe* (1719) and Johann Wyss's *Der Schweizerische Robinson* (*The Swiss Robinson*, usually known as *The Swiss Family Robinson*, 1812). The themes of shipwreck, survival under adverse circumstances in strange lands, and the recreation of civilized forms made an imperishable impression on his mind. The Robinson archetypes established by Defoe, and especially in the follow-up of Wyss, were Verne's favorite childhood reading, along with James Fenimore Cooper's *The Crater* (1847) and such now-forgotten imitations as *The American Family Robinson, The Twelve-Year-Old Robinson, The Robinson of the Ice-Fields,* and *The Robinson of the Desert.* As Verne explained, "The Robinsons were *the* books of my childhood and I retained an undying recollection of them. The frequent readings which I made of them could only strengthen this in my mind, even though I could never recapture the impressions of my youth in my later modern readings. There is no doubt that my taste for this kind of adventure instinctively led me toward the path which I would follow one day."[1] (Among the rare introductions to his books are two from his Robinsonades, included in complete English-language translations in the appendix to this volume.)

Verne was also convinced that *The Swiss Family Robinson* was ultimately the superior novel. "I am well aware that the work of Daniel Defoe has a weightier philosophy. It concerns a man in command of himself, a man alone, a man who finds one day a naked footprint in the sand. But Wyss's book, rich in facts and incidents, is more interesting for young minds. It has the family, the father, mother, the children

---

1.  Jules Verne, "Preface of the Author: Why I Wrote *Second Homeland*," translation by Sidney Kravitz from its appearance in Verne, *Seconde Patrie,* (Paris: Hetzel, 1900), n.p.

and their different aptitudes. How many years I passed on their island! With what ardour I involved myself with their discoveries. How much I envied their fate!"[2] The persistence of its impact was demonstrated when *The Swiss Family Robinson* became one of the two books to which Verne wrote sequels (the other was *Le Sphinx des glaces* [*The Sphinx of Ice*, 1897], a follow-up to Edgar Allan Poe's *The Narrative of Arthur Gordon Pym of Nantucket*; Poe was the other major influence on Verne). *Seconde patrie* (*Second Homeland*, 1900) continued the exploits of Wyss's heroes, and in his preface, Verne expressed his motivation.

> Really, wouldn't it be interesting to continue the recital of Rudolph Wyss, to again find this family in a new set of circumstances, with these four lads so well established, Fritz, enterprising and courageous, Ernest, a bit egotistical but studious, Jack, the mischievous and little Francois, to watch the changes in their character as they come of age after twelve years on this island?… Wouldn't the introduction of Jenny Montrose into this little world change their lives? Shouldn't there be a complete exploration of this rich island since only the northern part is known to them? Doesn't the departure of Fritz, François, and Jenny Montrose for Europe call for a story of their adventures until their return to New Switzerland?
>
> And so I could not resist the desire to continue Wyss's work, to give it a definitive conclusion, which, besides, would be done sooner or later.
>
> So then, driven on by my imagination, I plunge into my project, to live side by side with my heroes and it produces a phenomenon: it is that I have come to believe that New Switzerland really exists, that it is really an island in the northeast part of the Indian Ocean, that I have seen it on the map, that the Zermatt and Wolston families are not imaginary, that they live in this very

2.  "Souvenirs d'enfance et de jeunesse". *L'Herne* (Paris), no. 25 (1974), translation in Peter Costello, *Jules Verne: Inventor of Science Fiction* (New York: Scribners, 1978), 29.

prosperous colony…And I have but one regret, that my advancing years prevent me from joining them there![3]

Augmenting Verne's childhood reading was the experience of growing up in a seaport.

I lived in the maritime bustle of a big commercial city which is the starting-point and goal of many long voyages.

I still see the river Loire, whose numerous arms are connected by a league of bridges, its quays encumbered by freight…Ships two or three rows deep line the wharves. Others sail up or down the stream…In fancy I climbed their shrouds, tried their maintops, and clung to their sky-rakers.

I did venture to scale the netting of a three-master, while its watchman caroused in a neighboring wine shop.

I was soon on deck. My hand caught hold of a halyard that slid in its block. What joy was mine! The hatches were open, and I leaned over their sides. The strong odors that came from the hold went to my head; odors in which the pungent smell of tar mixes with the perfume of spices.

I rose, went back towards the poop and entered. The interior was filled with those marine scents which give to it an atmosphere like that of the ocean.

Yonder appear the cabins with their creaking partitions, where I should have wished to live for months, and those bunks, so hard and narrow, wherein I should have liked to sleep whole nights. Then there was the room occupied by the captain, a much more important personage in my opinion than any King's minister or lieutenant general of the kingdom.

I came out, mounted the poop, and there actually made so bold as to turn the wheel a quarter round! I fancied the vessel was about to leave its moorings; that

---

3.  Jules Verne, "Preface of the Author: Why I Wrote *Second Homeland*," translation by Sidney Kravitz.

its hawsers had been cast off, that its masts were crowded with sail, and that I, an eight-year-old helmsman, was about to steer it out to sea![4]

The center of Nantes, the Ile Feydeau, was completely surrounded by the river Loire, and Verne's childhood imagination was haunted by a fearsome and exciting old legend that it might be washed out to sea at flood time.[5] Such an event did not seem so unlikely to a lad; every spring the cellars were drenched. These memories led to the motif of floating islands that would appear in four Verne novels. At school, Jules listened eagerly to the tale of one of his teachers, Madame Sambain, whose sailor husband had shipped out shortly after their marriage, never to be heard from again; she imagined him stranded on some desert island waiting to be rescued—a situation Verne would recreate and resolve when decades later he wrote *Mistress Branican* (1891).

Verne recalled how the closest he came to becoming a real Robinson while sailing the Loire.

> One day I happened to be alone in a sorry yawl, which had no keel. I was some two leagues beyond Chantenay, when one of the planks was stove in, and the water came into the boat. There was no stopping the hole. The yawl went down head-foremost, and I had just time to save myself by swimming to an islet all covered with a thick growth of reeds, the tufted tops of which were swayed by the wind.
>
> I was enacting, on my little island, not the part of Wyss's hero, but that of Defoe's. I was already meditating the construction of a log-hut, the manufacture of a fishing-line with a reed, and of fish-hooks with thorns, and of obtaining fire as the savages do, by rubbing one dry stick against another.
>
> Signals? I should decline to make any, for they would be answered too soon, and I should be saved quicker than I wished to be.

4.  Jules Verne, "The Story of My Boyhood," *The Youth's Companion*, 64 (April 9, 1891), 211.

5.  Kenneth Allott, *Jules Verne* (London: Crescent, 1940), 6.

The first thing was to appease my hunger. But how? My provisions had gone down with the wreck. Go hunting birds? I had neither dog nor gun. Well, what about shell-fish? There were none.

Now, at last, I was made acquainted with all the agony of being shipwrecked on a desert island, and with horrors of privation such as the Selkirks and other personages mentioned in the *Noted Shipwrecks* had experienced—men who were not imaginary Robinsons! My stomach cried with hunger.

The thing lasted only a few hours, for, as soon as it was low tide, I had merely to wade ankle-deep through the water to reach what I called the mainland, namely, the right bank of the Loire.

I quietly came back home, where I had to put up with the family dinner instead of the Crusoe repast I had dreamed of—raw shell-fish, a slice of peccary, and bread made from the flour of manioc![6]

Although Verne as the eldest son was groomed to inherit the family law practice, he envied his younger brother's permission to undertake a maritime career. As I.O. Evans explained, "It was not only the sea, but also the freedom of the undiscovered island, which made him return to it, in his imagination, time and again."[7] The depth of his desire for adventure would become evident in his literature, as well as in his yachting around Europe and the Mediterranean.

Verne's Robinsonades encompasses nine principal works written over the entirety of his life. They include not only science fiction, but adventure stories, the genre that accounted for some half of his output, facilitating his production of one or two novels annually. His Robinsonades are *Un Hivernage dans les glaces* (*A Winter Amid the Ice,* 1855), *Le Pays des fourrures* (*The Fur Country,* 1873), *The Mysterious Island, Hector Servadac* (1877), *L'École des Robinsons* (*The School for Robinsons,* 1882), *Deux ans de vacances* (*Two Year Holiday,* 1888),

6.   Jules Verne, "The Story of My Boyhood," *The Youth's Companion,* 64 (April 9, 1891), 211.

7.   I.O. Evans, "Introduction," in *The Secret of the Island* (Westport, CT: Associated Booksellers, 1959), 10.

Robinsonade Ad in an early 20th century French Hetzel edition.

From *Le Chancellor* (*The Chancellor*, 1875).

*Second Homeland, L'Eternel Adam* (*The Eternal Adam*, 1910), and *En Magellanie* (*Magellania*, 1987), published in a different version in 1909 as *Les Naufragés du Jonathan* (*The Survivors of the Jonathan*). The Robinsonade also resonates elsewhere in Verne's canon. Castaways, islands, shipwrecks, and survival are central in *Le Chancellor* (1875, *The Chancellor*), *Un Capitaine de quinze ans* (*A Fifteen-Year-Old Captain*, 1878), *La Jangada* (*The Jangada*, 1881), *L'Île à hélice* (*Propeller Island*, 1895), *Bourses de voyages* (*Travel Scholarships*, 1903), and *Le Phare du bout du monde* (*The Lighthouse at the End of the World*, 1905). *Les Enfants du capitaine Grant* (*The Children of Captain Grant*, 1867), *Mistress Branican*, and *The Sphinx of Ice* are Robinsonades told from the point of view of the rescuers.

This group of Verne stories was even recognized during his lifetime with advertisements such as the one included here, from an edition of *Deux ans de vacances* published early in the 20th century, and which also included *A Fifteen-Year-Old Captain* along with the purer Robinsonades. In *A Fifteen-Year-Old Captain*, when ship's officers are first lost and then its course diverted by a renegade crew, the coast where the ship inadvertently makes landfall turns out not to be an island, but Africa, with perils from wildlife to slavers.

*A Winter Amid the Ice* and *The Fur Country* were stories of the arctic. This was one of Verne's favorite locales: the polar regions would also form the basis for *Adventures of Captain Hatteras* and *Sphinx of the Ice*, along with providing incidents in many other tales. Verne's dedication to the Robinsonade was demonstrated by turning to its formula for one of his earliest novelettes. *A Winter Amid the Ice* recounts the trials of a search party who set out to find a missing sailor but in turn are themselves stranded in the far North.

*The Fur Country* is more significant, dealing with the establishment on the North coast of Alaska of a New Hudson's Bay colony. Unknown to the settlers, the peninsula they inhabit is not part of the continent at all. It is an enormous iceberg which had become attached to the mainland and is broken off by a volcanic eruption. Discovering themselves adrift, the residents of *The Fur Country* lack any control over their island. It may carry them into the far reaches of the frozen North or take them through the Bering Strait and melt beneath their feet. This idea derived directly from Verne's boyhood belief that the Ile Feydeau could be uprooted and swept out to sea, and the simultaneous emotions it gave

From *Le Pays des fourrures* (*The Fur Country*, 1873).

him of both anticipation and anxiety, as noted by Verne biographer Kenneth Allott.[8]

In *Une Ville Flottante* (*A Floating City*, 1871), *The Jangada*, and *Propellor Island*, Verne told of man-made islands traveling the oceans and rivers of the world. The floating island provided an unparalled opportunity for leisurely travel and offered the longed-for isolation of the desert island, without its attendant feeling of desolation. *The Fur Country* merged this idea of the mobile island with the Robinsonade theme of survival.

Verne created his purest Robinsonade in *The Mysterious Island*, carrying the traditional Robinsonade to its ultimate extreme. The story is of five Union soldiers, imprisoned during the civil war, who escape by observation balloon but are caught in a violent storm that sweeps them to an uncharted, uninhabited Pacific island. This device, unlikely as it may be, serves to maroon the castaways much more thoroughly than those of previous authors, leaving them stranded with nothing more than the contents of their pockets and minds.[9] As the reviewer for *Scribner's Monthly* noted, "Verne is not content with De Foe's *Robinson Crusoe* and Wyss' *The Swiss Family Robinson*. They did well enough for simple, unscientific times, but now it is necessary to show how scientific castaways can manage to live, without a vessel to break up, and convenient domestic animals at hand, with other necessaries which 'turn up,' always at the right time."[10]

*The Mysterious Island* was a parable of the historical development of man and his technology, as the castaways recreate from scratch all the necessities, and eventually even some of the luxuries, of life over a four-year period. These modern Robinsons bend nature to their purposes with the aid of their knowledge, and from the island's resources they discover that almost anything can be made.

As pointed out by the author's grandson, Jean Jules-Verne, the characters represent stages in the evolution of mankind: a child; a victim of slavery's injustice; a sailor; a journalist; and an engineer.[11]

8.   Kenneth Allott, *Jules Verne* (London: Crescent, 1940), 168.

9.   Anthony Boucher, "Introduction," in Verne, *The Mysterious Island* (New York: Dodd, Mead, 1958), n.p.

10.  "Topics of the Time: Jules Verne's New Story," *Scribner's Monthly*, 7 (April 1874), 755.

11.  Jean Jules-Verne, *Jules Verne*, translated and adapted by Roger Greaves (London: MacDonald and Jane's, 1976), 110.

There are even two pets, a dog and an orang-utang. The leader of the castaways is a Renaissance man whose mind is a repository of all practical human learning, the engineer and prototypical American doer Cyrus Smith. (Readers should avoid the incomplete and inaccurate older translations that christen him Cyrus Harding; not until the 21st century were unexpurgated, accurate versions offered in English).

The Vernian castaways proceed further along the evolutionary trail than do those of Defoe or Wyss, and succeed in rescuing a fellow Robinson, the solitary Ayrton, abandoned on a nearby island to atone for his crimes, as recounted in Verne's *The Children of Captain Grant*. Ayrton had reverted to savagery during his years alone, and henceforth the "success of Smith and his men can be measured on the scale of Ayrton's failure," as noted by Pierre Macherey.[12] By bringing Ayrton to what they have named Lincoln Island, the Union castaways not only further vitiate their own status as Robinsons, but also enhance their credibility as colonists who are not only surviving but also preparing this area for future annexation by the United States. This theme is not abandoned even after the volcano destroys the island, but renewed on a namesake farm in Iowa, a utopian community funded by a gift from Captain Nemo.

None of Verne's other Robinsonades would be so concerned with the inclusion of technology as an important part of the plot. In this respect, and because of the inclusion of Captain Nemo as "the secret of the island," whose intervention at critical moments assumes the dimensions of providence, *The Mysterious Island* acquires some of the aura of science fiction. *The Mysterious Island* is widely regarded as perhaps the most important Robinsonade after the original Defoe and Wyss classics. As well, its fame has been augmented by numerous film and television adaptations since the days of silent films, often emphasizing the role of Captain Nemo and telling the story partly from his perspective.

Verne debunked his own fascination with the desert island myth by gleefully manipulating it, subjecting the formula to a light mockery in *The School for Robinsons*. A rich and wily American, in order to curb the wanderlust of his young day-dreaming nephew, buys an island and endows it with all the accouterments of a Robinson—spurious animals, actors to play savage natives, even a man Friday. A shipwreck is staged,

---

12. Pierre Macherey, "Jules Verne: The Faulty Narrative." In *A Theory of Literary Production*, translated by Geoffrey Wall (London: Routledge and Kegan Paul, 1978), 220.

From *Le Pays des fourrures* (*The Fur Country*, 1873).

stranding the lad, and for companionship, he is given the burden of providing for his hapless tutor of dancing and deportment. The would-be Robinson and those who arranged his adventure get more than they bargained for, however, when the island is invaded by fierce wild animals. *The School for Robinsons* was undoubtedly one of the liveliest and wittiest of Verne's Robinsonades, one that has justifiably won a unique reputation for its satire.

In *Two Year Holiday*, like the Robinsons before them, the castaways attempt to convert wildlife into pets (with a notable lack of success), find a fellow castaway on a Friday (in this case a woman), and must overcome an onslaught of pirates. However, the emphasis is no longer on survival, but on the process of establishing a society. In his preface to *Two Year Holiday*, Verne wrote, "In *A Fifteen-Year-Old Captain* I have undertaken to show what even a brave and intelligent child can accomplish when he is obliged to face the dangers and perplexities of a responsibility beyond his years; but…In spite of the infinite number of stories included in the list of Robinsons it has always seemed to me that to complete it there should be a description of the experience and adventures of a party of children from eight to thirteen years of age, cast upon an island, and struggling for subsistence in the midst of the passions and prejudices naturally aroused by differences of nationality."[13]

Rivalry inevitably arises between the oldest boys, aggravated by their divergent nationalities: two are French brothers and one an American among a largely English group; all had been attending school in New Zealand. The need for leadership creates tensions; while the elder French boy proves the most capable and caring leader, this arouses the chauvinistic instincts of the British, and requires the intercession of the more mature American.

*Two Year Holiday* reflected Verne's sentiments toward the dominant nations of his day. The eldest British boy is depicted as having the ability Verne was ready to admire, but also an innate haughtiness and excess of pride shown as characteristic of his countrymen. It is some of these British, themselves the ultimate imperialists, who refuse for a time to be governed by anyone not of their nationality, withdrawing to set up a separate colony of their own until the threat of a pirate invasion compels a reunification.

Today *Two Year Holiday* is read in a different context, because of a later book, William Golding's *Lord of the Flies* (1954). *Two Year Holiday* is its antithesis; Verne believed that, for better and worse, a group of boys would emulate European society, not revert to savagery. Verne's children carry on their studies, and create a school of their own, with the older boys teaching those who are younger, and eliminating elements of the education system that tended to breed social class consciousness.

Increasingly central to Verne's Robinsonades was the belief that the narrative should reveal the island's transformation into a society. Verne's characterization of the Swiss Family in *Second Homeland* shows them as uncertain over the relative merits of their past situation and the

---

13. Jules Verne, "Preface," *Two Year's Vacation* (New York: George Munro, 1889).

From *La Jangada* (*The Jangada*, 1881).

changes colonization will bring; for over a decade they have remained undisturbed and lacked for nothing. Now they must surrender their insular existence and prepare for an influx of settlers, a change in their island and its status that brings mixed emotions.

This anxiety became the central theme of one of his last works, the posthumously published *Survivors of the Jonathan*. All of Verne's stories published in the five years after his death were rewritten by the author's son, Michel, as was discovered when the original texts were unearthed in the 1980s. In this case, Michel took his father's novel, *Magellania*, and expanded it three-fold. Today, both versions have been translated and published in English, allowing the reader to compare the writing of father and son.

Although Michel's *The Survivors of the Jonathan* is a reflection of his own views, not those of his father, it is also a vivid, literary novel which comprehensively develops its many ideological crosscurrents. The elder Verne's *Magellania*, by contrast, reads like an outline rather than a polished book. Michel's determination to "flesh out" these limitations is understandable.

*Magellania* and *The Survivors of the Jonathan* have tremendous scope. A boatload of immigrants are shipwrecked on unpopulated Hoste Island, at the tip of South America. Initially failing in self-government, they turn to a benevolent dictator. Under his direction, they overcome strife caused by radicals and the depredations of a gold rush, ultimately developing a prosperous nation-state.

Jules Verne's hero in *Magellania* is the "Kaw-djer," a name meaning friend, benefactor, and savior to the Fuegians, with whom he shares his medical skills and knowledge. He begins as an atheist and anarchist, a self-exiled European nobleman who has abdicated his position because of his beliefs. Determined to exist apart from mankind, out of disillusionment rather than misanthropy, he is living in the Magellanes, one of the remaining uncolonized areas at the end of the 19th century.

Central to the Kaw-djer's success is his commitment to free trade as a means of attracting business. By contrast, the taxes and restrictions imposed upon a neighboring island by Argentina hamper development. Hoste Island becomes a new beacon of hope and freedom in the New World, economically and politically. The novel ends as the beams flash from the Cape Horn lighthouse, built according to the Kaw-djer's vision to save ships from future wrecks in the region. The demands of governing have forced him to renounce his impractical anarchistic theories, but he has found fulfillment in creating orderly government, with a dawning faith in God.

Jules Verne lauds the nationalism of Hoste Island and its commitment to self-determination; Michel Verne portrays these as failed goals in *The Survivors of the Jonathan*. He creates a novel as much of politics as adventure. He examines the different ideologies offered as panaceas to the community, and the various characters associated with each. Communism and capitalism come in for equally harsh treatment; they are promoted by unethical individuals who exemplify greed, cruelty, and the desire for power. Socialism is treated as ineffectual and backed by an incompetent who leads the island to the brink of disaster. Michel reveals his sympathy is with the Kaw-djer's anarchism, although ultimately, like his father, he puts his faith in pragmatism.

Michel presents the Kaw-djer as a figure of tragedy. When the Hoste Island immigrants are facing starvation, they turn to him as the only man who can lead them. Raging mobs induce the Kaw-djer to sacrifice his own belief that man does not need governing. Although the Kaw-djer succeeds in establishing a regenerating society, because of the necessary betrayal of his own principles, he believes he has failed. He leaves the island in the hands of a trained successor and the Kaw-djer exiles himself from humanity once more, this time where he will be truly alone, at the lighthouse at Cape Horn.

The question of the authorship of Verne's last Robinsonade, *The Eternal Adam*, is unclear; it may be by Michel, or Jules, or both, but critics are agreed that it is a masterpiece. *The Eternal Adam* reflects the disillusion of *The Survivors of the Jonathan*, with a belief humanity is not the result of a continual evolution toward the greater good—but is subject to a never-ending pattern of cycles that will forever keep him from attaining a higher existence.

*The Eternal Adam* offers a bleak glimpse into the indeterminate but far-off future. Centuries from now a savant, the zartog Sofr-Ai-Sr, from a civilization technologically inferior to our own, discovers an ancient manuscript. In deciphering it, the zartog realizes that his is not the final development of man's progress, but that prior civilizations, including our own—and others before us such as Atlantis--have reached higher levels. Nonetheless they have all been

From *La Jangada* (*The Jangada*, 1881).

completely destroyed in great calamaties of nature. By structuring the narrative in this way, according to André Winandy, "the reader, together with the zartog, is able to transcend time and imagine through the infinity of time the passing of all things in the universe and gain an intimate understanding of the time wheel, the eternal recurrence of events."[14]

*The Eternal Adam* carries the Robinsonade toward a vision of a global apocalypse that ends civilization and returns man to his barbaric state. The continents of the world suddenly sink, becoming overrun by the oceans, while from the bottom of the sea a new island the size of a continent appears, the only land now on the globe. A small group on a boat survive to land at this new shore.

Although the population flourishes in numbers, and are materially better off than the castaways of *The Mysterious Island*, their meager effort to recreate civilization fails. Vernian plots are typically constructed with careful attention to dates, times and seasons, and one of the first indications of the social descent of man in *The Eternal Adam* is losing track of time. Within a few years the process of retrogression has begun and before a generation passes, even speech has been forgotten. In the words of Verne theorist Michel Butor, "Instead of the vision of mankind's progress, we have the hideous record of its degradation, of its gradual return to animality which it will take thousands of years to overcome and even then, as always, only provisionally."[15]

Because of the recurrent global disasters, mankind's progress must be forever limited, taking place in a cyclical pattern doomed to be endlessly repeated and never overcome. This bleak view was not a new one with Verne; the same cycle was already foreseen in *The Mysterious Island* when, after all the castaways' achievements, their island once again returns to the sea, leaving them on a barren rock with as little as they had started with.

*The Eternal Adam* was not Verne's first Robinsonade to enter the realm of science fiction. Almost thirty years before, in *Hector Servadac* he had told of a comet glancing the Earth and carrying off a small portion of the Mediterranean, along with its inhabitants, on a two year round trip through the solar system.

*Hector Servadac,* named for its principal character, (but often known in English translations with titles that include the word "comet")

---

14. André Winandy, "The Twilight Zone: Imagination and Reality in Jules Verne's *Strange Journeys*," Translated by Rita Winandy, *Yale French Studies*, 43 (November 1969), 99.

15. Michel Butor, "The Golden Age in Jules Verne." In Richard Howard, ed., *Inventory* (New York: Simon and Schuster, 1960), 143.

is one of Verne's most ingenious and surprising tales, and perhaps the first modern science-fiction Robinsonade. It places the castaways in a locale even more remote than the archetypal uncharted desert island: the unexplored domain of outer space. As they learn to survive the heat of approaching Venus to the cold of nearby Saturn, the underlying theme is the immutability of human behavior. Despite the palpable emergency that draws together most of the travelers on the comet, a few castaways obstinately stand apart, refusing to recognize the change. They include an eccentric and selfish French scientist, a greedy moneylender, and the British garrison at Gibraltar. Even while observing the cataclysmic celestial alterations, the officers insist that the silence of England does not mean that word from home cannot be received; ultimately their fragment of the comet breaks off and goes into space on its own orbit, forever lost.

*The Eternal Adam* and *Hector Servadac* are among the very few Vernian science fiction works in which imagination is wholly unfettered. Verne's publisher required an educative aspect to his stories, and in the case of *Hector Servadac*, demanded the end be changed. Rather than the comet slamming into the Earth on its return, the story is explained as a vague dream. Yet the absurdity of this new ending is obvious, since all the castaways had the same dream, and their friends back on Earth have noted their long absence. As a result, when Verne decided to again write a story of going into outer space, he evaded the constraints of his publisher by writing it as a stage play, *Voyage à travers l'impossible* (*Journey Through the Impossible*, 1881, first translated under the auspices of the North American Jules Verne Society in 2003).

Jules Verne preferred *The Swiss Family Robinson* over *Robinson Crusoe* because Wyss's book was a social drama, not one of man alone. Verne was interested in providing his characters with companions and dealing with the interior politics of group interaction. This interest in the Robinsonade as a form for analyzing social interaction reflects an apparent disbelief on Verne's part in the underlying Robinson myth, that an isolated person could survive without turning savage. The only lone Robinson in Verne's canon is Ayrton of *The Mysterious Island*, who represents the opposite movement of the Robinsonade; without companions he regresses to primitivism. Even Captain Nemo abandons solitude to become father-God to the castaways of Lincoln Island.

Verne's Robinsons hope to establish on their islands an alternate society that would be impossible within the ordinary confines of civilization. The settlement of the traders in *The Fur Country* is an attempt to be sufficiently distant from the other trappers to have a commercial outpost. Under the Kaw-djer's leadership, Hoste Island eventually becomes a free nation; the castaways of Lincoln Island are proud of their settlement and hope it will some day join the United States. The description of New Switzerland in *Second Homeland* clearly implies a latter-day Eden, and Verne united the Robinsonade with the desire to create an idyllic community. Yet at the same time, there were Atlantean

From *L'Île à hélice* (*Propeller Island*, 1895).

perils: the refuges in *The Fur Country*, *The Mysterious Island*, *Hector Servadac*, and *The Eternal Adam* are ultimately destroyed by nature.

Verne's interest in islands was more than that of the romantic or adventurer; he sought to expand the realm encompassed by the Robinsonade to include political and social commentaries. Through the course of Verne's Robinsonades he steadily shifted the emphasis away from the basic theme of survival on the desert island. In *The Fur Country*, *The Mysterious Island*, *Two Year Holiday*, *Second Homeland*, *Magellania*, and *The Eternal Adam*, there is a hope for the island settlement to be permanent. The activities become those of exploration and preparation for colonization, subordinating and using nature to human needs, in the name of not only survival but also science, progress, nationalism and sometimes imperialism. Verne generally supported these endeavors from the perspective of one imbued with the expansionist impetus of the 19th century, although he argued against the displacement and exploitation of native peoples or the abuse of animal and natural resources (especially in *The Fur Country* and *Magellania*).

From *Deux ans de vacances* (*Two Year Holiday*, 1888).

Robinsonades and the desert island idea ignited Verne's imagination more than any other literary type, and were united with his overall geographical and utopian concerns. His own works of this type varied considerably, emphasizing analogies of man's evolution from a primitive to technological state, but also expanding beyond Defoe's concentration on survival to Wyss's interest in focusing on how a small group creates its own society and interacts in isolation. Verne elaborated on the Robinsonade, dwelling increasingly on the politicization that would take place under such conditions, especially as islands expanded from small, isolated, self-contained groups into full-fledged societies, culminating in *Magellania* and *The Eternal Adam*. While these used the adventure framework, other Robinsonades created alternate worlds paralleling and contrasting with our own, told in terms of modern speculative science fiction. In these ways Verne experimented with the Robinsonade, taking it in new directions, forever enlarging its potential.

The most unusual of Verne's Robinsonades, however, is the current volume. Like *Magellania*, the recently discovered manuscript of the volume previously only known under the version created by Michel Verne, *The Survivors of the Jonathan*, here is the first draft of what became *The Mysterious Island*. Verne began this original version back in 1861, provisionally calling it *L'Oncle Robinson* (*Uncle Robinson*), and revised it a decade later. However, it was never completed because of his publisher's negative reaction. While this kept Verne from returning to it later, or Michel from undertaking its completion, despite the promising premise, the book is much more than a curiosity or failure, both revealing a variation he did not return to, yet also a forecast of plot ideas Verne would later try in different contexts, most notably *The Mysterious Island*, *Two Year Holiday*, and *Second Homeland*. To avoid confusion with the subsequent novel Verne entitled *The School for Robinsons*, also translated over the years as *Robinson's School*, *The Robinson Crusoe School*, *The School for Crusoes*, *Robinson Island*, and *An American Robinson Crusoe*, and considering it was only published posthumously, *Uncle Robinson* has been retitled in this edition more descriptively for its plot, *Shipwrecked Family: Marooned with Uncle Robinson*. Moreover, while "Robinson" implies a character of Defoe's isolated type in the word's European usage, in English it is a common surname, and the new title provides the reader with an idea of Verne's plot (and also ensures no confusion with the Robinson family in the television show *Lost in Space*!)

*Shipwrecked Family* begins with violence, as a trans-Pacific voyage is interrupted by a mutiny. The nascent pirates dispatch Mrs. Clifton and her four children into a small boat, daring them to make the distant island. Fortunately one of the loyal crewmen, Flip, jumps into the sea after the Cliftons and guides them to shore. The island's location is undisclosed but seems to be in the northwestern Pacific, and the story arose from Verne's desire to set a story in this region.

Two-thirds of the way into the volume, the Clifton's father Harry is found mysteriously ashore, half-dead and similarly stranded by the pirates. This allows much of the narrative to demonstrate Flip's own knowledge of wildlife and skill in mapping the island. He is a strong central character, a man who has traveled the seas of the world, but also a natural philosopher. However, he is more than the traditional male hero, for Flip is also a nurturer, a man who can step into the paternal role for the children despite having never been a husband or father. Verne's choice of Flip's nickname, "Uncle Robinson," as a title for the book signifies his centrality as the only one who is not part of the actual nuclear family, but adopted in avuncular fashion.

Ultimately, both the father's education in science, and Flip's practical experience, become valuable assets in surviving on the island. No less significant is the mother's strength in keeping the family's hopes and arranging a home, despite the primitive conditions; she demonstrates the strong women to be found in the Verne canon when the narrative offers the opportunity for a female character.

With its collective, familial hero, *Shipwrecked Family* forms a sort of "missing link" in Verne's works of the genre, covering ground that he chose not to furrow again with his own original characters. (Only later, in sequel form, would he use the family castaway theme in *Second Homeland*.) Here, too, Verne's protagonists are multi-national but cooperate as one. Unlike the American flavor of *The Mysterious Island*, the Clifton family is from New England but have been living overseas, while Flip is French-American. As in *Two Year Holiday*, *Shipwrecked Family* is close in style to a young adult book as befits the intended audience.

Although slow paced, the characterizations are absorbing and the relationships are warmly sentimental. Despite their minimal resources, the family consciously only kill the wildlife necessary for their own food and clothing; the children feel disgust even when killing penguins for their own need, because the creatures are so

From *Les Naufragés du Jonathan* (*The Survivors of the Jonathan*, 1909).

helpless. Other aspects of *Shipwrecked Family* similar to *Two Year Holiday* are the continuation of schooling despite the interruption of their lives, and the importance in the different ages of the children, and its relation to their castaway experience, resulting in different levels of awareness of their perils.

The almost diary-style chronicle of each day's life and activities in *Shipwrecked Family* was replaced in *The Mysterious Island* by the gradual evolution of the castaway's lot as they recreated, step by step, the technology of modern civilization. *Shipwrecked Family* lacks the emphasis on the unexplainable mysteries of the island that helped give constant intrigue to the narrative of *The Mysterious Island*, while retaining the aspect by which both *The Mysterious Island* and *Shipwrecked Family* could be regarded as a veritable handbook for the castaway.

As in *The Mysterious Island*, *Shipwrecked Family* opens with castaways who have almost nothing in hand save a knife, a single match, and a kernel of wheat. Verne clearly believes his own is the more realistic account, while not sparing the familial themes that have made Wyss's classic so beloved. *Shipwrecked Family* is also similar to *The Mysterious Island* in the episodes of the discovery of Clifton and his dog, the creation of fire, growing of wheat, finding tobacco, Jup the orang, and the mysterious bullet that indicates possible habitation of their island, all providing clear parallels. There is other equivalence in characters: besides Jup, the dog remains, his name changed from Fido to Top. The knowledgeable Harry Clifton becomes Cyrus Smith, Flip turns into Pencroff, and young Marc becomes Harbert [sic]. However, the tone and intended readership of the two books could not be more different; *The Mysterious Island* appeals to readers of all ages, with the teen-age Harbert the only concession to youth.

What remains unknown is how the remainder of *Shipwrecked Family* would have developed, and to what degree it would have resembled other incidents in *The Mysterious Island*; another two volumes were intended of *Shipwrecked Family*, the same length as the three volumes of *The Mysterious Island*. Whether Captain Nemo would have become the *deus ex machina* required by various incidents, as he would turn out to be in *The Mysterious Island*, is unknown. Verne had completed *Vingt mille lieues sous les mers* (*Twenty Thousand Leagues Under the Seas*, 1869) when he began revising his 1861 draft of *Shipwrecked Family*. Certainly Nemo's interest in the Clifton family's

From *L'Île mystérieuse* (*The Mysterious Island*, 1874).

survival would have made a far stronger motivation for his intervention. There are, however, some hints, suggesting an intervention beyond the bullet found in wildlife, or Clifton's unexplained rescue. They find surprising flora and fauna on the island, and most curious is the discovery of a rooster with a horn implanted in its head, doubtless by the scientific hand of man. To the reader coming to Verne from Hollywood interpretations, this suggests that the genetic experiments on the island attributed to Captain Nemo in the 1961 movie, *Mysterious Island*, were not so distant from Verne's own conceptions—which in turn led to the North American Jules Verne Society's decision to dedicate the English-language edition of this book to the film's creator, Ray Harryhausen.

*Shipwrecked Family* has already had a curious history in English. In a November 1991 issue of *The European*, published by the Robert Maxwell Group, the discovery of the manuscript was delineated, and its English-language publication was announced. A portion of the first chapters were to be continued in the next issue. Then no more was heard; possibly the editors realized that the novel was incomplete!

The North American Jules Verne Society is pleased to bring to book publication this most unusual of Verne's Robinsonades, the one he never finished, and which evolved into a recognized literary classic, *The Mysterious Island*. The translation and notes are by Sidney Kravitz, who is also translator of the best version of *The Mysterious Island*, published by Wesleyan University Press in 2002, and we urge readers of this volume to also consult that landmark edition.

Kravitz gave freely of his expertise and dedication to the cause of promoting a modern understanding of Verne's books. The society is grateful to his estate for their permission to publish this translation. *Shipwrecked Family* joins the North American Jules Verne Society's series of books we have brought to English-language publication for the first time, volumes named for our late member Edward D. Palik, whose generosity helped to underwrite the project. Both Sid and Ed were united in their wish to bring the unknown Verne stories to readers, and it is fitting that their names are joined in this volume honoring their memory.

⊙

To
Ray Harryhausen,

Whose wondrous film of *Mysterious Island*
has introduced millions to Jules Verne's
desert island adventures

# Shipwrecked Family:
## Marooned with Uncle Robinson

From *Seconde patrie* (*Second Homeland*, 1900)

# Chapter I

The North Pacific Ocean—Abandoned boat—Mother and her four children—Man at the helm—Will of heaven be done!—Question without an answer.

The most deserted portion of the Pacific Ocean is this vast expanse of water bounded by Asia and America to the west and to the east, and by the Aleutian Islands and the Sandwiches to the north and to the south. Merchant vessels hardly ever venture on this sea. There is no port of call and the currents there are capricious. The ocean going vessels which carry the produce of Australia to the western part of America travel at lower latitudes; only the traffic between Japan and California enlivens this northern part of the Pacific but there is not much of that. The trans Pacific line which connects Yokohama to San Francisco follows a somewhat lower great circle route. The region between the fortieth and fiftieth north latitude can hence be called "the desert." Perhaps some whaler sometimes chances on this nearly unknown sea; but he hurries to cross the belt of the Aleutian Islands in order to reach the Bering Strait, beyond which large whales take refuge from vivid pursuit by fishermen's harpoons.

Do unknown islands still exist on this sea which is the size of Europe? Does Micronesia extend up to this latitude? This cannot be affirmed or denied. An island is a small thing in the midst of this large liquid area. Such a nearly imperceptible point could easily escape the explorers who venture on these waves. Perhaps some more important but still unknown island will be found one day. It is a fact that in this part of the globe two natural phenomena cause new islands to appear; on the one hand plutonic action can suddenly lift land above the waves.

33

On the other hand, the constant work of the infusoria are little by little creating coral banks which in several hundred thousand years will form a sixth continent in this part of the Pacific. However on the 25th of March 1861, the portion of the Pacific just described was not absolutely deserted. A vessel was floating on its surface. It was not the steamer of a transocean line, nor a warship keeping watch over northern fishing grounds, nor a commercial vessel trafficking the products of the Moluccas or of the Philippines which only a windstorm would have thrown off its path, nor even a fishing boat. It was a frail boat with a simple foresail. It was trying to reach land about nine or ten miles windward. Hence it was tacking and trying to make headway by sailing close to the wind against a contrary breeze. Unfortunately the rising tide, always weak in the Pacific, was of little help in this maneuver.

The weather however was fine though a little cold. A few light clouds were dispersed in the sky. The sun lit up the foamy crest of some waves here and there. A long swell rocked the boat without however subjecting it to too many strong shocks. The sail was completely unfurled in order to better catch the wind which occasionally listed the light vessel to the point where water grazed its railing. But it soon righted itself and moved into the wind while approaching the coast.

After due consideration, a sailor would have recognized that this boat was of American construction, made with Canadian fir. Besides, on its rear nameplate one could read these two words: *Vancouver-- Montreal*, which indicated its nationality.

This boat carried six people. At the helm was stationed a man between thirty five and forty years of age, certainly with much sea experience, who directed his vessel with an incomparable firm hand. He was a vigorously constituted individual with large shoulders, strong muscles and in the prime of life. He had the look of a Frenchman, the glance of an open-minded person. His expression showed great kindness. From his coarse clothes, his callous hands, something uncultivated was imprinted on his entire appearance, to the continual whistling which escaped from his lips, it was easy to see that he did not belong to the upper class. From the way in which he handled the boat, there was no doubt that he was a sailor, but only a simple seaman, not an officer. As to his nationality, one could more easily determine that. He certainly was not an Anglo-Saxon. He had neither the harshness nor the rigid movements of the men of that race. One saw in him a certain natural grace, not the course rudeness of the Yankee of New England. If this man was not a Canadian, a descendant of those hardy pioneers who left their Gallic imprint, then he had to be a Frenchman, a little Americanized doubtless, but definitely a Frenchman, one of those shrewd chaps, bold, kind, obliging, ready for any challenge, never inconvenienced by anything, naturally confident and insensitive to fear such as one often finds in the country of France.

This sailor was seated to the rear of the boat. His gaze left neither the sea nor the sail. He watched one and the other simultaneously: the sail when some fold indicated that it was carrying too much wind, the sea when he had to gently change the direction of the boat to avoid some wave.

From time to time a word or rather a suggestion escaped his lips and from his pronunciation one detected a certain accent which could never have been produced in the throat of an Anglo-Saxon.

"Put your minds at ease, my children," he said. "The situation is not very good, but it could be worse. Put your minds at ease and lower your heads, we are going to tack." And the worthy sailor brought his boat into the wind. The sail passed noisily over the bent heads and the boat inclined to the other side, approaching the coast little by little.

To the rear, near the vigorous helmsman, was a woman about thirty six years of age, who hid her face under her shawl. This woman was crying but she tried to hide her tears in order not to depress the children who were pressing close to her.

This woman was the mother of the four children which the boat carried with her. The oldest of these children was seventeen years old. He was a tall fellow who would one day become a vigorous man. His black hair and his face tanned by the sea breeze suited him. His red eyes were still moist with tears but anger as much as sorrow had brought on his tears. He was standing in the forward part of the boat near the mast, looking at the land still in the distance. Turning at times, he cast a sad and an annoyed look at the western horizon. His face then paled and he held back a show of anger. He then looked at the man at the helm, and the latter, with a smile, made a small reassuring nod.

The younger brother of this lad was not more than fifteen years old. His large head was crowned with reddish hair. He moved about, anxious, impatient, sometimes seated, sometimes standing. He could not calm down. This boat did not move fast enough for him; land was not approaching rapidly enough. He already wanted to set foot on this shore, even if it meant that he would want to be somewhere else as soon as he reached it. But when he cast a glance at his mother, when he heard the sighs which filled the chest of this poor woman, he went to her, he put his arms around her, he lavished his best kisses, and the unfortunate woman pressed him to her heart: "Poor child! Poor children!" she murmured.

She then looked at the sailor seated at the helm. The latter had never neglected to motion to her with a sign that very certainly signified: "But all goes well, Madam, and we will manage our affairs."

However, on observing the southwest, this man saw large clouds rising above the horizon, which foretold nothing good for his travelling companion and her young children. The wind threatened to freshen, and a very strong breeze would be fatal to this fragile undecked boat. But the sailor kept this worry to himself not wanting to reveal the fears that were bothering him.

The two other children were a small boy and a small girl. The small boy, with blonde hair, was eight years old. His lips were pale with fatigue, his blue eyes were half closed, and his cheeks, which should have been fresh and pink were drab from the tears. His small hands were painful from the cold and he hid under his mother's shawl. His sister near him, a seven year old girl, had her arms around her mother. She was overwhelmed by the jolts of the swell and half asleep, her head bounced with the rolling of the boat.

As noted, the weather was cold on this day of the 25th of March. The wind out of the north was a glacial wind. These unfortunates, abandoned in this boat, were very lightly dressed for resisting the cold. Evidently they had been surprised by a catastrophe, a shipwreck or a collision, which had forced them to throw themselves into this boat; besides, one could see that they carried few provisions with them, some sea biscuits and two or three pieces of salted meat placed in a box in front.

When the small boy, half awake, passed his hands over his eyes, he murmured these words: "Mother, I am hungry." The helmsman immediately got up and took a piece of biscuit from the box. He offered it to the child and with a jolly smile he said to him: "Eat, my child, eat! By the time this is all gone, we may have more!"

The child, thus encouraged, bit his fine teeth into the hard crust and then put his head back on his mother's shoulder.

However, the unfortunate woman, seeing that her two children were shivering under their clothing, had removed her own. She lifted her shawl to cover them with more warmth and then one could see her beautiful figure, her large black eyes solemn and thoughtful, her appearance so deeply marked with maternal tenderness and devotion. She was a "mother" in the full sense of the word, a mother who could have been the mother of a Washington, of a Franklin or of an Abraham Lincoln, a woman of the Bible, strong and courageous, a combination of all virtues and all tendernesses. But to see her so disheveled with all consuming tears, one would think she had received a mortal blow. She evidently struggled against this despair, but the tears in her eyes showed what was in her heart. Like her elder son she turned to the horizon from time to time, searching this sea for some invisible object: but seeing nothing but an immense desert she fell back into the boat, poor woman, her lips still refusing to pronounce these words of evangelic submission: "Lord, thy will be done!"

This mother covered two of her children with her shawl, but she was barely covered herself. A thin woolen dress could barely protect her against this biting March wind which easily blew under her wide-brimmed hat. Three of her children wore wool jackets, trousers, vests and oiled cloth caps. But over these clothes there should have been some well made jacket with a double lined cap and some traveling coat made with a thick material. However, these children did not complain of the cold. Doubtless they did not wish to cause their mother more despair.

As to the sailor, he wore a pair of cotton velvet trousers and a brown wool pea jacket, insufficient protection against the biting wind. But this worthy man possessed a warm heart, a veritable furnace allowing him to react vigorously against physical suffering. In fact, the distress of the others gave him more pain than his own. Looking at the poor woman who took off her shawl to cover her children, he saw that she was shivering and that her teeth were clacking in spite of herself.

Soon he returned her shawl, covering the mother's shoulders, and carefully placed his own warm jacket over the two children.

The mother resisted this action. "I'm overheated," the sailor simply replied, wiping his brow with his handkerchief as if he were steaming in sweat.

The poor woman extended her hand to this man which he fondly held without saying a word.

At this moment, the oldest of the children jumped up to the small upper deck which formed the front of the boat and carefully observed the western part of the sea. He put his hand over his eyes to protect them from the sun's glare and to see better. But the ocean scintillated from this direction and the line of the horizon was lost in this intense radiation. Under these conditions, a rigorous observation was difficult.

Nevertheless, the child kept looking for a rather long time while the sailor shook his head, seeming to say that if help should come their way, it would be from a higher source.

At this moment the young girl, just waking up, left her mother's arms, revealing her pale face. Then, looking at the boat's passengers, she asked, "Where is father?"

No answer was made to this simple question. The children's eyes filled with tears and the mother, hiding her face in her hands, began to sob.

The sailor looked silently on this deep sorrow. He could no longer speak his words of comfort to these poor abandoned people, but his powerful arm gripped the helm.

# Chapter II

The *Vancouver*—Engineer Harry Clifton—Boatload of Kanakas—
The Pacific Ocean—The second mate Bob Gordon—imprisoned—
Family at the mercy of the waves's devotion.

The Vancouver was a three-masted Canadian vessel displacing five hundred fluid tons. It had been chartered to take a group of Kanakas to San Francisco, emigrants who voluntarily hire themselves out for work abroad. One hundred fifty of these emigrants took passage on board the *Vancouver*.

Travelers ordinarily avoid crossing the Pacific in the company of these Kanakas, who are coarse people.[1] Their society is not desirable and they are always inclined to revolt. Mr. Harry Clifton, an American engineer, and his family had not planned to embark on the *Vancouver*. Mr. Clifton, who had been employed for several years in improving the approaches to the Amour River, was looking for an occasion to get back to Boston, his native city. He had made his fortune and he waited, there being almost no connections between North China and America. When the *Vancouver* arrived on the coast of Asia, Harry Clifton found the captain who commanded her to be a compatriot and a friend. So he decided to take passage on board, with his wife, his three sons and his small daughter. He had acquired a certain fortune and he aspired only to retire even though he was still young, barely forty years of age.

---

1.  "Kanakas" may also be correctly translated as Polynesians or as natives of New Caledonia.

His wife, Mrs. Elisa Clifton, felt some apprehension in boarding this vessel full of Kanakas: but she did not wish to oppose her husband, so eager to see America again. The crossing, besides, would be a short one. The captain of the *Vancouver* was experienced with these sorts of voyages, and this reassured Mrs. Clifton a little. So she and her husband embarked on the *Vancouver* with their three sons, Marc, Robert, and Jack, their young daughter, Belle, and their dog, Fido.

Captain Harrison, the vessel's commander, was a very competent sailor who knew that there was little danger on the Pacific Ocean. Mixing socially with the engineer, he carefully saw to it that the Clifton family would have no contact with the Kanakas who were lodged in the steerage.

From *Un Hivernage dans les glaces* (*A Winter Amid the Ice*, 1855)

The crew of the *Vancouver* was composed of some dozen sailors of no particular nationality. It was difficult to avoid this kind of crew when hiring in far away places. They were often in conflict with each other. The crew of this vessel was composed of two Irishmen, three Americans, a Frenchman, a Maltese, two Chinamen and three Negros hired for service on board.

The *Vancouver* left on the 14th of March. At first all went well but the wind was not favorable. In spite of Captain Harrison's skill, the currents and the wind from the south drove the vessel too far north. That presented no serious danger, it would only make the trip longer. The real danger came from certain of the crew who were inciting the Kanakas to mutiny. These scoundrels were encouraged to disobedience by Bob Gordon, second in command, a notorious rogue, who betrayed the captain's trust with whom he was travelling for the first time. Several times already the crew had heated discussions and the captain had to act with authority. These regrettable incidents would have disastrous consequences.

In fact, serious symptoms of insubordination were not long in declaring themselves among the crew of the *Vancouver*. The Kanakas were difficult to control. Captain Harrison could only depend on the two Irishmen, the three Americans and the Frenchman, a brave sailor barely Americanized, having lived for some time in the United States. This worthy man was a native of Picardy. His name was Jean Fanthome but he answered only to the nickname of Flip. This Flip had been everywhere in the world; all that could happen to a human being had happened to him but he still maintained his good humor. It was he who warned Captain Harrison of the dangerous conspiracies on board; he urged him to take energetic measures. But what could be done under these conditions? Would it not be best to be tactful while waiting for a favorable wind to drive the vessel in sight of San Francisco Bay?

Harry Clifton was informed of the second mate's intrigues and his anxieties increased each day. Seeing the alliances that were forming between the Kanakas and certain members of the crew, he seriously regretted going on board the *Vancouver* and exposing his family to the perils of this voyage; but it was too late.

The evil conspiracies began to turn into acts of violence and Captain Harrison ordered a Maltese who had insulted him into irons. This occurred on March 23rd. The Maltese's companions did not

From *Un Hivernage dans les glaces* (*A Winter Amid the Ice*, 1855)

oppose the execution of this sentence; they merely murmured while their companion was seized by Flip and an American and put in irons. The punishment by itself was a small thing; but, on their arrival in San Francisco the act of insubordination could have serious consequences for the Maltese. However, he did not resist, doubtless being certain that the *Vancouver* would not reach its destination.

The captain and the engineer often spoke about the regrettable state of affairs. Harrison, truly anxious, thought of arresting Bob Gordon, who did not hide his intention of taking control of the vessel. But this could provoke an explosion because the second mate was supported by a large majority of the Kanakas. "Evidently," Harry Clifton replied, "this arrest will accomplish nothing. Bob Gordon will be freed by his supporters and we will be worse off than before."

"You are right, Harry," replied the captain. "I know only one way to get him out of the way! That is to put a bullet through his head! And if he persists, I will do just that, Harry! Ah! If only the wind and current weren't against us."

In fact, the wind continued to blow the *Vancouver* off route. The vessel often labored. Mrs. Clifton and her two youngest children did not leave their cabin. Harry Clifton judged it best not to tell his wife what was happening on board, not wanting to alarm her unnecessarily.

However, with the sea so rough and the wind so strong, the *Vancouver* was steered with the staysail and its two topsails lowered.[2] During the 21st, 22nd and 23rd of March no observation was possible. The sun was hidden by thick clouds and Captain Harrison no longer knew to which part of the north Pacific the storm had driven his vessel. This was a new concern to add to those he already had.

On the 25th of March, about noon, the sky was a bit improved. The wind shifted a quarter toward the west which favored the vessel's progress. The sun showed itself. The captain wanted to profit from it by making an observation, made more necessary by the fact that land appeared some thirty miles to the east.

Land in sight in this part of the Pacific where the most recent maps showed nothing? Captain Harrison was astonished. Had his vessel drifted as far north as the Aleutians? It was important to verify this. He shared this information with the engineer who was no less surprised than he was.

Captain Harrison took his sextant, went to the upper deck and waited for the sun to reach its highest point so he could make his observation and determine the exact moment of noon at this place.

It was then 11:50 and the captain placed his eye to the lens of the sextant when shouting erupted from the steerage.

Captain Harrison rushed to the front of the deck. At this moment, about thirty Kanakas overpowered the English and American sailors and rushed out of cover uttering terrible cries of rage. The freed Maltese was in their midst.

---

2. The staysail is forward three-cornered sail closest to the foresail mast, while the topsails are the square sails on the topmast

Captain Harrison, followed by the engineer, immediately descended to the bridge, surrounded by those seamen of his crew that had remained loyal to him.

Ten feet from them, in front of the main mast, the coarse rebellious Kanakas stopped. Most were armed with anspect bars, awls, and mooring hooks. They brandished these arms and their frightful shouting blended with the cries of the Maltese and the Negros. These Kanakas wanted nothing less than to seize the vessel. This revolt was the result of the intrigues of the second mate, Bob Gordon, who wanted to make the *Vancouver* a pirate ship.

Captain Harrison resolved to finish with this scoundrel. "Where is the second mate?" he demanded.

No one answered. "Where is Bob Gordon?" he repeated.

One man moved out from the mutineers. It was Bob Gordon. "Why are you not on the side of your captain?" Harrison asked him.

"There is no other captain on board but me!" the second mate responded insolently.

"You wretch!" shouted Harrison.

"Seize this man," said Bob Gordon, pointing out the captain to the mutineers.

But Harrison, advancing a step, took his pistol from its holder, aimed at the second mate, and fired.

Bob Gordon moved aside and the bullet was lost in a wall.

The pistol firing was the signal for a general revolt. The Kanakas, incited by the second mate, rushed toward the small group surrounding the captain. It was a frightful scuffle whose outcome could not be in doubt. Mrs. Clifton was frightened and rushed out of the cabin with her children. The English and American mates had been seized and disarmed. When the crowd thinned, a corpse was slumped on the bridge. It was that of Captain Harrison, mortally wounded by the Maltese.

Harry Clifton wanted to rush on the second mate, but Bob Gordon held him down firmly and, on his order, was locked in his cabin with his dog, Fido.

"Harry! Harry!" Mrs. Clifton shouted, joined by her children's cries.

Harry Clifton could not resist. Judge his despair when he thought of his wife and his children at the mercy of this furious band... A few moments later he was imprisoned in his cabin.

From *Les Histoires de Jean-Marie Cabidoulin* (*The Yarns of Jean-Marie Cabidoulin*, 1901)

Bob Gordon then found himself master of the vessel. The *Vancouver* had fallen into his power. He could do whatever he wished with it. The Clifton family was a nuisance on board and the measures to be taken against the unfortunates would barely inconvenience anyone's scruples.

At one o'clock the vessel was nearing a land twenty miles windward. A lifeboat was brought out and thrown into the sea. The crew threw in two oars, a mast, a sail, a sack of biscuits and some pieces of salted meat. Flip followed these preparations, having been left at liberty. What could he, alone, do against the crowd?

When the boat was ready, Bob Gordon ordered Mrs. Clifton and her four children to embark, pointing first to the boat and then to the land.

The poor woman tried to sway the rascal. She cried and begged him not to separate her from her husband. But Bob Gordon banished her with a gesture. He would listen to nothing. Doubtless he wanted to deal with the engineer Clifton more firmly. He responded to the poor woman's prayers with only a single word: "Get in!"

Yes! Such was this rascal's design! He would abandon this woman and her four children in a frail craft on the high seas, knowing full well that without a sailor to guide them they would perish; as to his accomplices, as inflamed as he, they remained deaf to the prayers of the mother and the tears of the children! "Harry, Harry!" the poor woman repeated.

"Father! Father!" shouted the children.

The oldest, Marc, seized a rod, and rushed toward Bob Gordon but the latter brushed him aside, and soon the unfortunate family was dropped into the boat. Their cries were heartrending. Harry Clifton heard them from the cabin where he was imprisoned. His dog, Fido, responded with furious barks.

At this moment, at Bob Gordon's order, the rope that held the boat to the *Vancouver* was cast off and the vessel began to move away.

Valiant Marc, like a true sailor, stood at the helm in order to steady the boat, but the sail could not be hoisted. The boat, caught in a crosswind, threatened to founder.

Suddenly a body fell into the sea from the height of the poop deck of the *Vancouver*. It was the mate, Flip, who, throwing himself into the water, was swimming vigorously toward the boat in order to come to the aid of these abandoned people.

From *Seconde patrie* (*Second Homeland*, 1900)

Bob Gordon turned back. For a moment he thought of pursuing the fugitive. But he looked at the threatening sky. An evil smile was on his lips. He set up the foresail and the two top-gallants. Soon the *Vancouver* moved a considerable distance away from the boat which now only appeared as a point in space.

⊙

# Chapter III

**First moments—The storm—Flip's encouragements—They head toward the reefs—Aspect of the coast—Driven by the waves—Among the breakers—Flip uneasy—Landfall.**

Worthy Flip reached the boat a few fathoms away. Then skillfully and with perfect equilibrium he raised himself into the boat without tipping it. His clothes stuck to his body but that hardly bothered him. His first words were:

"Don't be afraid, my young lads, it is I!"

Then, speaking to Mrs. Clifton:

"We'll pull out of this together. We must be steadfast."

Then, speaking to Marc and Robert:

"Come and help me, my charming lads!"

Assigning a task to each, he hoisted the sail with the help of the two boys. He tightened the halyard [2], held the sail aft, took to the helm, and moved the boat close-hauled so as to approach the coast in spite of the contrary wind, but profiting from the rising tide.

Worthy Flip encouraged everyone in his small world, speaking with a confidence which came naturally to him, reassuring the mother, smiling at the children and watching over every motion of the boat. Nevertheless, he knit his brow, his lips contracted and an involuntary terror seized him when he saw the fragile boat, the coast still eight or ten miles in the distance, the unfavorable wind, and the threatening clouds above the horizon. He rightly said to himself that if they did not make landfall with this tide, they would perish!

After having asked again about her absent father, the young girl fell asleep again in her mother's arms, her brother also in slumber. The two older boys were active with the frequent tacking maneuvers. The unfortunate Mrs. Clifton thought of her husband separated from her and at the mercy of the mutineers. Her eyes filled with tears which fell on her children. She thought of the miserable fate that awaited them on this unknown coast, deserted perhaps, and perhaps inhabited by a cruel race! And yet they must land there or perish. In spite of her moral courage, she was left overwhelmed, unable to control her distress or give an example of courage or resignation. At each moment in the midst of her sobbing, the name Harry escaped from her lips.

But Flip was there. Mrs. Clifton pressed the hand of this brave man more than once. She said to herself that heaven would not abandon them since this devoted companion, this humble friend, was by her side.

During the trip on board the *Vancouver*, Flip had always exhibited great sympathy to her children, often taking pleasure in playing with them. Yes! the unfortunate woman said all that to herself but after looking again at the immense extent of the sea, more tears escaped from her eyes and sobs from her chest. Her head inclined on her hands and she remained inert, unconscious and overwhelmed.

At three o'clock in the afternoon, land showed itself distinctly, but it was at least five miles windward of the boat. Clouds were rising rapidly. The sun was setting in the west making the clouds appear still darker. The sea sparkled in places contrasting with the somber aspect of the sky. All these symptoms were frightening.

"Certainly," murmured Flip, "certainly, all this is bad. If I had a choice, I would choose better. Between a warm house with a good chimney and this boat, I would not hesitate, but I do not have a choice!"

At this moment a strong wave struck the boat crosswise covering it with water. Marc, standing in front, was struck by this wave and shook his head like a drenched dog.

"Good, Master Marc, very good Master Marc! It is only a bit of water, the good water of the sea, well salted! It cannot harm you!"

The skilful sailor moved his boat a bit to keep clear of the stronger waves. Resuming his monologue, he spoke to himself as usual, with these serious conjectures.

"If we were on land," he said to himself, "on this deserted land, instead of battling the waves in this nutshell, if we had a nice grotto to shelter us, that would be better, without doubt. But we are not there yet. We are on this sea that only wants to show us its rough character and we must endure it if we don't know how to avoid it."

The wind then blew with renewed violence. From afar they could see the breeze making a white foam on the ocean's surface, a liquid flowing above the large undulations. The boat then inclined to an alarming degree, which made the brave sailor knit his brow.

"Still," he resumed his thought, "since we have neither a house nor a grotto, still if we found ourselves on board a really solid vessel, well decked and able to resist the waves, we would have nothing to complain about. But no! Nothing but some fragile planks! However, as long as they don't break up, there's nothing to say. But, since this wind is so strong, this is not the time to control the sail with a rope!"

In fact, it became urgent to reduce sail immediately. The boat leaned over and threatened to fill with water. Flip put it standing into the wind, he unfurled the halyard, and with the help of the two boys, he put his sail on low reef. The boat, now less burdened, behaved better.

"Very well, my lads," shouted Flip. "Aren't these sails well designed? See how we fly across the waves! What could be better, I ask you?"

However, they were approaching the coast. Land birds were frolicking in the wind. Swallows and sea gulls swirled around the boat uttering sharp cries. Then, rising on an updraft, they flew away.

From *Le Chancellor* (*The Chancellor*, 1875)

The coast did not seem inviting. The land seemed arid and savage. There was not a tree and no vegetation brightened the background. It seemed made of high granite cliffs with the surf breaking against its base. The jagged rocks certainly made the shore inaccessible. Flip wondered how a boat could make landfall on this tightly enclosed tightly enclosed shore. There was not the smallest break in this curtain of granite. A high promontory, a mile to the south, hid the land behind it. They could not say whether this was a continent or an island. A mountain loomed up in the distance capped with a sharp peak of snow. From the distorted black rocks and the brown lava flows streaking across the mountain, a geologist would have assigned a volcanic origin to this land; he would have recognized it as a product of plutonian action. But this was not on Flip's mind as he searched this gigantic wall for a cove, an opening, any gap whatever to run his boat aground.

Mrs. Clifton lifted her head. She saw this barren land. She could not mistake its savage appearance and her eyes questioned the worthy sailor.

"A delightful shore! A delightful shore!" Flip murmured: "Beautiful rocks! Nature makes grottos with rocks like these, Madam! How comfortable we'll be once settled in some cavern with a good fire of dry wood and some soft moss to lie on!"

"But can we reach this coast?" Mrs. Clifton asked, casting a desperate look on the furious sea which raged around her.

"How is that! If we will reach it!" Flip responded, while skillfully dodging a large wave. "But look how fast we're moving! We have a good wind behind us and nothing in front of us, and we'll run aground in front of these high cliffs. I guarantee that once there we'll find a small natural port where our boat can take cover! Ah! What an excellent boat! She rose with the waves like a sea gull!"

Flip had barely finished speaking when a formidable wave washed across the entire boat and filled it three quarters with water. Mrs. Clifton screamed. Her two youngest children, suddenly awakened, pressed close to her. The two older boys, clinging to their seats held on when the wave struck them. Flip, with a quick movement of the helm, held the boat steady while shouting:

"Come, Marc, Robert, empty the water, empty the water! The boat! Empty the boat!"

And he tossed the boys his rawhide leather cap which could used in place of a baler. Marc and Robert went to work and quickly emptied the boat.

Flip encouraged them with gestures and with his talk: "Good, my lads! Very good! Hey! What an invention these hats are! Real cooking pots. We could boil our soup in them!"

The boat, now relieved, leaped anew over the waves. But the wind was now blowing from the west and it was so violent that Flip had to draw in his sail and tack the boat almost entirely to the end of the yard. The boat presented a small triangle of sail to the wind but that was sufficient.

Also, the coast was rapidly approaching and all its details were becoming distinct.

"A fine wind! a fine wind!" shouted Flip, all the while keeping an eye on the waves at the rear. "How it shifts to our advantage! It could be a little stronger, perhaps! But it will do as it pleases!"

At half past four the shore was barely a mile away. The boat seemed ready to dash against it. At every moment they thought they could touch it, an impression invariably produced when high lands appear submerged.

Soon Marc, who was at the stern, signaled black topped breakers which emerged in the surf. The sea was a foaming white. It was a moment of extreme danger; the boat had only to scrape these rocks and it would be dashed to pieces.

Flip stood up, steering with the helm between his legs. He searched for a passage among the foaming waves and, if he feared that the boat would break up at any moment, he did not let it show. On the contrary!

"These rocks are well designed!" he said. "I would say that these lifebuoys mark out a channel! We will pass through, we will pass through!"

The boat flew past the reefs at a frightful speed, the wind driving it headlong against an unbroken coast. Flip skimmed past the foaming rocks but he did not collide with them; he passed over the black patches which marked the shallows without touching them. His sailor's instinct guided him through these dangers, a marvelous instinct which is superior even to nautical science.

Flip then signaled the two lads to draw in the sail completely. They pressed it around the yard. The boat, driven by the wind, still moved at an excessive speed.

The question of a landing place still remained. Flip saw no opening among these high cliffs, closed tight like a fortified wall. To land at their base with a high sea was impractical. But barely two hundred fathoms separated the boat from the shore. He would have to move further along the coast if he could not land here.

Flip became anxious. While knitting his brows, he looked at this inaccessible land and mumbled some unintelligible words between his teeth. Already, with a tilt of the helm, he had slightly modified the movement of the boat and it changed direction rather than run to shore. But, in this situation, the boat went abeam, shipping water which Marc and Robert emptied with the leather hat.

Flip stood up on his seat. He tried to discover any opening whatsoever, a break in these cliffs, or at least a bit of shore on which to run aground. The tide being high, he could hope to drop the boat on dry sand. But still nothing. Always this high wall rising to a phenomenal height.

Mrs. Clifton also surveyed the shore. She understood the dangers of going aground. She plainly saw that this land, their only refuge, was inaccessible. But she did not dare to speak. She did not dare to question Flip.

Suddenly the sailor became animated and his confidence returned in a flash.

"A harbor!" he simply said.

In fact, a break appeared among the cliffs which seemed to have been separated by some powerful geological effort. The sea thrust into a small cove between the cliffs forming a rather sharp corner. Flip also saw that it was the mouth of a river into which the rising tide flowed.

Flip directed the boat towards the cove's entrance and, traversing it for a few hundred meters, he gently ran aground on a sandy beach.

# Chapter IV

**The unfortunates finally reach land! They touch solid ground! They have escaped the dangers of the ocean. But what awaits them on this shore? What resources does it offer?**

Flip jumped to shore. Marc and Robert followed him and together the three towed the boat onto the sand. Besides, the tide was going down and the boat was soon high and dry.

Flip took the two young children in his arms, put them on the sand, then he helped Mrs. Clifton step off the boat. The worthy sailor could not hide his joy on walking on this solid shore.

"All goes well, Madam," he repeated, "all goes well. We have only to settle in!"

The place where chance had left them was situated on the left bank of a river a hundred feet wide at this point. The sandy shore was rather narrow, not measuring more than twenty five feet. It was wedged in between the watercourse and the high granite wall. This wall, which was a continuation of cliffs on the coast, followed the left bank of the river and gradually sloped lower. At the landing site, its height was still more than three hundred feet. It was nearly straight and even vertical in some places. Thus, it was impossible to climb this face: Flip found this annoying because he wanted to survey the surrounding countryside from the top.

First he looked for some cavity or hole where the family could find shelter from the menacing rain on this first night. He searched along the granite wall but to his bitter disappointment he could not find the smallest grotto which could serve as a temporary encampment. The block was solid throughout and did not show the smallest crack. In one place, on the beach where the boat had run aground, tidal action had hollowed out a little shelter which gave some protection against the westerly winds blowing at the moment but it was an insufficient refuge which would become uninhabitable if the wind should shift even a quarter toward the north. Flip resolved to walk up river for several hundred feet to see what he could find. He told Mrs. Clifton about his plan.

"Do not be afraid, Madam," he told her. "I will not go far. I have tall legs and I will return promptly. Besides, your children will not leave you. You will watch your mother, Marc?"

"Yes, Flip," replied the young lad, who displayed an energy truly superior for his age.

"I am leaving then," said Flip. "Since I will go and return by the left bank, you cannot mistake the route if you have to go to meet me."

Flip conducted Mrs. Clifton and her two youngest children to the hollow he had found. Mother, Belle and Jack huddled there, while Marc and Robert stood watch on the beach. Night was coming on. They heard only the whistling of the wind, the noise of the surf, and the cries of the birds nesting high above in the massif.

Having settled his small world, Flip moved quickly. He followed the foot of the cliff which became lower bit by bit. After a half mile it reached the ground with a steep slope. Here the river measured only sixty to sixty five feet across. The right bank showed about the same layout as the left bank being limited by a rocky cliff.

Arriving at end of the wall, Flip saw a less savage countryside. There were green pastures which extended to the edge of some forest blurred by the oncoming darkness. "Good!" thought the sailor. "There will be no lack of firewood."

Flip went to the woods to get some firewood; as to a shelter, he could find nothing. He had to be content, for this night at least, with the temporary encampment. The sailor reached the edge of the forest. The view was blocked on the right. He noted the unevenness of the ground as it rose to a higher level toward an obscure interior. This land was dominated by a peak thirty miles in the distance whose presence first alerted the sailors of the *Vancouver* to this unknown land.

While tying the fagots, Flip thought about ways to manage the affairs of this family to which he was devoted. The question of an encampment preoccupied him.

From *Seconde patrie* (*Second Homeland*, 1900)

"After all," he repeated to himself, "we have plenty of time. We need not settle in at the shore. What we need first is fire, and to make a good fire: a good flammable wood."

It was easy to harvest it since a large quantity of dead wood, thrown down by storms, littered the ground. What species this wood was, Flip could not say, but he was content to assign it to the category of "burning wood," the only one which suited him at the moment.

But if there was no lack of fuel, there was no way to transport it. All the load Flip could carry—and he was a strong man—was not enough for one night. However, he must hurry. The sun had disappeared in the west behind some large red clouds. The atmospheric moisture, less harassed by the wind, condensed and rain began to fall. But Flip did not want to return without enough wood. "There must be a way to transport this load," he said to himself. "There is always a way to do everything! I have only find it. Ah! If I had a handcart, I would have no problem! What could take the place of a handcart? A boat? But I don't have a boat!"

Flip gathered his wood while immersed in thought. "But if I don't have a boat, I have the river, a river that moves itself. And floating rafts were not invented not to be used!"

Flip was enchanted with his idea. He loaded his shoulders with wood and went back to the river not one hundred meters away. There the sailor found still more dead wood. He gathered it and began to make a raft.

In a sort of eddy produced at one point of the bank which broke the current, Flip placed the largest pieces of wood and tied them together with dry creepers. He formed a raft on which he piled his harvest, a load for ten men. If the cargo arrived safely, there would be no lack of fuel.

In a half hour Flip finished his work. The sailor did not plan to float the raft in the river unattended, and neither did he intend to get on board to steer it. He would control it the way children do with their

From *Seconde patrie* (*Second Homeland*, 1900)

toy sailboats. But the cord? Doesn't every sailor have a belt around his body several fathoms long? He detached it while remarking to himself, and not without good reason, that belts had been specifically invented for towing wooden rafts. He attached it to the rear of his raft and by means of a long pole he shoved his apparatus into the current.

Everything went as hoped. The large load of wood that Flip held in check followed the river's current. The bank was steep so there was no fear that the raft would run aground. A few minutes after six Flip arrived at the landing place where he moored his floating train.

Mother and children ran up to him.

"Yes, Madam!" Flip shouted with joy, "I can bring you an entire forest and there will be more left over, believe me. No need to economize. The wood costs nothing."

"But what kind of land are we on?"... Mrs. Clifton asked.

"Oh! Very pleasant!" replied the worthy sailor, unruffled. "You will see that in full daylight. The trees are magnificent. When everything blooms, the countryside will be charming."

"But what about our house?" Belle asked.

"Our house? my dear little girl. We will make a house and you will help us."

"But what about today?" said Mrs. Clifton.

"Today, Madam," replied Flip, somewhat embarrassed. "Today we must stay where we are! I still have not found even the smallest grotto! The cliff is smooth like a new wall. But tomorrow, in full daylight, we will find what we need. Meanwhile, let us make some fire. It will clear our minds."

Marc and Robert began to unload the raft and soon the entire cargo was on the ground at the foot of the cliff. Flip chopped away like a man who knew his business. Mrs. Clifton and her two young children, crouching in the hollow, looked on.

When Flip finished, he reached into his pocket for his match box which was always with him because he was a confirmed smoker. He rummaged through his large pants pockets and to his deep amazement he could not find the box.

A shiver ran through his entire body. Mrs. Clifton stared at him without blinking.

"Imbecile!" he said, shrugging his shoulders, "my matches are in my jacket pocket."

His jacket was in the boat. Flip went on board, took the jacket and turned it inside out, no box.

The sailor paled. Perhaps the match box fell inside the boat when he covered the children with his jacket.

He searched the boat, rummaged through all the corners, under the small deck, between the frames. Nothing. Evidently the box was lost.

The situation was serious. The loss of this box was irreparable. Without fire, what would become of them? Flip could not hide his disappointment. Mrs. Clifton understood everything and went to his side. Without matches how could they make a fire? Flip could easily make flint sparks with his knife but he had no amadou. Burnt linen could replace amadou but he needed fire to get that. As to the method the savages use to make fire by rubbing two pieces of dry wood, he had to forget about that also not only because a special wood is needed which he didn't have, but also because he didn't have experience with it.

Flip remained thoughtful not daring to look at Mrs. Clifton with her unfortunate shivering children. She returned to the foot of the cliff.

"Well, Flip?" Marc said to the sailor.

"We have no matches, Marc!" Flip replied, lowering his voice.

Marc picked up the jacket. He turned it every which way. He rummaged through the inner and outer pockets. Suddenly he shouted.

"A match!" he said.

"Ah! One, a single one!" shouted the sailor, "and we are saved!"

Flip took his jacket and, as Marc had done, he felt a little piece of wood stuck in the lining. His large hands trembled. They clutched at the little piece of wood through the material without being able to pull it out. Mrs. Clifton came over.

"Give it to me, my friend!" she told him.

Then, taking the jacket, she removed the little piece of wood.

"A match!" Flip shouted! "It is a real match with sulfur and phosphorous! Ah! It as good as an entire cargo!"

And the courageous sailor jumped for joy, embracing the children and hiding the tears flowing from his eyes.

"Ah, so!" he said. "We have a match, that's good, but we must use it carefully and think twice before making a move."

That said, Flip carefully examined his single match and quickly assured himself that it was really dry. Then, that done:

"We need some paper," he said.

"Here it is," Robert replied.

Flip took the paper the young lad gave him and went toward the wood pile. He took additional precautions and crammed in a few handfuls of dry grass and moss gathered at the foot of the cliff. He arranged it so the air could circulate easily and quickly ignite the dead wood; then he rolled the paper into a cone the way smokers do in a high wind.

Next he took the match and picked up a dry stone, a rough pebble on which to rub the phosphorous. Then, crouching at the foot of the cliff, in a well protected corner, while Marc held his hat a short distance from the wall as an added precaution, he gently rubbed the match on the stone.

The first rubbing produced no effect. Flip had not applied enough pressure. But the poor man was afraid to rub off the phosphorous. He held his breath and could hear his heart beating.

He rubbed his match a second time. A weak blue flame spurted out producing a pungent smoke. Flip introduced the match into the paper cone. The paper caught fire a few seconds later and Flip introduced it under the hearth of grass and moss. A moment later the wood crackled, and a joyful flame, activated by the breeze, developed in the midst of the darkness.

# Chapter V

In front of this clear sparkling fire, the children shouted with pleasure. Belle and Jack opened their small pink hands to the flame. With this fireplace they considered themselves rescued. The present is everything at this age. Neither the past nor the future concerns them.

It must be said that the health of the abandoned family depended in part on this fire. Without fire, what would become of them? Flip, faithful Flip, had been overcome by the emotion he felt when he tried that last match. But this fire must never burn out; they must always keep some cinders to rekindle it. This needed only care and attention. At the moment they had enough wood and Flip promised to renew it on a timely basis.

"Now," he said, "let's go to supper."

"Yes! Let's eat," shouted Jack.

"There's no shortage of biscuit and meat! Let's live on what we have. Later we'll find what we don't have."

Flip went to the boat to look for the small reserve of food. Mrs. Clifton accompanied him.

"But afterwards, Flip?" she asked him, showing the sailor the sack of biscuit and salted meat.

"Later we will see, Madam," replied Flip. "From afar this land seemed barren but on the contrary, it is fertile. I saw this during my walk in the forest. This island will be able to support our little colony."

"Yes, my friend Flip; but we are abandoned without arms, without tools..."

"Arms we will make, Madam, and as to tools... Don't I have my knife? See—a fine "bowie knife" with a large blade. With this very instrument a man is never at a loss!"

Flip spoke with conviction, with such assurance and confidence in the future that the unfortunate Mrs. Clifton began to take hope.

"Yes, Madam," the sailor repeated while going back to the fire which sparkled at the foot of the cliff, "you should know that with a knife, a simple knife, we can make a house of wood or a boat! Yes, a vessel of a hundred tons! I could supervise the work from the keel to the top of the masts, given enough time of course."

"I believe you, my brave Flip," Mrs. Clifton replied. "but how can we replace the pot or the kettle we don't have? How can we prepare a warm beverage for these children to refresh them?"

"Tonight will be bad," replied the sailor, "but tomorrow we will find some coconuts or some gourds and I'll make you some things for the kitchen."

"And some vases that can be heated?" Mrs. Clifton asked.

"If the fire cannot go underneath the pot, it will go inside the pot," the sailor replied, "which will amount to the same thing. We will do what the savages do; we will heat some stones and these stones we will put into our gourds filled with water and we will get boiling water. Have confidence, Madam, have confidence! You will be astonished at what we can do when we have to."

Mrs. Clifton and Flip joined the children who were poking at the fire; the smoke was twirling higher in the dark, sending up a shower of sparkles. It was like fireworks and it filled the two younger children with wonder. Jack took a lighted stick and amused himself by tracing circles in the air. Marc and Robert set aside enough wood for the night. Mrs. Clifton prepared supper and soon everyone had a share of biscuit and salted meat. As for a beverage, it was water from the river, the tide having gone down sufficiently so that the water lost its bitterness.

Nevertheless, Flip was uneasy seeing the family without good shelter on this rainy night. He decided to visit the western face of the cliff that formed the coastline. He hoped to find some cavity hollowed out by the high winds but out of reach of the waves. The high tide had receded. Flip went along the shore to the mouth of the river, turned left, and followed the beach which extended between the high wall and the breakers. For several hundred meters he carefully examined this rocky substructure but its surface, smooth and polished by the waves, showed no opening.

Flip then returned, absorbed in thought, and nibbled on a piece of biscuit.

"They need a nest!" he thought.

A nest, in fact. Rain was already falling in fine droplets. The high winds pulverized the condensed vapors. Thick clouds made the night even darker. The heard the sea growling on the reef. The surf sounded like thunder.

Flip was not mistaken about these signs. He thought about the mother and these young children who would be chilled by the rain and frost. The wind shifted a little to the west and it was evident that the cliff would no longer protect

From *Les Naufragés du Jonathan*
(*The Survivors of the Jonathan*, 1909)

the encampment. The situation was becoming unbearable!

The worthy sailor, disconcerted, returned to the Clifton family. The children finished their meal, mother placed Jack and Belle on a bed of sand at the foot of the wall; but she could not keep the wind and rain away. Her eyes turned to Flip and she questioned him so intently that the honest sailor could not mistake her look.

Marc shared his mother's anxieties. He looked at the thick low clouds and held out his hand to see if the rain was getting heavier. At this moment he got an idea because he ran straight to Flip.

"Flip," he said.

"Marc."

"What about the boat!"

"The boat!" shouted the sailor. "The boat turned over! That's a roof! The house will come later! Come, my lads, Come!"

Marc, Robert, Mrs. Clifton and Flip ran to the boat! Flip declared Marc an industrious lad. He was a son worthy of an engineer! The boat turned over! He had not thought of that, he, Flip, with all his experience.

They had to bring the boat to the foot of the cliff to use the wall itself as a support. Fortunately it was a light boat made of fir, measuring but twelve feet long and four across. If they pulled together then Flip, the two boys, and Mrs. Clifton could drag it to the sand at the encampment. Flip, a strong fellow, braced himself on his knees and shoved with his shoulders the way fishermen do, giving the boat its initial thrust. It reached its destination in a few moments.

There, at small hollows in the wall, Flip set up two piles of large rocks, intended to support the two ends of the boat at a height of two feet above the ground. That done, the boat was overturned with the keel in the air. Already Jack and Belle wanted to dash underneath but Flip stopped them.

"Just a minute," he said, "what is it that fell there on the sand?"

In fact, while the boat was turned over, something rolled to the ground making a metallic sound. Flip bent over and got hold of it.

"Good!" he shouted. "We are rich."

And he showed an old iron kettle, a utensil so dear to every American and English sailor. The kettle was damaged, as Flip saw when he examined it near the fire, but it could still hold five to six pints of liquid. This was a priceless utensil for the Clifton family. "All goes well! All goes well!" the happy Master Flip repeated, "a knife, a kettle! We are well stocked. The dinners at the White House are not served better than ours!"

The overturned boat was then edged closer to the stone supports. The bow was soon resting on the right pile but it was quite an affair to get the rear up without a hoist or a screw jack.

"Bah! My lads" he said to the boys who were helping him, "when one is not strong he must be smart."

And little by little, by sliding thin wedge shaped pebbles under each other, Flip was able to bring the stern to the level of the bow. The left gunwale leaned against the cliff. To make this improvised shelter even more waterproof, Flip wrapped the sail around the sides of the boat making it reach the ground. This made it like a tent with a solid roof giving protection from the high winds.

In addition, Flip dug up the sand underneath the boat, throwing it outside and forming a weather stripping to keep out the rain.

In a few moments the children and he gathered a large quantity of moss which carpeted the lower part of the cliff, a sort of brownish androecium, which formed an excellent rock moss; it was a natural eiderdown which changed the sand on the ground into a soft bed. Flip, enchanted, did not stop talking about it.

"It's a house! A real house!" he repeated "and I begin to believe that we are mistaken about the purpose of boats: they are roofs except that we turn them over for indoor sailing! Come children, to the nest, to the nest."

"But who will watch the fire?" Mrs. Clifton asked.

"Me, me!" Marc and Robert said simultaneously.

"No, my young friends, don't argue," the honorable Flip replied, "let me have this task during our first night. Later we will organize our schedule."

Mrs. Clifton wanted to share this task with Flip, but the sailor would not hear of it and she had to obey him.

Before going inside the boat, the children huddled around their mother; they prayed for their missing father and invoked the help of Providence. Then after having embraced Mrs. Clifton and the good Flip, after having embraced each other, they snuggled up on their bed of moss. Mother shook hands with Flip and went into the boat in her turn. The attentive sailor watched this precious fire throughout the night while the rain and wind threatened to extinguish it!

# Chapter VI

The night passed without incident. It stopped raining about three in the morning. Mrs. Clifton's troubles had kept her awake. At daybreak she left the boat. Her children were sleeping soundly. She wanted to take Flip's place and the sailor, for better or for worse, had to get some rest under the boat for several hours.

At seven o'clock, Flip was awakened by the noisy children. They were already running around the beach. Mrs. Clifton was getting the younger children ready, washing them in the sweet water of the river. Jack, who was ordinarily unmanageable during this operation, did not resist this time. It was a real river and more amusing than a washbowl.

When Flip left his bed of sand and moss, he saw with satisfaction that the sky was serene. The clouds, high and scattered, showed large patches of blue sky. This fine weather favored Flip's plans for the day which were to explore the surrounding countryside.

"How are you today, my children?" he shouted with a happy voice. "And you, Miss Belle and you, Mrs. Clifton? And I was the last to get up, at my age!"

"Weren't you on the watch all night, friend Flip?" replied Mrs. Clifton, extending her hand to her worthy companion. "You barely slept two hours."

"That is enough for me, dear lady," replied Flip... "Ah! Talking about the household chores, there is the kettle already on the fire! But if you do everything by yourself, Mistress Clifton, what's left for me?"

While speaking, Flip approached the fire on which the old kettle was suspended between two rocks already blackened by the flames. Sparks were flying about.

"Hey! What water! What beautiful water!" Flip shouted, not sparing any admiration. "It is a pleasure to watch it! It chirps like a bird! So we don't have a few tea leaves or some coffee grains for a nice beverage; that will come in time! Come, my children, who wants to go with me to look around?"

"We, we!" the three boys shouted.

"Me too, I want to go with papa Flip," the young girl said.

"Good," replied the sailor, "My only problem is that I have too great a choice."

"Are you going far, Flip?" Mrs. Clifton asked.

"We will not go far, my dear lady, only a few hundred feet. Marc, Robert and I will explore the countryside."

"We are ready," said the two lads.

"As to Jack, he is a big boy we can depend on. I hope he will keep an eye on the fire while we are away and especially that he won't spare any wood."

"Yes! Yes!" shouted Jack, excited about the task assigned to him. "Belle will hand me the pieces of wood and I will throw them into the fire."

Already Marc and Robert were out on the road walking along the left bank of the river.

"You will be back soon?" said Mrs. Clifton.

"In an hour, Madame," replied the sailor. "I ask only for enough time to turn the cliff to examine the inlet where we landed yesterday. We will fail if we don't bring you back something to eat so we can economize on our meat and our biscuit."

"Go then, friend Flip. And if you get to the top of the cliff," Mrs. Clifton added with tears in her eyes, "look out to sea…"

"Yes! I understand, my dear lady! I have good vision! I will look! This is not the end of the matter and perhaps Mr. Clifton... Take hope, have faith, Madame, you must set an example of courage and resignation for us. Have confidence. Ah! The fire! The fire comes first! I believe that Master Jack will not let it burn out but keep an eye on it from time to time. I am going, I am going!"

That said, Flip took leave of Mrs. Clifton and soon joined his two young companions at the mouth of the river.

At this place, the cliff made an abrupt turnaround itself and ended in a sharp corner. It then ran north and south forming an elevated shore. The tide began to go down leaving behind a rocky and sandy dry beach which was easy to walk on.

"Won't we be blocked by the rising tide later?" asked Marc.

"No, my boy," replied Flip. "The ebb tide[1] is just starting and the sea will not be high again until six o'clock tonight. While crossing the beach, look around the rocks. Nature may have placed some good things here and there which we can use to our profit. As for me, I'll be looking for a ramp to help me climb this cliff but I will not lose sight of you, don't worry!"

Marc and Robert separated. Marc, being more observant, walked carefully and examined the beach and the cliff. Robert, being impatient, jumped around the rocks and leaped over the water puddles at the risk of slipping on the clumps of wrack.

While Flip went southward along the beach, he kept his eye on the two boys. The high wall continued for a quarter of a mile, always with the same uniformity and the same perpendicularity. Near the top of the cliff all kinds of sea birds fluttered about in particular various web footed species with long, compressed, pointed beaks, who were squalling and hardly afraid of the presence of man who, for the first time no doubt, was disturbing their solitude. Among these web-footers, Flip recognized several skua, a sort of sea gull, which are sometimes called stercorarius and also the voracious little sea mews which nested in the crevices in the granite. A gunshot fired into this swarm of birds would have killed a great number. But Flip had no gun and besides, these sea mews and these gulls are scarcely edible and even their eggs have a detestable taste.

Flip saw that the cliff extended yet another two miles to the south. It ended abruptly with a promontory covered by the surf's white foam. If they wanted to turn the promontory, would they have to wait another hour for low tide? This is what Flip asked himself when he found an opening in the wall produce by a rock fall.

"Here is a natural staircase," he thought. "I must use it to get to the top where I can observe both land and sea."

Flip began his ascension on the fallen rocks and thanks to his strong legs and his uncommon skill he reached the crest of the wall in a few minutes.

On arriving, his first care was to cast a glance at this land that developed before him. Three or four leagues away there rose a large snow covered peak. The area extending two miles from the shore up to the first ramps of the mountain was covered by vast woods with patches of taller evergreens. There was a green pasture bristling with clumps of trees at random between the forest and the wall of the shore. On his left, granite rocks were piled up in tiers along the right bank of the river, enclosing the horizon so he could not see beyond them. But toward the south, the wall receded in height, changing to isolated rocks, then sand dunes for a distance of several miles. There, the view was hidden by a cape boldly projecting into the sea. Did the land run east or west in back of the cape? Was it part of a continent? On the contrary, was the land rounded in the east making it merely an island on which chance had thrown this abandoned family?

Flip could not answer this important question putting it off for another time. As to the land itself, island or continent, it seemed to be fertile, pleasing in appearance, and varied in its output so one could not ask anything more of it.

After this quick look, the sailor turned his attention to the ocean. He looked at the sandy beach bordered by the breakers. At low tide, the emerged rocks resembled groups of amphibians sluggishly lying in the surf. Flip saw the two young boys who seemed to be searching for something among the rocks.

"They discovered something," Flip thought. "If it was Mister Jack or Mademoiselle Belle down there, I believe they would be gathering sea shells, but Mister Marc is a serious young man, so he and his brother are occupied with increasing our food supply!"

Beyond the reefs battered by the surf, the sea scintillated under the oblique rays of the sun which grazed the elevated ground of the shoreline. On this sea, this vast liquid surface, not a sail, not a craft in sight, nothing remaining of the passage of the *Vancouver*! Nothing to hint at the fate of the unfortunate Harry Clifton!

Flip took a last look at the beach below. He noticed an oblong islet offshore, a mile long, whose northern end was almost in line with the river and whose southern end was flush with the end of the cliff. Perhaps this end of the islet even extended further. This arid islet was rather higher than the waves so it protected the shoreline from the open sea. This left a tranquil channel between them in which vessels could easily find shelter.

After Flip carefully examined the countryside he thought of rejoining his young companions. They saw him and motioned for him to come down. Flip came down via the fallen rocks, leaving a complete exploration of the interior for another day. When he set foot on the beach, he came over to Marc and Robert.

"Come here, Flip," they shouted impatiently, "Come here. We collected a fine pile of edible mollusks."

"Which are edible and which we will eat," replied Flip, looking on as one of the boys used his teeth to detach some appetizing mollusks enclosed in a double valve.

"As for what's left, Flip, there's more than we can ever eat. Look at these rocks. They're covered completely and we can be sure we'll never die of hunger."

In fact, the rocks uncovered by the ebb tide were covered with oblong mollusks, firmly attached to the rock in clusters among the clumps of wrack.

"These are mussels," Marc said, "excellent mussels; I just noticed that they bore holes into the rock that supports them."

"Then they are not mussels," replied the sailor.

"I protest," Robert shouted, "the evidence of the eyes agrees with the taste."

"I repeat, Mister Robert," Flip replied; "It is a very common mollusk in the Mediterranean, but a little less widespread in American seas. I have eaten it so often that I can claim to know something about it. I guarantee that when you munch on these mollusks you will find they have a strong pepper flavor."

"That's right," Marc replied.

"Besides, notice that these valves form an oblong mollusk, nearly equally rounded at both ends, which is not found in the ordinary mussel. These mollusks are called lithodomes, but they are none the less good for us."

"Also," Robert said, "We have collected an ample supply for our mother. Let's leave!" the lad added, wishing he was back at the encampment.

"Hey, don't run so fast," Flip shouted on seeing Robert bolting across the rocks; but nothing came of his suggestion.

"Let him go," said Marc. "Our mother will be at ease that much sooner when she sees him return."

However, Marc and Flip returned to the shore and walked along the base of the cliff. It was about eight o'clock in the morning. The two explorers had no lack of appetite and a substantial meal would have met with universal approval. But these mollusks are not rich in protein. And Flip regretted that he could not bring Mrs. Clifton something more nourishing. But it was difficult to catch a fish without a string or a line or to catch some game without a gun or some noose. Fortunately, on following the granite wall, Marc found a half dozen bird's nests in the cracks on the lower sections of the granite.

"Good," said the sailor, "these birds are not sea gulls. See, Mister Marc, how they fly away at top speed! If I am not mistaken, this game is excellent to eat."

"What are these birds?" Marc asked.

"I recognize them by the double black band on their wings, by their white rump and their ashen blue plumage. They are wild pigeons also called rock pigeons. Later we will try to domesticate this species for our future poultry yard. But if the rock pigeon is good to eat, its eggs cannot be bad and if they would only let us get into their nest!..."

While speaking, Flip approached some of the cavities from which frightened pigeons were escaping. In one cavity he found about a dozen eggs which he carefully placed in his handkerchief. Decidedly, breakfast was complete. Marc gathered a few handfuls of salt from the rock hollows where the sea water had evaporated. They went back to the encampment.

A quarter of an hour after Robert returned, Flip and Marc rounded the corner of the cliff and saw the entire colony gathered around a sparkling blaze with a plume of smoke twirling into the air. The newcomers were welcomed. Mrs. Clifton had placed the kettle on the fire and soon the mollusks were gently cooking in several pints of sea water which would pep up its flavor. As to the pigeon eggs, they were greeted with joy by the two young children. Little Belle first wanted an egg cup; but Flip, not having one to give her, consoled her by promising to pick one off a tree that grew egg cups. This time they had to be content with hardening the eggs under the hot cinders.

Breakfast was soon ready. The fully cooked mollusks gave off an excellent sea odor. Even soup plates were not missing; because Mrs. Clifton had gathered a few dozen large sea shells to replace them. When the kettle was empty, Marc went to fill it with fresh water from the river. As usual, Flip livened things up by talking about his plans for the future, making a castaway's life seem enviable. It goes without saying that no one touched the biscuit or the salted meat, reserving it for extreme circumstances.

With breakfast over, Mrs. Clifton and Flip talked about improving their situation. It was indispensable to find a more secure shelter. This search would necessitate a serious exploration of the cliff. But Flip put this exploration off for the next day. He did not want to go far on this first day leaving Mrs. Clifton alone with her children. Besides, he wanted to keep up the supply of fuel.

He returned to the forest by way of the right bank of the river. He carried back several loads of wood using the raft. He even took the precaution of lighting two distinct fires so they would not be deprived in case one of them was extinguished.

The second day thus passed. Lithodomes and more eggs, gathered by Flip and Robert, assured the evening meal. Then night came on, a starry night, which the family passed under the shelter of the boat. Mrs. Clifton and Flip took turns in watching the fires. Nothing troubled their tranquility except for the distant howling of some wild beasts who once again frightened the poor mother!

# Chapter VII

The next day, the 27th of March, everyone was on foot at daybreak. The weather was fine, but a bit chilly. It was an opportune time for an excursion to the interior and Flip resolved not to postpone this important exploration. To survey the land, the nature of the resources within it, what the castaways could expect from it, to know if it was inhabited or not, to decide once and for all if the Clifton family could settle here, these were serious questions that must be resolved as soon as possible. As to this other no less interesting question to determine if this was an island or a continent, Flip did not expect to find the answer during this initial expedition. It probably was not an island, at least not a small island. The height of the peak and the buttresses that supported it made that unlikely. Certainly, if they could climb the mountain, they would probably know what they could count on; but the ascension of the mountain would have to be attempted later; they must think first of the most pressing matters; food and lodging.

Flip, making his plans known, obtained Mrs. Clifton's approval. As a strong and courageous woman, she was able to control her sorrow. She placed her confidence in God, in herself, and in Flip, knowing that providence would not abandon them. When the worthy sailor consulted her on the necessity for this exploration of the interior, she well understood that her two youngest children could not join the expedition and that she must remain alone with them. A vivid emotion seized her heart at this thought, but she surmounted it and replied that Flip must leave without delay.

"Very well, Madam!" Flip replied, "let us start breakfast and we will decide later which of the young gentlemen will accompany me!"

"Me! Me!" Marc and Robert shouted.

But Flip announced that only one of the two older boys would accompany him with the other guarding the family during his absence. And, while saying this, Flip looked at Marc in a way that the brave boy could not mistake. He understood that it was incumbent on him, as the oldest, to watch over his mother, his brother and his sister. This child was the head of the family; better suited than impetuous Robert, he understood the gravity of the situation and the responsibility placed upon him. Flip did not need to say another word.

"I will stay with you, Mother. I am the oldest and I will watch our camp while Flip is away."

Marc chose his words well because Mrs. Clifton began to cry.

"A thousand devils!" shouted the worthy sailor, becoming emotional. "You are a brave boy, Mister Marc, and I would like to embrace you."

Marc ran into Flip's arms and pressed against his chest.

"And now, let's eat," he said.

It was seven in the morning. They ate lightly. Mrs. Clifton did not want the explorers to leave without sufficient provisions for the trip. She insisted that they take some of the biscuit and salted meat. Flip had to give in, but the question of food did not worry him. He counted on nature to provide. He regretted only one thing, that they didn't have the proper weapons. How could they hunt for game without weapons or protect themselves against attacks from men or wild beasts? He cut off two sticks, sharpened one end and hardened them in fire. No doubt a primitive device but a formidable weapon in Flip's hands. With his stick on his shoulder, Robert assumed a challenging posture which made his brother smile.

It was agreed that Mrs. Clifton and the children would not roam far; Marc would go along the shore only to gather more mollusks and pigeon eggs; but, with Flip's express instructions: watch the fire, watch it constantly. Marc and his mother were especially directed to keep up the fire.

At eight o'clock, Robert embraced Mrs. Clifton, his brothers and his sister. They were ready to leave. Flip shook their hands, he reminded them again of their duties, and he started off along the left bank of the river. He did not pause when he reached the place where he had constructed the raft. Little by little the river narrowed and the grassy banks became hemmed in. The right bank was bordered by a granite cliff which was higher than the cliff on the other side and it extended beyond the forest. They would not be able to survey the countryside toward the north. But Flip could explore the right bank of the watercourse at a later time, limiting this exploration to the south countryside.

At a mile from the encampment, Flip and his young companion saw that the river disappeared under the double arch of the forest. The evergreen trees presented a gloomy appearance. They must now cross the woods and Robert, always impatient, wanted to run on ahead, but Flip suggested that he should not leave him.

"We do not know what we will encounter in this forest," he said. "I beg you then, Mister Robert, not to go far from me."

"But I am not afraid!" the young lad replied, waving his sharp stick.

"I know that," the sailor replied with a smile, "but I will be scared if you leave me alone."

Without abandoning the path formed by the bank, both entered under the dome of trees. Fresh water flowed on their left. The sun, already high in the sky, traced shadows of the foliage across the dark river. Flip and Robert did not follow the riverbank without encountering a few obstacles, here some bent trees with stumps soaked in the river, there some creepers or thorns which they broke with a stick or the knife. Robert often pranced about the broken branches with the agility of a young cat, and he disappeared into the forest, but Flip called him back.

"Mister Robert," he shouted.

"Here I am, here I am, Mister Flip," the young lad replied, showing himself through the shrubs with his face red as a peony flower.

Nevertheless, Flip surveyed the surrounding area. The soil was flat on the left bank of the river; wet in places it took on a marshy appearance. They felt an underground network of streams which, by some subterranean fault, flowed toward the river. At times a real brook flowed through the brushwood which the two travelling companions crossed without difficulty. The opposite bank was more varied and the valley more sharply patterned. The embankment, covered by trees of various sizes, formed a curtain which obstructed their view. On the

From *L'Île mystérieuse* (*The Mysterious Island*, 1874).

right bank, walking would have been difficult because of the abrupt cavities in the ground and because the trees, curved to the surface of the water, seemed to hold on only by a miracle of equilibrium.

Needless to say, this forest showed no signs of any human touch. Flip only saw traces of animals. Nowhere the mark of a pick or an axe. Nowhere an extinct fire. The sailor was happy about this because cannibals frequent this part of the Pacific. He dreaded the presence of man more than he desired them.

Flip and Robert were moving along but slowly. After an hour they barely covered a mile. They did not leave the watercourse which would show the way to return out of this labyrinth. They frequently stopped to look for game. Flip, who had travelled the entire world from the frigid zones to the torrid zones, hoped to find some edible fruit. But up to this point their search had been fruitless. The trees of this forest generally belonged to the conifer family, which grow in all the regions of the globe from cold climates to the tropics. A naturalist would have especially recognized the deodar species which are seen as far away as the Himalayan. These trees emit an agreeable fragrance. They saw numerous clusters of maritime pines whose opaque parasol boughs were widely spaced. In the midst of the tall grass, their feet crushed dry branches which crackled like fireworks.

Several birds were chirping and flying about under the foliage, but they showed themselves to be extremely elusive. In a marshy part of the forest, Robert recognized a bird with a sharp and elongated beak which anatomically resembled a kingfisher. However, what distinguished this bird was its rather rugged plumage which was coated with a metallic brilliance. Robert and Flip really wanted to get hold of it, one to bring to his brothers, the other keeping its edible qualities in mind. But they could not get near.

"What bird is this?" Robert asked.

"This bird, Mister Robert," replied the sailor, "I think I have already encountered in the forests of North America where they call it a jacamar."

"How fine it will look in a henhouse," the young lad shouted.

"And in a stew!" Flip laughed. "But this roast is not in a humor to be caught!"

"What does that matter!" Robert shouted, pointing to a flock of birds scattered across the foliage. "What pretty plumage! What a long tail and what sparkling colors. But they are small! They rival the hummingbird's size and color!"

In fact, the birds indicated by the lad sluggishly scattered across the branches but their loosely attached feathers fell to the ground in a fine down. Flip gathered some of these feathers and examined them.

"Are these small creatures edible?" Robert asked.

"Yes, my boy" replied the sailor. "These little birds are much sought after because of their delicate flesh. I much prefer a guinea fowl or a heather cock; but with a few dozen of these charming birds we could make a presentable meal."

"And what birds are these?"

"Couroucous," replied Flip. "I have captured thousands of these in northern Mexico, and if my memory is not mistaken, it is easy to approach them and kill them with a stick."

"Good!" said Robert, dashing forward.

"Not so fast, Mister impatient!" shouted the sailor, "not so fast. You will never become a good hunter if you are so quick tempered."

"Oh! If I only had a gun..." Robert said.

"Gun or stick, you must be cunning. When you are well armed, do not hesitate to fire or strike. But right now, stay calm. Watch! Imitate me and try to bring Mrs. Clifton a plate of couroucous."

Flip and Robert glided through the tall grass until they came to the foot of the trees whose lower branches were covered with these small birds; these couroucous were waiting for the passage of insects that made up their diet. They could see their feet, covered with feathers up to their toes, grasping the branches that supported them.

The hunters had arrived at their theater of action. Robert controlled his impatience but he promised himself he would deliver a sharp blow. He was disappointed when he realized how insufficient his stick was against these peaceful birds. Hiding in the tall grass, Flip gave a signal. He stood up in a flash and razed entire files of couroucous. The birds, dazed and stupefied by this sort of attack, did not think of fleeing. They calmly allowed themselves to be slaughtered. About a hundred littered the ground when the others decided to fly away.

Robert finally got permission to act. If it was not in the role of a hunter at least it was worthy of a hunting dog. This role suited him and he did it well. He leaped across the brushwood, dashed over tree stumps and scooped up the wounded birds huddling in the grass. Soon nine or ten dozen were piled up on the ground.

"Hurrah!" shouted Flip. "That will make a commendable dish. But it is not enough. The forest must be rich in game. Let's look further!"

The couroucous were strung up on a bulrush and the hunters continued their journey under the shelter of the green trees. Flip noted that the river curved slightly to the south. The sun was now shining from the side whereas before it was directly in front proving that the river's direction had changed. But in his opinion the river could not continue long in this direction because its waters evidently came from the foothills of the mountain, supplied by the melting snow which covered the sides of the central peak. Flip then resolved to continue along the river bank, hoping soon to leave the thick forest behind so he could explore the open countryside.

The trees were magnificent but Flip did not stop to admire them. Still no edible fruit. The sailor searched in vain for some of those precious palm trees that find so many uses in domestic life, and he was surprised at not finding any since they grow from the fortieth degree north latitude to the thirty fifth degree south latitude. But the conifer family of trees were the only ones in this forest. The Douglas trees resembled those admirable fir trees that grow in northwest America measuring sixty centimeters in diameter at their base and growing to sixty meters in height.

"What beautiful trees!" Flip shouted, "but we can't put them to use!"

"Perhaps!" Robert replied, suddenly getting an idea.

"What is your idea?"

"To climb to the top to examine the countryside."

"Can you do that?"

Flip had not finished speaking but the lad had already climbed to lower branches of the colossal fir tree. He climbed with unrivalled agility. The arrangement of branches facilitated his ascension. Flip urged caution but Robert barely heard him. But his agility was so remarkable and he seemed to have experience with this exercise so Flip felt reassured.

Robert soon reached the top of the tree. Getting a good grip, he looked around. Flip heard him clearly.

"Nothing of interest," he said, "nothing but trees; a shoreline, a peak that dominates the countryside; and a scintillating line that must be the ocean. All is in order."

"I did not say no," shouted Flip, "but go down carefully."

Robert obeyed and reached the bottom without mishap. He repeated what he had said: the forest was covered with fir trees like the one he had climbed. "Never mind," Flip replied, "let's continue along the river and if we don't reach the end of the forest in an hour we will go back."

Around eleven o'clock, Flip remarked to Robert that the sun's rays were no longer striking them from the side but from the back. The river's direction was now toward the sea. There was no inconvenience to the hunters in following the river. They were on the inside curve but they had had no occasion to cross to the other bank. They continued on their way. They still had not caught some larger game. However, several times Robert had flushed out some invisible animal while running in the tall grass. The lad was not able to get hold of it and he often regretted that his dog Fido was not there to do the job!

"Fido is with Robert's father!" Flip thought, "and perhaps it is better that way!"

They caught a glimpse of a new flock of birds pecking away at aromatic berries. Flip recognized that they were juniper berries. Suddenly the sound of real trumpets resonated through the forest. Robert cocked his ear expecting a cavalry regiment to appear. But Flip recognized that this strange fanfare was made by gallinules which are called grouse in the United States. Soon the saw several couples, with a variety of brown and fawn colored plumage, and with a brown tail. The males were recognized by the two pointed fins formed by the feathers raised on their neck. Gallinules are larger than a chicken and Flip knew that their flesh is as good as that of a hazel hen. He decided to capture a few of these grouse. In spite of Flip's ruses, in spite of Robert's skill, they were not able to get hold of them. The sailor was at the point of striking one of the grouse with his pointed stick but a sudden movement by Robert made the bird fly away.

Flip looked at the lad and pronounced these words which affected him deeply: "Mrs. Clifton would have been very happy to share a wing of this fowl with her small children!"

Robert, with his hands in his pockets and eyes to the ground, walked behind the sailor and followed him without saying a word.

By noon, the hunters had gone about four miles from the encampment; they were exhausted not so much from walking along the bank but from their walk across the obstructed forest. Flip decided not to go any further but to return by the left bank of the river in order not to go astray. But he and Robert were hungry. They both sat down under a clump of trees and started to eat with a good appetite.

With the meal ended, the sailor got ready to return to the encampment when he heard an unusual sound. He turned and saw an animal crouching under the brushwood. It was a kind of pig, about eighty centimeters long, blackish brown but not as dark on the underside, having tough but thin hair. The animal's toes, which were then gripping the ground, seemed to be united by membranes. Flip immediately recognized this animal as a capybara, one of the larger rodents.

The capybara did not move. It stupidly rolled its large eyes which were deeply imbedded in a thick layer of fat. Perhaps it saw man for the first time and did not know what to expect!

Flip held his stick firmly. The rodent was ten feet from him. Flip stared at Robert. Robert did not move any more than the capybara did. He crossed his arms on his chest and made every effort to control himself.

"Good!" Flip said to him, making a sign that he should not move from his place.

He then walked in small steps around the brushwood while the animal remained immobile. He soon disappeared into the tall grass. Robert stood as if rooted to the soil; but his chest heaved with rapid movements. He stared at the rodent. Five minutes passed and then Flip appeared in back of the brushwood. The capybara, sensing danger, turned its head; but suddenly Flip's formidable cudgel struck it from behind like lightning. The capybara let out a vigorous grunt and, being seriously wounded, it ran forward, knocked Robert over and escaped into the woods.

Hearing Flip shout, Robert got up still stunned from his fall, and ran after the wounded rodent. He soon spotted him. Just as he was about to pounce on the animal the latter made one last dash and overshot the boundary of this endless forest which unfolded not onto a prairie but a vast body of water.

To Robert's great surprise, the capybara plunged into this lake and disappeared. The lad stood still, his stick raised, looking at the bubbling water. Flip soon appeared. He did not even look at the new scenery. He thought only of his capybara. He asked about his capybara.

"Ah! How clumsy I am!" Robert shouted. "I lost him!"

"But where is it?"

"There! Under the water."

"Let us wait for it! Mister Robert. It will soon come to the surface to breathe."

"Won't it drown?"

"No. It has webbed feet. It is a capybara and I have hunted more than one of them on the banks of the Orinoco. Let's watch for it."

Flip paced back and forth this time more impatient than Robert. In his mind it was a priceless rodent. It was the *pièce de résistance* of a future dinner. But Flip was not mistaken. After a few minutes the animal emerged from the water at least a meter from where Robert was stationed. The lad dashed towards the capybara and grabbed him by a leg. Flip ran over and strangled the capybara.

"Well done!" Flip shouted. "You will become a real hunter, Mister Robert. Here is a rodent which we will gnaw to the bone and which will conveniently substitute for the grouse that escaped us. But where are we?"

The surroundings were worth looking at. This large expanse of water was a lake shaded by fine trees on the eastern and northern banks. The river served as a spillway for the lake's overflow. There were a few arid ramps south of the lake where only clumps of trees grew. The lake measured about a league along its larger diameter. An island emerged a few hundred feet from the edge of the forest. Toward the west, across a curtain of trees among which Flip recognized some coconut trees, the scintillating horizon of the sea appeared.

The sailor threw the capybara over his shoulder and, followed by Robert, he walked alongside the edge of the lake for about two miles. There the lake formed a sharp corner with only a large verdant prairie separating it from the shoreline of the ocean. They need only cross this prairie to reach the coast and Flip counted on the new route to reach the encampment. He was not mistaken. They crossed the large carpet of greenery as well as the line of coconut trees. The two hunters found themselves at the southern end of the cliff whose summit Flip had reached on the previous day. The long islet he had already seen extended in front of him with a narrow channel separating it from the shore.

But Flip was impatient to rejoin Mrs. Clifton and her family. Robert and he turned the small promontory formed by the corner of the cliff, walking across the sand. They had to hurry because the tide was coming in and the tops of the rocks had already disappeared under the rising sea. They made haste and at about two thirty they reached the encampment where they were greeted with joyous cries from the entire family.

⊙

# Chapter VIII

No incident worthy of note occurred during Flip's absence. The fire had been carefully maintained and Marc had renewed the supply of eggs and mollusks. Flip brought over the capybara and the dozens of couroucous. There was no worry about food for the time being.

Before telling about his trip, the sailor want to prepare a meal, an urgent task since the two hunters had sharp appetites. They decided to save the couroucous for the next day and eat the capybara, a real *pièce de résistance*.

But first they had to cut up the capybara. Flip took charge of this task in his capacity as a sailor, that is to say as a "jack of all trades." He skinned the rodent with remarkable skill. The chops from the capybara were placed on the burning wood. At the same time, the mollusks were cooked in the kettle and the eggs were placed under the cinders. That made a fine dinner. Mrs. Clifton intended to smoke the rest of the capybara early the next day.

Soon the odor of roast chops filled the air. Mother was ready with her dinner plates, that is to say her seashells. In the shadow of the cliff, the dinner guests gathered round the kettle on this fine day. Although the mollusks appeared to be ordinary, they were their usual success; the capybara chops were declared to be without rival in the entire world. If one were to believe the honest Flip, they had never had such a meal! He proved it by devouring anything left over.

When the dinner guests had satisfied their hunger, Mrs. Clifton begged Flip to tell about his exploration. But the sailor left that pleasure to his young traveling companion. Robert eloquently told what had happened during the excursion, a little impetuously perhaps, in short phrases and in poor grammar. He described the walk through the forest, the hunt for the couroucou, the capture of the capybara and the return by the lake and the southern cliff. He did mention their clumsy maneuvers with good grace and he minimized only a little his victory in his memorable battle with the amphibious capybara. But what he did not say, Flip said for him.

Mrs. Clifton was proud of her son. She embraced him tenderly while shaking Marc's hand. Perhaps the latter was a bit jealous of his brother's success. In this way Mrs. Clifton thanked her oldest son for watching over them during Flip's absence.

Then the sailor repeated, in detail, Robert's story; he emphasized certain important points principally about the discovery of the lake with potable water.

"There, Madam Clifton," he said, "if we can settle in between the lake and the ocean, we will have a real Garden of Eden. We should not live far from the sea and here it will always be in view. The lake will furnish all our needs because it is frequented, I imagine, with flocks of aquatic birds. Further, the trees are much more beautiful than those on the shore and I saw coconuts, which have many uses."

"But how can we settle there?" Mrs. Clifton asked.

"The worst part," Flip replied, "will be to substitute the shelter under the boat for a cabin under a roof. But even that would not make an acceptable shelter. We must respect a castaway's dignity. We will surely find a grotto, an excavation, a hole, a simple hole..."

"That we can make bigger!" said little Jack.

"Yes, with my knife," Flip replied, smiling at the child.

"And where we can play!" Belle added.

"Yes, my pretty lady, without gun powder, only with a little bang, and we will have a charming place, dry in the winter and cool in the summer!"

"I would like a beautiful grotto, with diamonds on the walls like in the fairy tales."

"We will make one, Miss Belle, just for you!" Flip replied. "The fairies will take their orders from pretty ladies like you!..."

Belle clapped her hands and the worthy sailor was very happy to spread a little gaiety and hope among these young spirits. Mrs. Clifton looked at him with half a smile on her pale lips.

"Then," Flip said, "we will visit the neighborhood of our new home; not today, it is too late for that, but tomorrow."

"Is the lake far?" Marc asked.

"No. Only two miles away. Tomorrow morning, with your permission, Mistress Clifton, I will take, for two hours only, Mister Marc and Mister Robert and we will examine this place."

"All that you have done has been good, friend Flip," Mrs. Clifton replied. "Aren't you our Providence?"

"A pretty Providence!" shouted the sailor. "A Providence that has only a knife to carry on our affairs!"

"Yes," Mrs. Clifton added, "only a knife, but a strong hand to grasp the knife!"

With this project agreed upon, it only remained to rest up while waiting for the next day. Flip rested in his usual way, by renewing the supply of wood.

Night then came on. The fire was prepared for the night. A clear sky indicated that it would be cold. But moss, dried with the fire, was prepared by Mrs. Clifton herself and the children huddled like fledglings in their nest.

Mrs. Clifton wanted to watch the fire and with difficulty she was able to get Flip to take a few hours of sleep. He obeyed her but decided to sleep with only one eye shut. Mother remained alone this dark night in front of the sparkling fire, attentive and thoughtful at the same time. Her stray thoughts focused on the ocean and on the outcome of the mutiny!

The next day, after a quick breakfast, Flip gave his two young companions the signal to depart. After embracing Mrs. Clifton, Marc and Robert went on ahead and turned the corner of the cliff. Flip soon joined them. While passing the bank of lithodomes they agreed that they had an inexhaustible supply. On the other side of the channel, on this long islet that protected the shoreline, numerous flocks of birds promenaded solemnly. These animals belonged to the division of divers; they were penguins, easily recognizable by their disagreeable cry which reminds one of the braying of a donkey. The flesh of these birds, although blackish, is quite edible. Flip knew this, and he also knew that these penguins, sluggish and stupid, could easily be killed with blows from a club or a stone. He promised himself that one of these days he would cross the channel to explore the islet so abundant in game. But he did not tell the two young lads about his plan. Robert would not have hesitated for a moment to throw himself into the water with the intention of giving chase to the penguins.

A half hour after leaving the encampment, Flip, Marc and Robert arrived at the southern end of the cliff with the tide ebbing at the moment. They had reached the large area between the shore and the lake which was familiar to Flip from his exploration of the previous day. Marc found the countryside charming. Clumps of coconut trees grew majestically at midway, tilted a little backwards. A curtain of fine trees grew on an uneven soil. These were beautiful conifers, some pines and larches among others, about thirty superb specimens of the ulmaceae family known under the name of Virginia elms.

Flip and his two young companions explored all of this part of the coastal area where the lake formed its eastern boundary. The lake seemed to be swarming with fish. But to exploit this resource, they would need lines, hooks and lines; Flip promised Marc and Robert that he would make these fishing devices after the small colony settled in.

While following the western shore of the lake, Flip discovered the footprints of some large animals who probably came to quench their thirst at this large reservoir of potable water. But he saw no trace of the presence of man. They were exploring land unsullied by humans.

Flip then returned to the southern part of the cliff where it was perpendicular to the sea and ended only a few feet from the clumps of elms.

This wall was carefully inspected. They hoped to discover a rather large cavity to house the entire family. This search had a happy result. It was Marc who discovered the long sought grotto. It was a real cavern cut into the granite, measuring thirty feet in length by twenty feet in width. A fine sand, bristling with mica, covered the ground. The cavern was more than ten feet high. Its sides, rugged near the top, were smooth and polished at the base as if the sea had at one time smoothed out its rough spots. The opening to this cavern was cut in an irregular shape, forming a sort of triangle, but there was sufficient daylight for the interior. In any event, Flip would not be inconvenienced by it. He would enlarge it.

On entering the grotto, Marc did not allow himself to jump or run on the sand—it was bound to happen with Master Robert. The latter's jumping about destroyed large traces etched in the ground. Flip examined these traces. They were large footprints, evidently

From *Seconde patrie* (*Second Homeland*, 1900).

made by an animal that plainly moved on the soles of its feet, like the mammal racers do, and not on its fingers. The locomotive organs of the plantigrade that had left these footprints were powerful ones with pointed nails that made clear marks on the sand.

Flip did not want to frighten his young friends. He erased the footprints saying that they were of no importance. But he asked himself if this cavern which was frequented by a large beast could ever offer sanctuary to people who had no defensive weapons. However, having made this observation, he thought, not without reason, that even if it was visited by an animal, it was not the animal's den. He saw no trace of excrement or of gnawed bones. They could hope that this chance visit would not occur again. Besides, if they obstructed the opening with blocks of stones, this grotto could be secure. In addition, fires could be kept burning night and day to keep ferocious beasts at a distance since fire is one of their great fears.

Flip then decided to make this spacious excavation his principal encampment. After examining the inside he looked at the exterior of the cliff. It was a solid mass a hundred and fifty feet high at this point. Its upper part receded like the high roofs that covered brick houses in Louis XIII's century. The grotto was situated three hundred meters from the shoreline and two hundred meters from the lake. It was sheltered in part by a granite block which protected it from the rainy west winds. As to the grotto itself, they would not have a full view of the ocean but only a side view which extended to the promontory in the south. The central peak which rose to the rear of the cliff was not visible from the grotto; but otherwise they would have a fine view, the blue sky reflected in the lake, the wooded banks to the right, the piled up dunes, and the far away horizon with everything in between! It was a charming landscape!

The grotto was in a good location between the lake and the sea, at the edge of this green prairie covered with beautiful trees. Flip decided to bring Mrs. Clifton and her family here on this very day. This plan appealed to the young lads. They started back to the encampment.

They did not return without fishing and hunting on the way. The boys did not want to return with empty hands. While Robert gathered pigeon eggs, Marc collected mollusks. He was even able to capture an enormous crab, a toothed carapace weighing at least five pounds with powerful claws he skillfully avoided. It was a fine piece of meat. On his part, Robert collected about a dozen eggs after breaking a few in his hurry to snatch them up. But he knew he wouldn't break all of them.

At ten o'clock, Flip and his two travelling companions returned to the encampment. A smoke from the fire was rising gently into the air. Jack and Belle, charged with keeping up the fire, had done their job well.

Mrs. Clifton quickly made lunch with the crab prepared fresh. She had to cut it into pieces to get it into the kettle. Cooked in sea water, it was as tasty as lobster or crayfish from European seas.

Flip told Mrs. Clifton about his plan to move and she was ready to follow him. However, after the meal, the equinox winds which are so unpredictable during the final days of March burst into a violent rainstorm. Flip was forced to forgo his plans to move on this day. The gusts of wind, coming from the northwest, blasted directly against the cliff and threatened to sweep through the bed of moss under the boat. Flip worked constantly to prevent a flooding. The Clifton family was poorly protected and suffered a great deal from this squall which lasted all day and into the night. The fire was maintained only with the greatest difficulty. Never was their need for an enclosed and dry home felt so urgently.

# Chapter IX

It was cloudy the next day but the rain had stopped. Flip and Mrs. Clifton decided to leave immediately after breakfast. After this wet night everyone was anxious to get to the new place.

After getting Jack and Belle dressed, Mrs. Clifton made breakfast. During this time, the two young children were frolicking on the sand even though their mother told them they risked damaging their clothes which would be difficult to replace. Jack especially, who looked up to Robert because of his vivacity, gave his sister deplorable examples of unruliness. Mrs. Clifton was right to worry about clothing. They could find nourishment and keep warm on this deserted shore but wouldn't it really be difficult to clothe themselves?

During the meal they naturally talked about how they would make the move.

"Have you some ideas, Mister Jack?" the sailor asked the young lad who was taking a little interest in the discussion.

"Me?" replied Jack.

"Yes," said Flip, "how will we get to our new house?"

"We'll walk," Jack replied.

"At least," laughed Robert, "we won't be taking the Fifth Avenue bus."

Robert, by mocking, was making allusion to the system of loco-motion used in the larger American cities.

"The bus!" repeated Belle, looking at Flip with large astonished eyes.

"Instead of a joke, Robert," said Mrs. Clifton, "you would do better to make a serious response to the question our friend Flip asked in earnest."

"But it is really very simple, mother," replied the young lad, slightly blushing, "our furniture is very light! I will be in charge of the kettle. We will take the road past the cliff and we will easily reach the grotto."

Robert was already on his feet impatient to leave.

"One moment," Flip shouted, seizing the youngster by the hand! "Not so fast! What about the fire?"

In fact, Robert had completely forgotten about the precious burning fire that must be transported to the new encampment.

"Well then, have you nothing to say, Mister Marc?" the sailor asked.

"I think," Marc replied after some thought, "I think that without inconveniencing ourselves, we can use another means of transport. Since sooner or later we must drag the boat to its new port, why don't we use it to transport all of us?"

"Well said, Mister Marc!" shouted the sailor, "that is an excellent idea you have there, and I would never have thought of it. We will take the boat, load it with fagots placed over a bed of hot cinders and we will set sail for our new lake home."

"Good, good!" shouted Jack, eager for this chance to sail on the ocean.

"What do you think of my proposal, Madam Clifton?" Flip asked.

Mrs. Clifton was ready to follow Flip. The sailor, wanting to profit from the rising tide which, according to his observations, would carry them from north to south between the islet and the shore, soon made preparations for a departure. He first had to take the boat off its supports; the rocks that supported it were removed one at a time and the operation was easily completed. The boat was then turned over and as soon as its keel and sides were firmly on the ground everyone, old and young, pushed it toward the river. There it was prevented from drifting with a line held down with a large stone. The wind was good—blowing to the northeast—and Flip decided to rig his foresail. Marc skillfully helped him to get underway. The sail was rolled out ready to be hauled up to the top of the mast.

They then began to load the boat. They piled up all the wood the boat would hold, but with a plan, placing the heaviest pieces at the bottom to serve as ballast. Then Flip spread out a layer of sand at the rear which he covered with a layer of cinders. On this double bed, Marc placed some glowing embers and charcoal. While at the helm, Flip expected to keep an eye on his travelling fire in case it needed more fuel. As an extra precaution, the fire at the encampment was not extinguished. On the contrary, Robert revived it by throwing on large fagots in a way that would make it possible to find some embers should the fire on the boat die out. Marc even suggested that he remain behind to watch the encampment fire while the rest of the family went through the channel; but Flip judged it useless to act this way, not wanting to leave anyone behind.

At nine o'clock everything was loaded, the kettle, the sack of salted meat and biscuits, the capybara ham that Mrs. Clifton had smoked on the previous day, the mollusks and the eggs. Flip took one last look around him to see if they had forgotten anything. How could these poor people ever forget this poor place? Then the signal to start was given. Marc and Robert were in front. Mrs. Clifton, Jack and Belle were seated on a little deck near the rear. Flip posted himself by the helm near the burning embers and charcoal, watching it like a vestal at a sacred fire.

At a command from the sailor, Marc and Robert pulled on the halyard, hoisting the sail to the top of the mast. Flip drew in the rope that anchored the boat. He turned the sail to catch the wind. They reached the entrance to the channel and the incoming tide swept the boat along rapidly.

The sea was calm. The light boat moved rapidly. The panorama of cliffs moving past them filled the young travellers with wonder. Thick clouds of birds passed over the water, filling the air with their deafening cries. The agitated fish jumped out of their element. Flip saw a timid seal and a capricious porpoise. The boat entered the right end of the channel several meters from the islet. They could see hundreds of stupid penguins who did not even think of fleeing. The islet was two fathoms above sea level forming an enormous flat and dry rock thrown up as a barrier between the shore and the ocean.[1] Flip thought that if he could enclose one end of the channel, it could become a natural port for a flotilla of vessels.

The boat moved rapidly. Everyone on board was silent. The children looked at the large cliffs that towered over them. Flip paid attention to his fire and, helping Mrs. Clifton, he surveyed the open ocean, looking at the silent horizon. Not a sail in sight! The ocean was deserted.

After travelling for a half hour, the boat reached the southern end of the cliff and he turned to avoid the submerged rocks that formed the point. The rising tide caused a strong surf by the meeting of two currents, the current from the channel and the current which drove to shore.

---

1. A fathom equals six feet.

From *Les Naufragés du Jonathan*
(*The Survivors of the Jonathan*, 1909).

Once the point was doubled, all of the beautiful countryside came into view, the clear lake, the green prairie, clumps of trees thrown about at random, dunes to the south, forests in the background, and the majestic peak that dominated everything. "How beautiful! How beautiful," the young children shouted. —"Yes," Flip replied, "this is a delightful garden that Providence has given us!"

Mrs. Clifton, with a sad expression, observed this part of the coastal area. She too was affected by this beautiful countryside. Flip, unfurling his sail, brought his boat almost to a standstill. These beautiful scenes were made only by nature, speaking to the children's imagination; they had suffered and the worthy sailor wanted his small colony to be carried away by its beauty.

He then looked for a cove in which to direct his boat. He ordered his two young novices to bring the sail to mid-mast and, skillfully maneuvering through the narrow passes left free by the rocks, he gently grounded the boat.

Robert jumped to shore. His brother and Flip followed immediately. Then the three of them hauled in on the mooring rope, placing it rather high so the tide could not reach it and drag on it.

Mrs. Clifton, Belle and Jack disembarked immediately.

"To the grotto, to the grotto!" Robert shouted.

"Wait, my young man," said Flip, "and let us first unload our boat."

Flip was concerned about the fire before anything else. The cinders were carried to the base of the cliff and with a few fagots they established a temporary fire. The firewood was then unloaded and each of the children did their share carrying food and utensils. The small troop then went to their new home following the southern face of the cliff.

What was Flip thinking of? While walking he thought of the footprints on the sand of the grotto that he had carefully observed on the previous day before erasing them. Would they again find new traces in the sand? This really worried him because the grotto must no longer remain a den frequented by wild beasts; in that case what should Flip do? Without defensive arms would he dare to occupy the cavern and drive out these ferocious inhabitants? The worthy sailor was at a loss, but since he had told no one about his fears, he kept his thoughts to himself.

The small group finally arrived at the grotto. Robert, who was in front, was about to enter, but Flip stopped him with a word. He wanted to examine the floor of sand before it was trampled on.

"Mister Robert," he shouted to the young man, "do not go in, do not go in, I ask you. Mrs. Clifton, I beg you, tell him to wait for me."

"Robert," Mrs. Clifton said, "listen to our friend, Flip."

Robert held back.

"Is there some danger in going into the grotto?" Mrs. Clifton asked.

"None whatsoever, Madam," the sailor replied, "but in case some animal has taken refuge there, it would be best to take some precautions."

Flip quickened his pace and soon joined Robert, waiting at the entrance of the excavation. He entered and, without saying anything about the undisturbed sand inside the grotto, he soon came out.

"Come, Madam, come," he said, "your home is ready to receive you!"

Mother and children entered their new dwelling. Jack rolled in the sand. Belle wondered why no diamonds were embedded in the walls, but she was content with the mica stars that were shining here and there like points of fire. Mrs. Clifton could only thank God; she and her children were sheltered, and she began to hope.

Flip left Mrs. Clifton at the grotto. He returned to the boat in order to bring back some firewood with Marc and Robert's help. On the way, Marc asked the sailor what his reason was in being the first to enter the grotto; and since he could tell Marc everything, Flip told him about the footprints he had seen on the previous day, begging him not to speak to anyone about it. It was important to note that the animal that had already visited the grotto had not returned and Flip hoped that this chance visit would not occur again.

Marc promised the sailor that he would be silent, but he asked him, in the future, not to conceal from him any dangers to the family. Flip promised him, adding that Marc was worthy enough to know everything and that henceforth he would treat him as the head of the family.

At seventeen years of age, head of the family! These words reminded the young man of all that he had left behind on board the *Vancouver*, all that he had lost!

"Father! poor father!" he murmured to himself, holding back his tears. Then, with a firm step, he walked to the water's edge.

Arriving at the boat, Flip took on a heavy load of firewood asking Marc to carry two or three lighted sticks and to shake them while walking so as to keep them burning.

Marc obeyed and when he arrived at the encampment the sticks were still burning. Flip looked for a convenient location outside the grotto for his fire. He found a corner formed by some rocks which would shelter it from strong winds. There he placed some flat stones intended as an ash box and, above them, some elongated stones to act as an andiron. Over these stones he loaded a large log crosswise that Robert found in the boat and thus prepared the furnace was suitable for all domestic uses.

This very important installation required a certain amount of time. Soon the children were crying of hunger. They developed an appetite during the morning journey. Marc went to the lake to fill the kettle with fresh water and Mrs. Clifton quickly prepared a sort of capybara stew which refreshed everyone.

After the meal, Flip judged it best to spend the rest of the day gathering wood. It was a distance from the encampment to the edge of the forest and this time the river was no longer there to move the raft. But everyone, children and adults, did their share with this important occupation. Dead wood was everywhere. The woodsmen had only to tie the fagots. Guided and encouraged by Flip, the children worked until evening to carry this indispensable fuel. The wood was placed in a dry corner of the vast grotto and Flip calculated that this new supply would last for three days and three nights on the condition that they would not turn up the heat.

Seeing her children so busy with this laborious and fatiguing occupation, Mrs. Clifton decided to prepare a fortifying dinner. She sacrificed one of the four smoked capybara legs. The leg, roasted over a sparkling fire, was gnawed to the bone. Flip resolved to devote several hours of the next day to hunting and fishing in order to bring the food supply to a normal state.

At eight in the evening everyone was asleep with the exception of Flip who was outside keeping an eye on the fire. The night was cool and clear. About ten in the evening the reddish moon set behind the mountain shedding its gentle light over the ocean. At midnight young Marc took Flip's place.

# Chapter X

The next day the weather was favorable for an excursion. Flip decided to explore the shores of the lake. He asked Mrs. Clifton if she wanted to accompany him with her young children.

"I thank you, friend Flip," the mother replied. "Since someone must stay behind to watch the fire, it is better that I should be in charge of this task. Marc and Robert will be more useful than I, as hunters and as fishermen. During your absence, I will use the time to arrange things in our new home."

"Then you don't mind remaining here alone?" the sailor asked Mrs. Clifton.

"Yes, Flip."

"If you want, Mother," Marc said, "I will stay with you and Robert can go with Flip."

"As a hunting dog," Robert joined in.

"No, my children," Mrs. Clifton replied. "Both of you go with Flip. Mustn't I get accustomed to staying alone some of the time? Besides, don't I have big Jack to protect me?"

Master Jack stood heroically on his two feet on hearing his mother speak. However, to speak frankly, this little boy was not very brave. Whenever night came on, he did not dare to venture outside alone in the shadows. But in full daylight, he was a hero.

They respected Mrs. Clifton's decision. Flip, Marc and Robert prepared to leave. Not wanting to prolong his absence, the sailor agreed to limit his exploration to the western and southern shores of the lake.

Knowing that Mrs. Clifton intended to smoke the three remaining legs of the capybara, Flip installed an apparatus proper for this operation before leaving. Three stakes united at the top like a tent and fixed in the ground at their lower extremities formed the apparatus. The hams would be suspended over a fire of green wood and the thick smoke would penetrate the meat. They would use a few branches from aromatic bushes which would give the meat a delicious aroma and since there was no lack of these bushes in the vicinity, Mrs. Clifton would put the finishing touches on her culinary operation.

At eight o'clock, after a quick breakfast, the three hunters, armed with their pointed clubs, left the encampment and crossed the prairie to the shore of the lake. In passing, they admired the magnificent

From *Un Capitaine de quinze ans* (*A Fifteen-Year-Old Captain*, 1878)

groves of coconut trees and Flip promised his young companions that before long they would harvest the nuts.

When the sailor reached the lake, instead of going left along the circular shore that led to the forest already explored, he turned right to go south. In certain places the shore was marshy. Many aquatic birds were there including several couples of kingfishers. Perched on some stone, solemn and immobile, they were on the lookout for passing fish. From time to time they dashed and plunged under the water making a sharp cry, then they reappeared with prey in beak. Robert naturally wanted to try his skill at hunting these birds either with his club or by throwing a stone; but Flip stopped him; he knew that the flesh of these birds is detestable; so why destroy these inoffensive creatures?

"Let them live around us," he said to the two young boys. "These animals break our solitude and charm us. Remember, Mister Robert, that we must never spill the blood of an animal for no reason. That is the act of a bad hunter."

After walking for half an hour, Flip and his two companions reached the extremity of the lake. The western shoreline, following an oblique line, turned away from the coast; from this point the ocean was not even visible and a succession of dunes, bristling with bulrushes, cut short the view. At the point where the travellers then found themselves, the southern bank ran from the southwest to the northeast. It was rounded, making the lake look like the point of a heart directed southward. The waters were beautiful, clear, a bit blackish and, from the bubbles and the concentric circles that criss crossed each other at the surface, there was no doubt that these waters were full of fish.

South of the lake the ground was uneven, rising abruptly and forming a succession of hills. The three explorers crossed this new countryside. Marc immediately noted that a large number of tall bamboo trees were growing there.

"Bamboos!" shouted Flip. "Ah! Mister Marc, here is a precious discovery."

"But we can't eat bamboos," Robert said.

"Good," replied the sailor, "aren't there other uses besides eating? Besides, I can tell you that in India I have eaten bamboos like asparagus!"

"Asparagus thirty feet high!" shouted Robert. "And were they good?"

"Excellent," Flip responded unruffled. "Only to be frank, it was not the thirty foot high stalks but the young shoots. You should also know, Mister Robert, that the pith of the new stalks, pickled in vinegar, makes a very appreciated condiment. In addition, these bamboos, which are suitable for all sorts of economic uses, exude a sweet liqueur between their nodes which Miss Belle will find very tasty."

"What else can be done with this precious vegetable?" Marc asked.

"With its bark cut into flexible lath, Mister Marc, we can make bread baskets and bins. This bark, macerated and reduced to a paste serves to make rice paper. From the stems, according to their size, we can make canes and water pipes. The largest bamboos are an excellent construction material, light and strong, which are never attacked by insects. Finally, and this is what we will use them for, we will make vases of different sizes."

"Vases! But how?" Robert asked.

"By sawing the bamboo internodes to a convenient length, and keeping for the bottom a portion of the transverse partition which forms the node. In this way sturdy and handy pots are obtained which are very much in use by the Chinese."

"Ah! Our mother will be happy!" Marc said. "Her poor kettle is her only utensil!"

"Well, my young friends," said Flip, "it is useless for us to load up now with these bamboos. On our return we will pass by here and then we will collect them. Let's be on our way."

The walk through the hills was resumed. The hunters, always on the alert, soon saw the scintillating ocean past the capricious line of dunes. From this elevated point they could easily distinguish the end of the cliff, the one with the excavation that now served as the family's home.

The boys looked carefully toward the coast but at this distance of five miles across a curtain of trees they could not locate the exact position of the encampment.

"No," said Marc, "I cannot see the grotto in which our mother, Jack and Belle are sheltered at the moment. But look, Robert, don't you see a small line of bluish smoke rising above the trees? Isn't that a sign that all is well down there?"

"Yes, I see it," Robert shouted.

"And in fact," said Flip, "this small smoke is a good sign and we need have no fear for those we have left behind. But, if you please, my young gentlemen, if we keep looking at the shore we won't be getting much hunting done. I would rather find out if these hills of the southwest have game. Let us not forget that our duty as hunters comes before our explorations. Let's think of our cupboard."

Flip's suggestion was a good one to follow. They still had no game. Flip and his young companions went down toward the ocean and they discovered some small prairies hidden among the sand dunes; the lightly moist soil was covered with aromatic herbs that perfumed the air. Without difficulty, Flip recognized groups of thyme, serpolet, basil, savory, all sweet smelling species of the labiate family. It was a natural warren only lacking in rabbits. In this area, at any rate, they saw none of the holes that riddle the grounds frequented by these rodents. However, Flip could not admit that the guests would be missing when the table was set for them. He decided to explore this warren with greater care and they continued their walk among the hills and the prairies. Robert ran and jumped about like a child, gliding among the sandy declivities at the risk of tearing his clothes.

This exploration was continued for another half hour but rabbits or other representatives of the rodent tribe did not appear. However, although there were no animals, a naturalist would have had the occasion to study several specimens of the vegetable kingdom. Marc, who was rather fond of natural history and botany, saw certain plants that could be useful in a household. Among others, he recognized various plants of didymous monardas which go under the name of Oswego tea in North America.[1] Marc remembered their agreeable taste when taken as a tea. He gathered a certain quantity as well as basil shoots, rosemary, melissa, betony, etc., and others which possessed therapeutic properties for use as cough mixtures, astringents, antifebriles, others antispasmodics, or antirhumatics.[2] These prairies contained a fortune for a pharmacist.

However, since no member of the small colony was nor wished to be sick, Flip was not paying too much attention to these medical resources when he heard Robert calling about fifty paces ahead.

---

1. Labiate which have two lobes in the embryo of their grain and have non parallel veins in their leaves.

2. Betony is a labiate with purgative properties for the inducement of sneezing, and antifebriles reduces a fever.

Flip rushed over and realized that he had not been mistaken in his feelings. He saw hundreds of sandy mounds riddled with holes.

"Burrows!" Robert said.

"Yes!" Flip replied.

"But are they inhabited?"

"That is the question" replied the sailor.

The question was not long in resolving itself. Almost at once, bands of small animals resembling rabbits fled in all directions but with such speed that they could not hope to follow them. Being good runners, Marc and Robert went in pursuit but the rodents easily escaped them. But Flip resolved not to leave the place before capturing a half dozen of these animals. First he wanted to supply the pantry and then to domesticate those that they would take later. But when he saw Marc and Robert returning exhausted and with empty hands, he realized that since they could not take these rodents on the run, they must try to take them at the burrows. With a few collars hung at the openings to the burrows the operation would likely succeed, but with no collars and no way to make them, that compounded the difficulty. They resigned themselves to visiting each burrow, to pry with a stick, doing with patience what they could not do any other way.

For an hour the three hunters visited a large number of burrows, taking care to plug earth and grass into those that were not occupied. Marc was the first to find one of these rodents crouching in its burrow; with a little difficulty he captured the animal with a blow from his stick. Flip recognized the rodent as a rabbit resembling its European congeners and who are commonly known under the name of "American Rabbits" because they are found in the northern parts of that continent.

Marc's success made his competitors hungry. Robert did not want to return to the encampment without at least two or three of these rodents as his share, but since he had more energy than patience, he allowed a half dozen rabbits to escape him after surprizing them in their burrows. After an hour, Flip and Marc captured four rabbits and he not a single one. He gave up prying into the burrows and began to chase them on foot but the agile rodents easily dodged his stones and stick. When Flip gave the signal to leave, the unfortunate lad mumbled something about his disappointment.

Flip, however, was enchanted with his success. He could not be more pleased. Four rabbits, that was a good catch especially under the conditions it was obtained. Besides, the sun indicated it was noon time and the stomachs of the hunters spoke urgently. Flip decided to get back to the grotto. He suspended his two rabbits at the end of his stick; Marc imitated him; and both, belittling the need for collars, took to the road past the lake. Robert preceded them, whistling as if he didn't care at all.

"I am sorry that Robert didn't catch anything," Marc said to his friend Flip.

"Mister Robert is a little bitter," the sailor replied, "but he will mature in time."

At half past twelve, Flip and his companions reached the southern end of the lake. They then turned left towards the bamboo groves. While prying about here and there in a marshy area, Robert caught sight of a bird that quickly flew away. The young lad's self-esteem came into play and he decided to catch this bird at any price. He dashed off in pursuit. Flip didn't have time to call him back. The thoughtless boy was already splashing about the mud; but with a skilfully thrown stone he wounded the bird. With its wing broken, the creature was struggling in the grass a few meters away.

Not wanting his prey to escape, Robert went deeper into the marshy area. In spite of Flip's shouts, he went to the bird and captured it. But the soil was soaked and little by little he began to sink. It was fortunate that he had the presence of mind to place his stick crosswise; then, pulling on clumps of grass, he hauled himself out of the marsh at the expense of ruining his clothes now covered with black mud.

He was triumphant. He paid little attention to Flip's reprimands nor the danger he had undergone, nor the condition of his clothes which would be difficult to replace. He had no regrets whatsoever.

"I caught my bird! I caught my bird!" he shouted while gesticulating.

"You didn't act wisely," Flip replied. "Besides, what kind of bird do you have there? Is it edible?"

"It is good," Robert answered back, "I would like to see someone find fault with it."

The sailor examined the bird that Robert gave him. It was a coot, belonging to the group of macrodactiles that form the transition between the order of waders and those of the web footers. The coot is a good swimmer, grey colored with a short beak, an eminent frontal bone, fingers stretched in a scalloped frame, distinguished by a white edge on its wings, about the size of a partridge. Flip easily identified it and, shaking his head, he gave it up as poor game, unworthy of a respectable roast or stew. But Robert belonged to that group of hunters humorously called "carnivorous imbeciles" who care nothing about which animal they eat as long as they have killed it! Since Robert considered his coot to be edible and since a discussion in this regard would fall on deaf ears, Flip did not pursue it, and he continued on his way to the coconut groves.

There, using his knife, he cut a half dozen different sizes of these vegetables belonging to the armidinaria bamboo species which from afar resemble small palm trees because numerous branches full of leaves come out of their nodes. Flip and the boys shared in carrying the bamboos and, taking the shortest route, they reached the encampment around two in the afternoon.

Mrs. Clifton, Jack and Belle went forward a quarter of a mile to meet them. The hunters were welcomed with joy and the rabbits with the honors they deserved. The housewife was happy to know that this warren could always furnish her family with healthy nourishing game.

On arriving at the encampment, Flip found the fire in perfect condition, because Mrs. Clifton had taken care to add wood after he left. The capybara legs were smoked in thick vapors which escaped from a pile of green branches. Flip immediately began to skin one of the four rabbits. A stick, acting as a spit, pierced the rabbit from head to toe. Two forked branches, dug into the ground, held the stick in place. A flaming fire was maintained under the future roast. Master Jack was put in charge of turning the apparatus and a food hound would not have discharged his duties with more intelligence.

On seeing Robert's clothes soiled with mud, mother looked at him without saying a word. But the boy understood the meaning of this silent reproach. He carefully brushed his clothes since the dry mud had turned into dust. As to his coot, he did not want to admit his mistake. He quickly plucked it, tearing off some of the meat with the feathers, then, after tearing half of the crop with the entrails under the pretence of cleaning it, he put it on the spit and watched the roast himself.

The rabbit roast was ready and dinner was served on the sand outside the grotto. The rabbit, perfumed with the odor of all the herbs that served as its regular nourishment, was found to be excellent and was gnawed to the bone. Little would have remained if another one of the rabbits had been passed around. But a dozen pigeon eggs completed the meal. As to Robert's coot, after it was only half roasted, it was cut into pieces to be served all around. Little Jack decided to taste a piece. But at the first mouthful, he made a terrible face and had to spit it out. The flesh tasted muddy and marshy and it was impossible to swallow it. Robert, however, with his self esteem at stake, was stubborn. He courageously ate every last piece just to show that there was nothing wrong with it.

Flip and Mrs. Clifton devoted the next day to getting things in order and settling in. The sailor used the day to make vases from the bamboo internodes. He used his knife to skilfully cut this hard material. A saw was the proper instrument for this task but Flip used the point of the knife and he was able to give the family a dozen finished vases which were placed in a corner of the grotto. The largest were immediately filled with fresh water and the smallest were used as drinking glasses. Mrs. Clifton was very satisfied with her wood glassworks which were worthy for use in Bohemia or in Venice. "Even better," she said, "we needn't fear that these glasses will break."

During the day Marc discovered a sort of edible fruit which would fortunately vary the regular menu. These fruits, or rather these grains, came from a pine tree they frequently came across at the edge of the prairie. It was the pine kernel which produces an excellent almond that is very esteemed in the temperate regions of America and Europe. The ones Marc took to his mother were in a perfect state of maturity. Henceforth the children helped their brother gather an abundant supply of these kernels. They didn't have to beg. As compensation, their mother let them nibble at a few of them.

So then, the family's situation improved day by day. Little by little hope began to return to this poor woman so cruelly tried. But for how long a time had this family been cast on this land? Neither Mrs. Clifton, nor Flip, nor any of the children could say for sure. That night Jack asked, "What day is it?" prompting them to think of past events.

"What day?" Flip repeated. "My word, I am forced to admit that I don't know."

"What," said Robert, "we don't know how many days we've been here?"

"I can't say!" Mrs. Clifton replied.

"I don't know any more than mother does," Marc added.

"Well, I, I know," said little Belle.

Everyone turned to the little girl and they could see her taking some stones out of her pocket and placing them on a seashell.

"Little Belle," her mother asked her, "what is the significance of these stones?"

"Mother," the child replied, "every day since we have been here, I put one of these stones in my pocket so all we need to do is to count them."

They welcomed the little girl's declaration. Flip congratulated her for having thought of this mineral calendar and he embraced her for her trouble.

They counted the stones; there were six. It was six days since the abandoned family had set foot on this land. Now it was on Monday, the 25th of March that the boat had left the *Vancouver*. Today was Saturday, the 30th of March. "Good!" shouted Jack, "tomorrow will be Sunday."

"Yes, the 31st of March," Mrs. Clifton replied, "and this Sunday, my children, will be Easter Sunday!"

The next day was devoted to rest and prayer. Everyone thanked heaven for having so obviously protected them and they did not forget to pray for their absent father who was always in their thoughts.

# Chapter XI

Flip used the days that followed to get the Clifton family settled in. The question of their survival was practically solved. This land could provide everything the small colony needed. The question of their health remained; but Flip did not despair in resolving that likewise.

During the week the sailor acquired large quantities of firewood. The fire must be constantly watched, it was his most urgent task. Keeping a constant eye on the fire was an exacting obligation. Flip, Mrs. Clifton and her children could not venture far from the grotto as a group. It was impossible to undertake a large expedition to the interior. Flip, who did not show emotion easily, trembled at the thought of finding the fire extinguished. He remembered his fears when he tried that last match! Flip still had not found a suitable vegetable replacement for the amadou, and not knowing how to obtain fire by rubbing two pieces of wood together the way the savages do, they had to keep a constant watch on the grotto fire. In an excess of precaution, the sailor even thought of lighting additional fires for the night; these were torches made of resinous wood which, driven into the ground several meters from the base of the cliff, burned for several hours.

During this second week, several excursions allowed them to explore the neighborhood but within a limited area. Flip, did not want to leave Mrs. Clifton alone for the night, exposed to attacks from wild beasts, so he made it his duty to return to camp every night. Thus he still could not settle this important question of knowing if the land which served as a refuge for this abandoned family was a continent or an island.

Little by little the utensils of the colony were perfected by the ingenious sailor with skilful help from Marc and Robert. There was no lack of bamboo vases which they could easily make in all sizes. Marc even discovered a tree on the northern shore of the lake from which they could obtain an assortment of readymade bottles. This tree belonged to a species of calabash trees, very common in the tropical zones of two continents, but rarely found in the temperate climates.

"This leads me to believe," the lad said to Flip, "that this land is at a lower latitude than we think."

"In fact," Flip replied, "the presence of these coconut trees tends to confirm that opinion."

"But you, Flip," said Marc, "you could not have known the position of the *Vancouver* at the time when the scoundrels abandoned us on the ocean?"

"No, Mister Marc. These things are the concern of the captain, not the crew. We sailors maneuver the vessel, but we do not decide in which direction it will go. But considering the products produced by this land, I think as you do, Mister Marc, that it is at a relatively low latitude, something like the Balearic Islands in the Mediterranean, or even the provinces of French Algeria."

"However," Marc replied, "this month of March is very cold for this low latitude."

"Well, my lad," Flip said, "don't forget that in some years, even African rivers are frozen over. In February, 1853, I saw ice at Saint-Denis-du-Sig in the province of Oran. Besides, you very well know that in New York, which is at the same latitude as Madrid or Constantinople, on the 40th parallel, the winters are extremely rigorous. The climate depends a great deal on the nature of configuration of the land. It is thus possible that the winters here will be very cold even if we are at a low latitude."

"It is unfortunate that we cannot determine it," said Marc.

"Yes, it is unfortunate, Mister Marc," replied the sailor, "but we have no instrument which will allow us to determine this position, and we will have to be content with guessing. In any case, whether the calabash trees have or do not have the right to grow here, they are growing here and we must profit from it."

While chatting, Marc and Flip returned to the cliff; They brought back about a dozen calabash fruits, a sort of gourd, which could advantageously replace bottles. Flip placed them in a corner of the grotto, because they still did not have shelves or cabinets or walls to separate the area into distinct rooms. However, Mrs. Clifton's methodical mind was able to imagine certain lines in the sand as divisions for the dining room here, the bedrooms there, over here the pantry, over there the kitchen, but above all, everything was neat and tidy.

Mrs. Clifton, holding back her constant grief, worked feverishly to organize her small colony. This mother, we must realize, worked not for herself but for her dear children. She worked hard for them. She did not forget but she controlled herself. Flip observed her and understood her efforts to resist despair. Marc perhaps also noticed it because at times he took her hand, kissed it and said in a low voice:

"Courage, mother, courage!"

And Mrs. Clifton, pressing beloved Marc to her bosom—the living image of his father, his face already showing the gentle intelligence that characterized the engineer—Mrs. Clifton covered him with passionate kisses!

During this week Flip, to the great joy of the children, managed to make some fishing devices, for better or for worse. He had very fortunately discovered a species of leguminous plants whose pines could serve as a fish hook. It was an acacia whose sharp thorns he detached. He bent them over a fire and attached them to the end of some coconut threads. When he made a few of these lines, he baited them with small pieces of meat and, followed by the children and their mother, he went to the lake.

Considering how rudimentary these devices were, Flip was not over confident. The lake was swarming with fish. Most of the fish that nibbled at the bait succeeded in detaching it from the hooks. Marc was very patient. A few fish lunged at the bait just as Marc gave a well-timed jerk on the line. They were thrown out of the water on to the ground. One of these resembled a trout whose silvery sides were covered with small yellowish spots. Even though the meat of this animal was very black, it was declared excellent when grilled on the fire. Other fish of the same species were caught on the following days because, being extremely voracious, they rashly threw themselves on the bait. They also caught a large number of smelts which were a treat for the colony's gourmands.

And so they had healthy and nourishing food—for meat, capybaras and rabbits from the warren—for fish, smelts and trout, mollusks, crabs and lithodomes—for fruits, pine cone almonds—and rock pigeon eggs. They lacked vegetables and especially bread. At each meal, little Belle did without bread.

"The baker is not coming," honest Flip invariably said. "He is late, my charming lady, this wicked baker, and we will most certainly fire him if he continues his bad service."

"Good!" said Jack. "We can do without bread. It is not so good!"

"It will be good when you eat it," Flip replied.

"And when will that be, please?"

"When we have some of it!"

Mrs. Clifton looked at Flip when he said this. He was a worthy man who doubted nothing. He was sure he could make bread one day or as he would say "something like it!"

And so the week passed. Sunday, the 7th of April arrived. It was religiously observed. Before dinner, everyone took a stroll along the top edge of the cliff to a point above the old encampment at the border of the river. From this point they could see far over the Pacific, an immense desert to which Mrs. Clifton gave her attention. The courageous woman had not lost all hope. Flip encouraged her. According to him, the *Vancouver* mutineers had no reason to take Mr. Clifton's life, or the engineer would be landed on a nearby island, or he would escape from the *Vancouver*. His primary concern would then be to search for his wife and children. However vague was his information, it would put this intelligent and audacious man on the right track. The devoted husband and father would surely find their refuge even if he had to search every island in the Pacific.

Mrs. Clifton made no comment to Flip's reasoning. Even admitting that the sailor was right, what about the dangers her husband would encounter and could they themselves survive on this unknown land.

"Besides," said Mrs. Clifton, "if the *Vancouver* mutineers did not intend to kill the engineer, why did they separate him from his wife and children? Why didn't they put him in the same boat that had carried them to land?"

Flip stammered but he had no answer.

During the week beginning Monday, April 8, they increased their food supply. They felt that famine would never be a problem. While working, Flip taught the children about practical things. He tried to make them as skilful and ingenious as he was. He had promised them bows and arrows as soon as he would find the right wood; but in the meantime, he taught them how to set bird traps, by making a noose from coconut threads placed over three fragile sticks arranged in the form of a "4." These nooses were even used with success at the rabbit warren. The rodents were caught with slipknots placed at the entrance to their burrows. Mrs. Clifton suggested that Flip try to domesticate some of these rabbits and gallinaceans; but first they would have to build a poultry yard and there was no time for that as yet.

While making traps and nooses, Flip taught the youngsters to act as decoys to lure birds by imitating sometimes the cry of the female, sometimes the cry of the male. They would turn leaves into a cone shape and blow through them to reproduce bird songs or rustle them to imitate the flight of various species. The children, especially Robert, became skilful in this activity. Little Jack likewise succeeded at it, with his cheeks puffed up looking like an angelic clown. The birds were attracted to it and often caught.

During all these activities, Flip always kept his eye on the fire because there was no way to protect it from a windstorm or a rainstorm. He would have wanted to place the hearth inside the grotto but the thick smoke would make the place uninhabitable. As to making a pipe to let the smoke escape outside, that was a difficult task. Without tools, a pick or pickax, how could he cut a path through the granite wall? If he found some crack, perhaps he could take advantage of it, but the wall was a compact mass and no knife could cut into it. Under these conditions he would have to give up his plan for a chimney inside the grotto and put his hearth outside. However, the sailor did not despair about executing his project one of these days. It nurtured in his brain along with two or three other ideas and he often talked about it with young Marc.

It was at the beginning of the third week, Monday, April 15th, that Flip, Marc and Robert made a new and important excursion into the forest. It was their intention to visit the right bank of the river and the thick woods which covered the slopes. But without a boat or a bridge, it was not easy to cross the waterway either near the lake or at its source. They decided to go around the west and south shores of the lake to reach the river's right bank. This was a trip of three leagues but Robert and Marc barely felt it. There was lots of time. The three excursionists had left early in the morning carrying provisions for the entire day not expecting to return until nightfall. Mrs. Clifton consented to this absence with apprehension.

At six in the morning Flip and the two boys reached the edge of the forest on the lake's eastern shore. The soil was very uneven here. The trees were entangled and formed a green dome that allowed no sunlight in. The moist air under the foliage was in constant shade. Everywhere they saw junipers, larches, firs and maritime pines belonging to the conifer family.

The boys and their companion entered the woods. They walked with difficulty across a path blocked by a network of branches and creepers. They cut and broke these plants with every step. Frightened birds flew away in the dim light. Several quadrupeds, disturbed in their shelters, escaped through the tall grass. To Robert's great disappointment, they could not recognize them let alone capture them.

After a half hour's walk, Marc, who was in front, suddenly stopped and shouted.

"What is it, Marc?" Flip asked, running to the lad.

"The river, friend Flip."

"Already," cried the sailor, in surprise.

"Look," Marc replied.

They saw deep dark water flowing along. The river measured sixty feet across at this point. Large trees, stretching from one shore to the other, formed a gigantic canopy. Both shores were uneven and hidden by the vegetation. The river, thus hemmed in, meandered through a narrow gorge and picturesque ravine. It was a savage area. In some places broken trees formed a clearing where the sun streamed in under the foliage and seemed to set the forest aglow. The air was perfumed with a good healthy odor from the woods enhanced by the balsam of the conifers. The vegetation there was semi-tropical. Intertwined creepers choked the trees under the excess foliage, a nest for reptiles which they must guard against.

Flip and the two lads looked at this ensemble with mute admiration. One thought however was on the sailor's mind. How did they reach this river which, according to his estimate, they should not have reached for yet another hour? He could not explain it. Marc and Robert did not understand it either.

"This river," Marc then said, "is not one we have already explored."

"That is evident," said Flip. "I recognize neither the color of these waters nor the rapidity of its current. These waters are blackish and move with the violence of a rapid."

"You are right, Flip," Marc replied.

"Let's follow its course," and we will soon see that it will not lead us to the sea."

"This river must go somewhere," said Robert.

"In fact," replied Marc, "why couldn't this river be an affluent of one we have already explored."

"Let's move on and we'll find out," said Flip.

The boys followed their companion and a hundred paces further, to their extreme surprise, they found themselves at the western shore of the lake.

"You spoke well, Marc," shouted the sailor. "This river empties into the lake instead of leaving it. The other river overflows from it, as we've seen. The two rivers are but one river, which crossing the lake, reaches the ocean a little below our first encampment."

"I am certain of that," Marc replied. "There are many examples in nature of rivers which follow their course across vast bodies of water."

"Yes," shouted Robert, "and the place where this river comes out of the lake, where my capybara disappeared under the water, it is there, a little to our right, not two miles from here! I see it distinctly, and if we had a raft to get to the right bank, we would have less than an hour's walk to get home."

"Doubtless," replied Marc, "only you forget on thing, my dear Robert."

"What, Marc?"

"It is that after crossing the upper river, we would still have to cross the lower part of the river."

"A wise thought," said Flip.

"Well then," replied Robert, "since we must return by the road we've already taken, and since that's a long ways, let's eat."

Robert's suggestion was accepted. Flip, Marc and he sat down on the shore in the shadow of a magnificent group of acacias. The sailor took some pieces of cold meat from his bag, some hard boiled eggs and a handful of pine kernel almonds. The lake furnished fresh clear water and the meal was soon finished with appetite.

Flip, Marc and Robert then got up and took a last look around. They could see the entire lake.

About a league away, a little to the right, there was the cliff in front of which Mrs. Clifton must be at this moment. But at this distance they could not see her nor even the smoke rising from the hearth. Beyond the watercourse, the shore of the lake, gently curved, was framed in vegetation. Above this there were wooded hills topped by a rounded peak of snow. This poetic scene, the peaceful water, the wind from the forest which came in ripples, the murmur of the wind through the large trees, the contour of sand which stretched from the warren to the sea, the ocean blazing under the sun's rays, all of this nature excited the boy's imagination.

"We must take mother here to admire this magnificent spectacle," said Marc.

From *L'Île mystérieuse* (*The Mysterious Island*, 1874)

"Yes!" replied Robert. "We will bring Jack and Belle along, if we had a boat on the lake."

"But couldn't we move our boat here?" Marc continued, "or even ascend the river with it?"

"A good idea!" shouted Robert. "Then we could explore the upper part of the river. Ah! what a charming excursion that would be, friend Flip!"

"All in good time!" replied the worthy sailor, enchanted to see Marc and Robert so enthusiastic. "But a little patience, my boys. At the moment, two waterways are blocking our way so I suggest that we go home."

It was the best thing to do and Flip gave the signal to leave. The three, with clubs in hand, followed the shore of the lake, which was much easier than the barely practical passages of the forest.

The excursionists, having finished their task, hoped on their return to resume their role as hunters. They would have returned with empty hands but for the fortunate blow struck by Marc against a small hedgehog half asleep in its burrow. This animal had a longer head and a smaller tail than its European congeners. It was also distinguished by its long ears and appeared to be of a species of flesh eating insectivores commonly found in Asia. In short, this hedgehog was rather mediocre game but it was game and as such, Marc suspended it from his club. Besides its quills, hard and sharp, could be used in different ways principally to arm arrows.

At three in the afternoon, Flip, Marc and Robert arrived in front of the grotto. They did well to press home because a few drops of rain were already falling from the cloudy sky. The wind was blowing hard and there was bad weather ahead.

Mrs. Clifton was not sorry to see Flip and her two sons return. During their absence she had not received any unwelcome visit but she heard howling close by. Did this indicate the presence of wild beasts in the vicinity of the grotto? When Mrs. Clifton told Flip about this, he thought that these noises could be coming from apes. Nevertheless, he resolved to put them on their guard. He had already formed a project in his mind to defend the entrance to the grotto with a strong palisade but with only his knife, how could he fell the trees and cut them into girders and planks?

During the week of the 16th to the 21st of April they did not attempt any new excursions. The rain fell incessantly with hardly a clear moment. Very fortunately the wind blew from the northwest and so the grotto was not exposed to its direct gusts. What suffering would the abandoned family have been exposed to under the insufficient shelter of their first encampment? Of what use would the overturned boat have been against the violent rain which struck like a sharp whip? On the contrary, in this solid and impenetrable grotto neither wind nor rain had access. Flip constructed a few channels which prevented the water from reaching the grotto's bed of sand.

The only worry, in fact the only difficulty, was to keep up the flame in the exterior hearth. The resinous torches were also at risk of being extinguished by the showers. Several times eddies of wind struck the cliff threatening to scatter the burning wood. Flip was always on the watch and took every precaution his inventive mind suggested. But he was very uneasy.

During breaks in the weather, the sailor and the two boys rushed to the forest to renew the supply of wood so the reserve did not diminish even though they did not spare the wood. Mrs. Clifton's kitchen suffered from the these atmospheric disturbances. The pot on the fire was overturned more than once. The housewife had to prepare her meals inside the grotto, but to avoid the smoke she only used hot charcoal to grill fish and meat. Little belle helped her with intelligence and papa Flip always complimented her.

Papa Flip however was never idle. He made cord from coconut fibers. This material, in the hands of a cord maker working with specialized tools, can be made into cord of high quality. But Flip, even if he was a bit of a cord maker as all sailors are, did not possess the proper tools. However, with the help of a large revolving drum that he constructed, he succeeding in giving the fibers sufficient strength. He obtained fine strings in this way which he wanted to use to make bows and arrows but the elasticity of the cord was not proper for this application. Flip then thought of using suitably prepared animal catgut for string and so he postponed the fabrication of the bows for the time when he could get some of it. He then spent his time in making some fixed benches to run along the length of the grotto wall. He drove stakes into the sand and used planks taken from the upper deck of the boat which the vessel could spare. He also installed a table in the center of the grotto. These few pieces of furniture were very much appreciated by the household and for the first time, it was on a Friday, the family could finally "set the table."

However, the bad weather did not let up. The showers and the winds continued without respite. Flip wondered if this land had a rainy season that could last for several weeks. That would curtail their hunting and fishing and they would have to work something out.

The rainstorm doubled in violence during the night of the 21st to the 22nd of April. Flip had taken every precaution to safeguard his fire. He did not believe there was any danger since the wind was blowing from the northeast. Only gusts of wind were to be feared. Ordinarily, Flip spent the night watching the fire so that Mrs. Clinton and the children could sleep in the grotto. But for some time now Marc was permitted to share this task with him. The courageous sailor could not go without some sleep and, for better or worse, he agreed to Marc's request. Flip and the young boy, in whom he had total confidence, took turns every four hours.

Now, on this detestable night of the 21st to the 22nd of April, Flip had turned over the watch to Marc and went to lie down on his bed of moss. The fire, furnished with lots of wood, burned brightly. There was no lack of wood piled up at the entrance to the grotto. Marc, protected by some rocks, was doing his best to protect himself from the rain which fell in torrents.

During the first hour there was nothing new. The wind and the sea howled in unison but the weather did not get any worse.

Suddenly, about one thirty in the morning, the wind abruptly changed direction from northwest to southeast. It seemed that a waterspout of air and water mixed with sand struck the cliff.

Marc, blinded for a moment, immediately ran to his fire. There was no fireplace. The storm had scattered the stones. The resinous torches were blown out. The incandescent embers rolled on the sand and threw off their last flame.

Poor Marc was desperate.

"Flip! Flip!" he shouted.

The sailor, suddenly waking, ran to Marc. He understood everything! The lad and he tried to get hold of some of the burning wood thrown about by the storm! But, blinded by the rain and thrown back by the wind, they had no success. In despair, they huddled at the base of the cliff in the darkness.

⊙

# Chapter XII

The situation had become terrible. A gust of wind had sufficed to compromise the future of the unfortunate family! Without fire, what would become of the small colony? How would they prepare the food necessary for their existence? How would they resist the rigorous frost of winter? How would they even protect themselves at night against an attack from wild beasts? Poor Flip did not know what to think. In spite of his courage, he was overwhelmed. He remained there, immobile, silent, his clothes soiled with mud and soaked from the rain.

As to Marc, his despair was indescribable. He was in tears.

"Forgive me! Forgive me!" he murmured.

Flip could find no words to console him.

"My mother! My poor mother!" Marc kept repeating.

"Let us not wake her," the sailor said to him. "She is sleeping! Her children are also sleeping. Let us not wake them! Tomorrow we will find a way to repair this misfortune."

"It is irreparable!" murmured Marc.

"No..." replied Flip, "no... perhaps!... we will see!"

The honest sailor could not find the words to express what he himself did not believe!

He tried to get Marc to go back to the grotto because the rain was falling in torrents. The unfortunate child resisted.

"It's my fault! It's my fault!" he repeated.

"No!" Flip replied. "No, my boy! It was not your fault. Had I been there, the same thing would have happened. No one can fight this

125

storm. In your place, I could not have saved a single spark from this fire. Don't carry on like this, Marc. Let's go back!"

Marc had to give in. He threw himself on his bed of moss. Flip did likewise but the worthy sailor, overwhelmed and in despair to the bottom of his heart, could not find a moment's sleep and for the rest of the night he heard the poor child crying.

Daybreak came at about five in the morning. A feeble light appeared in the grotto. Flip got up and went outside. The storm had left marks of its passage. The wind had piled up the sand into real dunes. Some trees were broken and others uprooted. The ground was scattered with burnt wood. Flip could not restrain a gesture of anger and despair.

At this moment, Mrs. Clifton left the grotto. She took the sailor by surprise. She came up to him and saw his face in pain. He was not able to deceive her.

"What is it, my friend?" she asked.

"Nothing, Madame, nothing!"

"Speak, Flip. I want to know everything."

"Well Mrs. Clifton..." Flip said and hesitated.

"Friend Flip," Mrs. Clifton repeated in a distressed voice, "what other misfortune has struck us in addition to the others we have already endured?"

"It is but one, Madame, only one!" the sailor replied in a low voice.

"And what is that?"

"Look!"

And while speaking, he led Mrs. Clifton to the destroyed fireplace.

"The fire! The extinct fire!" the poor woman murmured.

"Yes," replied Flip. "A storm... during the night!..."

Mrs. Clifton clasped her hands and looked at Flip.

"And you could not prevent it?..." she asked.

"No...Madame," replied the worthy man, evasively. "It was a clumsiness on my part...a default of surveillance...I forgot myself for a moment."

Marc came out of the grotto. He saw his mother. He heard what Flip told her. He understood that Flip wanted to take full blame. He ran to his mother and shouted.

"It wasn't Flip, mother. It was I!, It was I!"

The unfortunate mother opened her arms to her child. She covered him with kisses, but Marc was in despair.

"Don't cry, my child, don't cry," she said to him. "You are breaking my heart."

Robert, Jack and Belle came to Mrs. Clifton. Robert did not spare tender words for his brother. Jack and Belle put their arms around him. This touching scene was made for tears.

"Come, come!" said Flip. "Let's show a little courage, my children. In any event, no one is to blame! There's no fire? Well, we'll make some and get over it!"

"Yes, let us resign ourselves!" murmured Mrs. Clifton.

From *Seconde patrie* (*Second Homeland*, 1900)

But Flip was not a man to resign himself. At any cost he wanted to spend the day to rekindle the fire he had lost. He tried many ways.

There was an abundance of flint on the beach and it would be easy enough to get some sparks out of them using his knife. But sparks must ignite something. Nothing is better suited for this purpose than amadou, which is made from certain fleshy, spongy, velvety mushrooms of the genre polypore. This substance, properly prepared, is extremely flammable especially when saturated with cannon powder or mashed with nitrate or potassium chloride. Perhaps these mushrooms could be found here. Perhaps other mushrooms in the same genre could give them a suitable amadou. They must look for them. But as for directing these sparks onto dry moss—Flip tried this—he had to give it up. Mosses are not flammable!

After several vain attempts, the sailor tried the method used by savages which consists of rubbing wood to produce a flame. But—as has already been noted—the savages use a particular kind of wood Flip was not familiar with. Besides, they use two different methods in rubbing two pieces of wood against each other, either to move one piece of wood in and out through a cavity in the other piece or to rapidly rotate one against the other. Either method requires much practice for success.

Flip tried both methods. Marc, Robert and Jack imitated him without obtaining any result other than scraping their hands. The wood hardly heated from the rubbing.

Flip had to give up this procedure for making fire. He had only one hope, only one idea: to find the polypore mushroom or some other vegetable of the same species whose pulp can replace the amadou.

Four days had passed since this deplorable incident. The abandoned family lost its confidence. They were silent. No more chatter between the children and Flip! No more planning for the future! No more projects in mind for the ingenious sailor!

Their material life showed the effects of these things. They lived off the reserves of smoked meat and fish but their reserves noticeably diminished. Besides, what was the point of renewing them? Why hunt or fish? Without fire they could not use the products of hunting and fishing. Excursions were almost completely suspended. Each day Flip was content to gather the vegetables needed for that day's food supply.

Among these edible vegetables the most precious, without question, was the coconut fruit. These coconuts were gathered with care and became the main part of the family's regular food. The nuts, though not at full maturity, contained a milk of excellent quality. The children pierced one of the three openings at the tail end of the nut which enclosed a soft wood. Then they drank the liquid with extreme pleasure. In addition, when this liquid is enclosed in a bamboo vase or in a gourd for a period of time, carbon dioxide forms giving it an agreeable taste but very intoxicating. When the coconut is fully ripe, the milk hardens supplying a nourishing and healthy almond.

So then, the fruits of these coconuts, numerous in the vicinity of the grotto, could supply and feed this family deprived of meat. Marc and Robert, with the help of cords made by Flip, easily climbed to the top of these high coconut trees. From there, they threw the nuts to the ground but not all of them broke there because they have hard shells. They then had to break them with heavy stones, to the sailor's regret, because if he had had a saw he could have made various kitchen utensils from them.

Another vegetable discovered by the sailor was soon added to the regular food supply of the small colony. It was a marine plant eaten in large quantity by people living along Asian shores. Flip distinctly remembered having eaten it in the past. It was a seaweed belonging to the fucaceae family, a sort of sargasso found abundantly on the rocks at the extremity of the cliff. On letting this seaweed dry, it formed a gelatinous material, rich in nutrients, but with a disagreeable taste. However, they became accustomed to it. The young children at first made faces but they found it excellent and had no trouble eating it.

The mussels and some other shellfish, eaten raw, was a bit of a variation from the ordinary and introduced some protein which the body must have. Besides, at about this time, Marc was fortunate to discover a bank of very useful mollusks along the southern coast below the grotto.

"Mister Flip," he said one day to his friend, the sailor, showing him an oyster shell.

"An oyster bed," Flip shouted.

"Yes, Flip, and if it is true that each oyster produces fifty to sixty thousand eggs, we have an inexhaustible supply."

"You have made a useful discovery, Marc, and tomorrow we will visit this bank. They are delicious but I don't know if they are very nourishing."

"No," replied Marc, "these mollusks contain only a trace of protein and if a man tried to live on them exclusively he would need to eat at least fifteen to sixteen dozen daily."

"Well," shouted Flip, "if the bank is inexhaustible, then we will eat dozens upon dozens! These mollusks are easy to pick up from the bank and I have never heard anyone getting indigestion from them."

"Good," said Marc, "I will bring the good news to my mother."

"Wait, Mister Marc," replied the sailor. "Let's visit the oyster bank first and then we will be sure of our business."

The next day, the 26th of April, Marc and Flip went along the western shore in a southerly direction, crossing the line of dunes. At three miles from their encampment the shore became rocky. Enormous blocks were piled up in a picturesque fashion. Rocks like these are often found along the shores of Brittany where they form deep dark abysses or "chimneys." The rising tide engulfed them with a thunderous noise. A range of reefs rendered this shore unapproachable even by small boats. Everywhere the surf foamed against the rocks. The line of reefs extended up to the extremity of the southwest promontory.

To the rear of these rock piles and at a higher elevation, there were vast plains, real moors, with spiny shrubs and heather growing there. Their savage aspect was in sharp contrast to the cliff area where evergreens grew at the summit. A curtain of trees grew in the background for several miles from the shore up to the first high ground connected to the central mountain system. The country had a desolate appearance.

Flip and Marc went further south, walking near each other but speaking little. The sailor had some vague thoughts forming in his mind. He was obsessed with one special concern. Empty shells by the millions were crackling under his feet. Masses of edible marine snails were there under flat rocks that would be covered by the rising tide. They were excellent mollusks but they required a long cooking. They must think about making use of them.

It was the same for a reptile they were pleased to encounter. It was a magnificent specimen of the order of chelonia, a tortoise of the genus mydase, whose shell has a pleasing green luster.

Flip was the first to see this tortoise sliding among the rocks trying to get to the sea.

"Help, Marc, over here," he shouted.

"Ah! What a fine animal," shouted the lad, "but how will we get hold of it?"

"Nothing is easier," replied Flip, "we will turn it over on its back. Take your stick and imitate me."

The reptile, sensing the danger, withdrew into its shell and into its breastplate. They could no longer see its head nor its paws. It was as still as a rock.

Flip and Marc placed their sticks under the breastbone of the animal and, working together, they were able to turn it on its back. This tortoise measured a meter in length and weighed at least two hundred kilograms.

The overturned reptile allowed only a glimpse of its small flat head which widened further back by the large temporal fossa of the skull hidden under a bony arch.

"And now, Flip," asked Marc, "what will we do with this animal?"

"This is what we will do, my boy. I really don't know what we will do with it! Ah! If we only had a fire to cook it with, what delicious and nourishing food this superb beast would give us. It is a fully grown tortoise. It feeds on this excellent marine plant called zostere. Its flesh is delicate and sweet! With this we could make the celebrated tortoise broth..."

Truly, if the situation had not been so serious, one would think from the tone of the disappointed connoisseur that the sailor was ready to laugh. With what eyes he looked at the tortoise and what sharpened white teeth he showed while looking at it. Worthy Flip must be pardoned for his gluttony!

Marc listened to his companion. He understood the significance of his reticence. He thought again about the scene during the storm and felt guilty.

"Let's go," said Flip, striking his foot on the ground. "There is nothing more for us to do here. Let's leave."

"But what about the tortoise?" replied Marc.

"In fact," replied Flip, "it is not its fault if we cannot eat it. And it is useless and it would be cruel to let it die this way without profit to anyone. Let's use our sticks."

The sticks were used once more as levers and the reptile was put back into its normal position. Flip and Marc moved a few feet away. At first the tortoise did not move. Then, hearing no sound, it showed its head, its large eyes looked at the sea, and its oar shaped flat paws left its shell. Finally the animal moved with a sluggishness one would call "the gallop of a tortoise." It went toward the sea and soon disappeared under the waves.

"Bon voyage, tortoise!" shouted Flip, in a tone both piteous and comic. "You're a lucky reptile so don't brag."

Marc and the sailor resumed their journey interrupted by this encounter. They soon arrived at the area the lad had discovered. It was a series of flat rocks, broken and covered with oysters. Flip said that there would be no difficulty in gathering these mollusks. The bed was immense and they counted thousands of oysters. They were of medium size but excellent as Flip and Marc discovered while enjoying a few whose valves were half-opened. It reminded them of the oyster beds of the French channel port of Cancale, one of the world's best edible varieties. As to the exploitation of this bank, nothing was easier.

"With the boat," Flip said, "when the sea and wind are calm, I will go round the reefs and drop anchor a cable from the bank.[1] We will load the boat with these excellent mollusks and transport them to the foot of the cliff. They will be there within reach and we will make a handsome profit from them."

On this day, Marc and Flip gathered a few dozen to bring to the encampment. The harvest was quickly completed and three quarters of an hour later, they entered the grotto.

The mollusks were well received to serve as the main dish for the next meal.

The problem was to open these oysters without breaking their only knife. This was Flip's responsibility and with good reason. If the hearth still had had a few hot cinders then these oysters, held above the embers, would have opened by themselves, but—this difficulty was the consequence of their lack of fire.

Flip took it upon himself to use his knife to open the oysters. The children, standing around him, naturally took an interest in what he was doing.

At the eighth oyster his knife did not wedge in properly and made a sharp noise.

The blade, cracked at mid-point, fell on the table.

"Curses!" shouted the sailor, in a moment of anger.

No fire! Now his knife broken! What else would happen? What would become of these dear people to whom he was devoted body and soul?

---

1.　A cable equals 125 meters.

# Chapter XIII

**W**as heaven itself now against these poor wretches? They could well believe it after these two incidents of the extinguished fire and the broken knife!

After this last mishap, Flip left the grotto and threw away this useless part of the knife. Without saying a word, the children stood where they were. They understood the import of this irreparable calamity.

After the sailor left, Mrs. Clifton got up. Her eyes were red with fatigue and grief. She went outside.

Flip, with arms crossed, was staring at the ground. She went to him and called him by name.

Flip didn't even hear her.

Mrs. Clifton gently touched his arms.

Flip turned around. Flip was crying! Yes! Large tears were running down his cheeks.

"Flip, my friend," she said to him in a calm gentle voice. "When we first arrived here, when I was desperate and about to succumb to my anguish you came to me and restored me with your words! You taught me that it was my duty to survive for my four children! Well today, now that you have made me strong, is it not my duty in turn to give you strength and make you listen to the same words that you spoke to me and so I say to you: Friend Flip, do not despair."

On hearing this woman, this mother express herself in this way, the worthy sailor was overcome with tears. Seeing that her efforts were effective, Mrs. Clifton continued to speak to him quietly with encouragement. She reminded him the her children and she had not lost confidence in him. She added that if he lost hope, then everything would be over for them. They would perish!

"Yes," the sailor finally said after he had regained possession of himself, "you are right, Mrs. Clifton. It would be unworthy of me especially when you, a woman, show such force of character! Yes! I will fight and overcome this contrary feeling. Your children are my children. I will struggle for them as their courageous father would have done. But you must forgive me for this moment of depression! It got the better of me, but now it is over! It is over!"

Flip shook hands with Mrs. Clifton. Without adding another word, he picked up his broken knife and returned to the grotto. There he lifelessly opened the oysters with what remained of the blade, since it could still be used for that purpose.

The unfortunates ate because they were starving. The mollusks appeased their appetite a bit. The meal was completed with sargassum weeds and pine almonds. But they were silent and one could sense the loss of hope not only in the children but also in the mother and the worthy sailor. They had already met with so many misfortunes.

During the days that followed, April 27th, 28th and 29th, Flip and the children worked courageously to renew the supply of coconuts and sargassum. Twice the sailor used the boat to go to the oyster bank by doubling the shore. He transported several thousand of these mollusks. It was his plan to pack them into a natural pen formed by a few immersed rocks at the foot of the cliff. This new oyster bed would be only a few meters from the grotto. Together with the sargassum, it was their basic food from now on. Their bodies suffered from this meager menu but the brave children never thought of complaining in fear of causing their mother more pain.

But Mrs. Clifton was not able to misjudge the causes of this wasting away, so visible in young children. Flip was not affected as much. But the poor man no longer knew what to do next. He was at the end of his resources. All that was humanly possible to do he had done, but human strength has a limit. The family could no longer count on help from Providence. But would Providence intervene. "We had help from heaven before," Flip thought to himself. "Couldn't heaven help us just a little?"

About this time, Flip resolved to attempt an exploration to the north of the shore. If by chance this land was inhabited, he had to know about it without delay. But Flip wanted to make this reconnaissance alone. The children were weak from undernourishment and could not keep up with him because he intended, if need be, to cover a considerable distance. It was likely that he would not return the same day. It that case it would be better if the boys stayed with their mother for the night.

Flip told Mrs. Clifton about his plan. She approved. If Flip's trip could lead to help, however small this chance, then they must not overlook it.

It was at noon on Tuesday, the 29th of April, that Flip said goodbye to the family and took to the road. For food he cohered only some pine almonds, but he expected to follow the shoreline where he could gather shellfish, mussels and other things.

The weather was fine. A gentle breeze barely made waves on the sea.

Marc accompanied Flip for a quarter of a mile and then prepared to leave him.

"Watch the children, Marc," the sailor said to him, "and if I do not return by nightfall, do not worry about it."

"Yes, Flip. Adieu, Flip," said the lad.

Marc retraced his steps along the cliff and Flip followed the shoreline to the mouth of the river which he soon reached. There he found traces of their first encampment and cold cinders with an extinct fire. There was not an ember or a spark where the boat came ashore and he could not restrain a sigh. His heart was filled with hope then, and now!...

"Still, if I was alone!" he said to himself. "But I'm on a forgotten land with a mother and her children!"

Flip ascended the left bank of the river. He intended to swim across. A swimmer such as he was would have no difficulty. While walking along the river's bank, he saw that the opposite side was very steep with a fault that would allow him to easily climb to the top of the cliff. From this higher elevation, he would be able to observe the ocean on one side and on the other side he would be able to see over the plains that border this part of the coast.

Getting ready to cross the river, he began to take off his clothes to put them into a compact pile over his head. He had just removed his jacket when, on folding it, he felt a small packet in one of the pockets.

The packet was wrapped in a large elm leaf neatly tied with a coconut fiber. He did not know what to think. Very surprised, he untied the cord, unraveled the leaf and saw a piece of biscuit and a bit of meat which he was about to put into his mouth!

But he stopped himself. Mrs. Clifton, seeing that he was going to leave without enough food, had taken this bit of biscuit and this bit of meat from her reserve, the last of it perhaps!

"This good wonderful woman!" he shouted. "But did she think that I would eat this biscuit and this meat when she and her children have nothing!"

That said, Flip wrapped up the small packet and put it back in his pocket to return it to them. Then, undressed, with his clothes on his head, he went into the water.

The water was refreshingly cool. He enjoyed the dip. In a few strokes he reached the right bank. He set foot on a narrow strip of sand and let the breeze dry him a bit. He then dressed and climbed to the summit of the cliff which at this point measured three hundred feet in height.

First Flip looked at the ocean which was always deserted. The coastline extended to the northwest curving in the same way as it did below the river. It formed a sort of bay with a two to three league perimeter. The river emptied into this bay. It really was a kind of open harbor exposed to the winds and waves of the high seas.

The top of the cliff was horizontal for two or three miles and then it seemed to vanish. It was impossible to know what lay beyond.

He saw large tracts of vegetation at the eastern border of the plateau, that is to say opposite the sea. They were the first of the forest stages leading to the central peak. Above that, he saw powerful butresses which converged toward the mountain. All of this land was magnificent, covered with forests and prairies. Its fertility contrasted with the southern region which was arid, savage and desolate.

"Yes!" Flip thought. "We could live well here on this land. A small colony such as ours could prosper! A few tools and a bit of fire and I would guarantee the future."

With this thought, Flip moved on a rapid pace. He looked the countryside over very carefully but without leaving the cliff's edge. After an hour's walk he reached the end of the cliff. Here the cliff formed a cape which was the terminal point of the north of the bay. The shore continued a little to the east and formed a very pointed promontory.

Below the cliff, about two hundred feet from Flip, the ground was a marsh, in fact a vast marsh with large patches of stagnant water, a league in length and width. He saw the capricious outline of the shore, indicated by a long line of dunes that ran from south to north four or five hundred feet from the ocean.

Instead of going around the marshes and heading into the interior, Flip decided to follow the sandy border. A part of the cliff sloped downward which allowed him to reach the lower ground without difficulty.

The soil here was formed of siliceous clay mud mixed with vegetable debris. There were green algae, bulrush, sedge, club rush and, here and there, layers of pasture covering them. Many ponds sparkled under the sun's rays. Neither rain nor unexpected river overflows fed these reservoirs. One had to naturally conclude that these marshes were fed by infiltrations from the soil. That was the case.

Above these aquatic plants, above the stagnant water, a world of birds flew about. A hunter would not have wasted a single shot. Wild duck, teal and snipe lived there in flocks and since they had no fear, it would be easy to approach them. Flip could have killed them with the throw of a stone!

But for what purpose? These appealing specimens of water fowl could only make the sailor feel regretful. He turned away and hurried across the narrow slopes that must lead to the sea. With his stick he probed the vegetation that covered the puddles to avoid falling into the mud. But he made no misstep and moved quickly.

At half past three he finally reached the western limit of the marshes. He now had an easy path between the dunes and the sea. It was a fine sand, strewn with shells, and firm underfoot. He moved quickly, nibbling on some pine cone almonds and quenching his thirst from streams that overflowed from the marshes to the sea. There were no rocks on this part of the shore and consequently no mussels or other mollusks that Flip found so pleasing to eat. But the sailor had a philosophical attitude of mind and stomach and knew how to forego what he didn't have.

And so he continued his exploration to the north. What did he hope to find on these deserted beaches? Some native hut, the debris of a vessel, a wreck he could profit from? No. It would be more correct to say that the worthy sailor, discouraged in spite of himself, moved on mechanically, without a goal, without a thought to distract him and, we must add, without hope!

And so it went for several miles. There was no change in the appearance of the land. The sea was on the one side and the marshes on the other. There was nothing to indicate that this was going to be any different further on. Why should Flip continue his exploration? Why tire himself for no purpose? Anything he didn't already find he could discover another time.

Flip sat down on the sand between two clumps of sharp bulrush whose roots held the dunes from shifting. He stayed there for a half hour with his head resting on his hands without looking at the waves. Then he got up intending to return to camp.

At that moment he heard a bizarre cry that attracted his attention. It was not the clucking of a wild duck but more like a yelping.

Flip climbed to the top of a dune and looked over the marshes. He saw nothing, only flocks of birds rushing to the high trees.

"There must be some animal out there," Flip said to himself, "some reptile scaring these birds!"

Flip looked carefully but there was no movement in the tall grass. The cry did not repeat. The marsh, abandoned by the birds, did not seem to conceal any living being. The sailor listened for a few minutes. He observed the plain, the shore and the line of dunes. In fact, the sand could hide some dangerous visitor. Flip grasped his stick firmly, ready for any attack, but there was no movement in the bulrush.

"I was mistaken," Flip thought. He climbed down from the dune, went to the shore and turned southward.

But the sailor had barely walked for five minutes when he heard the yelping once more and closer.

Flip stopped. This time there could be no mistake. It was definitely a bark, but a stiffled bark, the bark of an exhausted dog.

"A dog here?" Flip wondered.

He listened again and heard two or three yelps.

"Yes, it's a dog," Flip said to himself, retracing his steps, "but not a wild dog. A wild dog doesn't bark like this. What is it trying to say?"

He could not explain the emotion that seized him. Why was a dog here? Did some natives or castaways live here. He must find out at any price.

Flip climbed back over the small chain of dunes. He heard the barking again. He ran past the bulrush, up and down the hillocks of sand. He could not see the dog but it could not be far off.

Suddenly the bulrush parted a little at the edge of a pool of stagnant water. Flip saw the animal. It was an emaciated dog, mere skin and bones, spattered with mud, worn out and barely able to walk.

Flip went toward him. The dog seemed to be waiting for him. It was a large animal with drooping ears and a short tail, its silky hair covered with mud. He belonged to the intelligent race of spaniels. But what was his condition, with bloody feet and his snout spattered with a muddy slime! But when he saw his kind sweet eyes and his affectionate look, Flip knew that he had nothing to fear from this animal.

The dog crawled toward Flip. He seized Flip's pants between his teeth and tried to drag him to the shore.

Suddenly Flip stopped and knelt on the sand. He looked carefully at the dog's head to see if he could recognize him under the mud. Then he let out a cry.

"He, he! No, this is not possible!"

He looked and looked again. He wiped the animal's head...

"Fido!" he finally shouted.

On hearing his name the dog became agitated. He wagged his tail and tried to jump for joy. He had been recognized!

It is very easy to understand Flip's amazement when he found Fido here on this deserted shore. Fido was the loyal companion of the engineer, Clifton, and a friend of the young children, a dog he had often petted on board the *Vancouver*. He knew Fido well!

"But he did not come here alone," Flip shouted. "What happened on board the *Vancouver*?"

It seemed that Fido understood the sailor's question. He seemed to want to answer. He barked and tried to pull Flip forward at the risk of tearing the sailor's clothes. This intelligent pantomime could not be mistaken.

"There is something here," he said. Let's go.

And he followed the shrewd animal.

Flip and Fido, one leading the other, crossed the dunes and descended to the shore. Flip seemed revived and ran ahead of Flip and came back. The sailor was overexcited. He was full of hope but he could not say what this was based on. He did not dare to put his thoughts in order. He went into the unknown. He forgot his fatigue and the long journey he had already made and the long way back!

It was five o'clock in the evening when the sun was already low on the horizon that Fido stopped at the foot of a rather elevated dune. Then, looking at Flip one last time, he yelped strangely and dashed through a narrow passage between two dunes.

Flip followed him. He turned around a large clump of bulrush and let out a cry when he saw a man stretched out on the ground.

He ran toward him and recognized the engineer Clifton.

# Chapter XIV

**W**hat an encounter! By what chance?... or say rather that divine providence brought this about! What a change in the situation of the Clifton family. Father and husband restored to them. Their deprivations and present misery are of no importance. They can now look to the future.

Not for one moment did it occur to Flip that the body lying stretched out on the sand might be a corpse. Harry Clifton's face was turned skyward, pale, eyes shut, mouth half open with his tongue between his teeth. His body, with hands extended, was completely immobile. His clothes, spattered with mud, showed traces of violence. Flip saw an old flint gun, an open knife and a grappling hook lying near the engineer.

Flip leaned over the engineer's body. He undid his clothes. The body was warm but horribly emaciated from the deprivations and suffering. Flip lifted Clifton's head. He then saw a large wound on the skull covered by a thick blood clot.

Flip held his ear against Clifton's chest. He listened.

"He is breathing! He is still breathing!" he shouted. "I will save him. Some water! Some water!"

A few feet away Flip saw a small brook on a bed of sand flowing from the marsh to the sea. He ran there, dipped his handkerchief into this fresh water and returned to the invalid. First he bathed his head and delicately detached the dried blood sticking to the hair. Then he wet the engineer's eyes, lips and face.

Harry Clifton moved a bit. His tongue moved slightly between his swollen lips and Flip thought he heard this word: "Food! Food!"

"Ah!" Flip shouted, "the unfortunate! He is dying of hunger! Who knows how many days he has not eaten!"

But how should he correct this misfortune? How should he revive this life about to escape him?

"Ah!" Flip shouted, "the biscuit and the meat that Mrs. Clifton... It was an inspiration from heaven that made the worthy woman do this!"

Flip ran to the spring and carried back a little water in a shell. Then he mixed a bit of the biscuit into the fresh water making a sort of soup of it and carried a handful of it to the wounded man's mouth.

Harry Clifton could swallow one or two handfuls of the bread soup only with difficulty. His contracted throat barely allowed food to pass through. However he succeeded in swallowing a bit of this dissolved bread and he seemed more alive.

During this while, Flip spoke to him like a mother speaks to her sick child. He lavished the most encouraging words on him. A half hour passed and Harry Clifton half opened his eyes. His look had a deep effect on Flip. He recognized the honest sailor—that was evident—because his lips tried to form a smile.

"Yes, Mister Clifton," Flip said to him, "it really is me, the mate from the *Vancouver*...You recognized me well! Yes! yes, I know what you would like to ask me! But do not speak! It is not worth the effort!. Only listen to me. Your wife, your children... everyone is well. They are happy! Very happy! And what joy when they see you again! What rapture!"

Flip immediately understood the slight movement of the injured man's fingers. Flip took the engineer's hand and gently squeezed it.

"It is understood, sir, it is understood," the sailor repeated, "but don't trouble yourself! Don't mention it! On the contrary, it is I who must thank you for coming to find us. That was a nice thing to do."

And jolly Flip laughed. He gently patted the injured man's hand. Fido joined in with his caresses, licking his master's cheeks.

Suddenly Flip shouted.

"I'm thinking. You must be dying of hunger, Fido! So eat then, mister, eat. Your life is still more precious than mine!"

While speaking, Flip gave the loyal dog a few small pieces of meat and biscuit. Fido jumped up and devoured it. Flip gave him more. This was a day to be lavish. Besides, he seriously believed that, with the father found, he need no longer worry about the well being of the small colony.

However, Harry Clifton had to gather all his strength to swallow the moist biscuit. While he was eating, Flip examined his wound. The bone of the skull was merely bruised. Flip had experience with this. Twenty times he had occasion to treat it himself. Other than this, there was nothing wrong. Fresh water would be the way to treat this fracture. A compress, made with Flip's handkerchief, was applied to Clifton's head. Flip then prepared a bed of grass and marine plants which he arranged on a slope of sand. The wounded man was carried to the improvised couch. Flip covered him with his jacket and his woolen shirt to protect him from the cold of the night.

Clifton could only thank him with a glance.

"Don't speak. Don't speak!" Flip kept repeating. "I do not need to know how you came here. Later you will tell us. The important thing is that you are here and, merciful heaven, you are home!"

He then whispered into his ear. "Can you hear me, Mister Clifton?" he asked.

Harry Clifton made an affirmative sign with his eyes.

"Listen to me, then, " Flip repeated. "Night is coming on and judging from the sky, it will be a fine night. If you could walk a bit or even if I could carry you for a mile or two, we would leave together; but to follow the irregularities of the shoreline, four leagues separate us from the encampment where we will find your wife and your children, in good health, I repeat. That's a valiant woman you have there, Mister Clifton, and courageous children."

With a look, Clifton thanked the worthy sailor. He was revived by hearing those he loved so much spoken about in this way.

"This is what I am going to do," Flip said. "The most pressing concern is that you be taken to the grotto where there will be no lack of attention. I will leave you here for a few hours. I put next to you in this shell a little moist biscuit and some small pieces of meat in case you have the strength to eat. Fido will not disturb it. He promised me that. In another shell you will find some sweet water to wet your lips. Very good. You hear me. Good. I am leaving. It is eight o'clock. In two hours at the most, I will be back at the grotto because I have good legs. Once there, I will take the boat, you know which one, the boat from the *Vancouver*, which these honest rascals from the *Vancouver* gave us. There's a good wind blowing from the southwest and in not more than an hour and a half after that I will be back at your side. So it will

From *L'Île mystérieuse* (*The Mysterious Island*, 1874)

be for three and a half hours, mister engineer, make it four hours, that I ask you to wait for me. I will be here at midnight. Together we will wait for the morning low tide which will favor our return. At eight in the morning you will be lying on a bed of moss, warm and comfortable, surrounded by your dear family. Is this arrangement to your liking?"

"Yes, Flip," Harry Clifton murmured.

"That said," the sailor replied, "I am leaving, Mister Clifton, wait for me with confidence and you will see that I will return exactly when I said."

Flip made some last minute arrangements. After carefully putting a border around the wounded man's bed, he once again pressed his hand. Then he addressed the faithful dog.

"As for you, Fido, keep a good lookout my boy, watch your master and don't eat his food!"

Doubtless Fido understood him because he barked in a way that sounded like a "yes" and Flip was satisfied. Then the worthy man left at a good pace.

With what energy and enthusiasm Flip ran back to the encampment! What joy sustained him. He forgot all about the fatigues of the day. No. He would not return to the grotto with empty hands. He no longer thought about his broken knife or his extinct fire. Wouldn't an engineer like Harry Clifton know how to handle that? He could make everything from nothing. Flip now thought of thousands of projects and did not doubt that they would be accomplished one day!

However, night came on. Land and sea blended into the darkness. The moon, then in third quarter, would not rise before midnight. Flip had to count on his instinct and ingenuity to find the wretched route. He could not move in a direct line for fear of getting entangled in the marshes. He must follow the shoreline to the beginning of the cliff. Once arrived at that point, the difficulties would begin. He would have to recognize the narrow foot paths that winded through the pools. Flip could not afford any wrong move. He even laughed about it but he did not resent this obstacle. At every step, aquatic birds were awakened and flew away across the weeds.

"Bah!" Flip repeated. "This soil is like a swamp. But the holes are only holes and I have seen better ones than these in my time. I have already sunk into holes deeper than these and there is no marsh that can hold me back!"

With this kind of reasoning, one can accomplish many things! Flip, soaked from head to toe, covered with mud, kept moving forward. He reached this breach from which he had earlier descended to the marshy plane from the cliff's summit. Twenty others would not have recognized the way to this practical path in the darkness. But Flip was not mistaken about it. He had night vision like a cat. He climbed the breech as swiftly as an antelope hunter.

"At last," he said to himself, "I'm on solid ground! This lousy marsh has worn me out. I even think I'm a bit tired... Ah! I can still run at full speed!"

And Flip did just that. With elbows close to his hips and chest pushed forward, he ran like a professional racer. In a few minutes he crossed the granite plateau and reached the right bank of the river. Taking off his clothes, that is to say his trousers and his thick wool shirt which he made into a pack placed on his head, he dashed into the water crossed the river, dressed himself on the other side, all in a minute. He reached their first encampment, crossed the beach and ran directly to the grotto.

Flip turned the last bend a few minutes after ten o'clock. He was hailed by a voice he immediately recognized.

"Hi, Flip!"

"Hi, Mister Marc," he replied.

The sailor and the lad were soon united.

Marc was not able to sleep. He was anxious about Flip's absence. While his mother was asleep, he went outside to guard the family and wait for his friend's return. It seemed that this night passed without Flip would never end.

But the sailor had not expected Marc to be awake. For a moment he hesitated to tell him that he must immediately return to bring his father back. Would this unexpected news be too much of a shock?

"But no," Flip thought, "this young lad has the strength of an adult and besides, good news is never fatal."

"Well, Flip," Marc asked, his heart pounding, "what happened?…"

"There is something new, Mister Marc," the sailor replied.

"Ah, Flip," the lad shouted, "can we give me mother something to hope for? These are difficult trials for a woman. She will collapse from them.

"Mister Marc," replied Flip, "if you do not thank heaven for the news I am about to give you, you will be an ingrate."

"What is it, Flip? What is it?" the lad asked, trembling with emotion.

"Be calm, sir," replied the sailor, "and listen to me. I found Fido."

"Fido! Our dog! My father's dog?"

"Yes! Fido, emaciated, exhausted, dying; but he recognized me."

"And then…" said Marc, his voice changed, "and then… speak Flip. Fido… you did not bring him?…"

"No, Mister Marc, I left him… down there… to watch someone…"

"My father?"

"Yes!"

Marc would have collapsed if Flip had not seized him. The lad cried in the sailor's arms. In an emotional voice Flip told him all that had transpired during his encounter. Ah! What joy! His father! His father alive!

"Let's leave," he shouted, tearing himself from the sailor's arms. "He must be brought here."

"Yes," replied Flip, "and there is not an instant to lose. Here is what I propose to do, Mister Marc."

Flip told the lad of his plan to take the boat to sea and sail it to the place where he left Fido to guard Harry Clifton. He wanted to keep his promise to return at midnight. The tide was rising which would be in their favor and he wanted to profit from it to sail more rapidly to the north.

"And my mother," said Marc, "shouldn't I warn her?"

"Mister Marc," replied the sailor, "this is a delicate matter. Listen to the dictates of your heart. You must prepare Mrs. Clifton little by little..."

"Then I'm not to go with you, Flip?" the lad asked.

"In the interests of your mother, Mister Marc, I believe that you should stay here."

"But my father! My father who is waiting for me!"

"No, my boy. You are the oldest of the family. You must watch over them in my absence. Besides, remember that we will be returning not later than eight o'clock in the morning. I ask you to be patient for only a few hours."

"But," the lad still argued, "what if my poor father collapses from his suffering and I am not there to..."

"Mister Marc," the honest sailor replied seriously, "I told you about a living father and it is a living father I will return to his family!"

Marc had to give in to Flip's logic. In fact, they agreed that Marc's presence at the grotto was necessary not only to keep watch on its hosts but also because the lad was the only one who could skillfully prepare his mother for the immense joy that awaited her. Besides, Marc could not leave without telling Mrs. Clifton about his departure and he did not have the courage to interrupt her sleep.

So Marc went to help the sailor get the boat ready. The sail was still in place because Flip had recently used the boat to pick up the oysters. He hauled it into the water.

At this moment the current between the islet and the shore flowed northward. In addition, the southwest breeze favored the boat's movement. The night was dark, it is true, and the moon would not rise for another two hours. But that did not prevent a sailor such as Flip from guiding it in the dark. Flip placed himself to the rear of the vessel.

"Embrace my father," the lad shouted.

"Yes, Mister Marc," replied the sailor, "I will embrace him for you and for everyone."

Flip hoisted the sail and soon disappeared in the shadows.

It was half past ten in the evening. Marc remained alone on the shore, in agitation. He could not decide whether to return to the grotto. He wanted to come, to go, to breath the fresh air of the night. No! He would not wake his mother at any price. What would he say to her? Could he hide his thoughts from her, could he keep silent in her presence?

But why keep silent? Hadn't Flip recommended that little by little he should prepare Mrs. Clifton for seeing the person she thought was lost forever? His father returned to him, husband to his wife, and this would happen in a few hours. But what to say, what to think, what to do?

Walking back and forth between the shore and the grotto, Marc was absorbed in thought. Soon the night's darkness cleared up a bit. A gentle light appeared vaguely outlining the high points of the coast, leaving a line between sky and sea. It was the moon rising in the east. It was now past midnight. If Flip had completed his trip, he would now be at Harry Clifton's side. Marc visualized his father with a friend watching over him. This thought calmed him a bit. In his excited mind, he imagined the worthy sailor lavishing devotion on his father and he wished that he could lavish it himself.

Then Marc thought of what he must say to Mrs. Clifton. He would have to tell her that Flip returned during the night and left with the boat and why he did this. He decided to tell her that during his excursion Flip had discovered an island near shore that appeared to be inhabited and that, for better or worse, he wanted to reach it before dawn. He would then add that in Flip's opinion, this islet might be a refuge for some castaways because the sailor thought he saw a mast erected at a high point to attract the attention of navigators. Marc would then hint that these castaways could well be the men from the *Vancouver*.

In fact, with this vessel lost and wandering, deprived of its captain, maneuvered by an ignorant second mate and a crew in revolt, could it not have given way against the reefs of the island? He would leave his mother with this possible hypothesis.

Marc thought about this for a long time afraid of saying too much or saying too little. However, the moon passed the meridian and vague light appeared in the east, announcing the coming sunrise. Full light comes rapidly at this relatively low latitude.

Marc was seated on a rock absorbed in his thought when, raising his head, he saw his mother standing in front of him.

"You didn't sleep, my child?" Mrs. Clifton asked.

"No, mother," Marc replied, getting up, "No. I could not sleep while Flip was away. It is my duty to watch over everyone."

"Dear Marc, my dear child," Mrs. Clifton said, holding the lad's hands. "And what about Flip?" she added.

"Flip?" said Marc, hesitating a bit. "Oh, Flip returned."

"Returned!" Mrs. Clifton replied, looking around her.

"Yes," Marc said, "returned... and left. He took the boat."

Marc was stammering. His mother looked straight into his eyes.

"Why did Flip leave again?" she asked.

"Mother, he left again..."

"What is it, Marc? Are you hiding something from me?"

"No, mother, I wanted to say... I'm not sure, but there's hope..."

Mrs. Clifton took her son's hand and said nothing for a few moments.

"Marc," she said, "what happened?"

"Mother, listen to me," Marc said.

Marc then told Mrs. Clifton about the fictional incidents of Flip's trip. Mrs. Clifton listened without interrupting him. But when her son spoke about the castaways from the *Vancouver* and the possibility of finding them on this island, Mrs. Clifton let go of his hand, got up and went to the shore.

At this moment she was surrounded by her other children. They threw themselves into her arms. Mrs. Clifton, without knowing why, without saying anything, embraced them passionately. Then, without asking for any new explanations from her eldest, but with her heart agitated with an inexpressible emotion, she got Jack and Belle ready for breakfast.

As for Marc, he continued to walk along the shore. He decided not to say anything else or his secret would soon leave his lips. However, he had to say something to Robert who saw that the boat was no longer in its usual place and asked what had become of it.

"Flip took it last night so he could pursue his exploration further to the north."

"Then Flip came back?"

"Yes."

"And when will he return?"

"Most likely this morning, about eight o'clock."

It was then seven thirty. Mrs. Clifton, now back at the shore, said:

"My children, if you like, we will go to the cliff to meet our friend, Flip."

They agreed. Marc did not dare to look at his mother. He paled at the thought of saying anything more to her and he felt all his blood returning to his heart.

Mother and children went to the shore. Soon, Robert saw a white speck on the horizon. It was a sail, there was no mistake about that. It was Flip's boat. With the help of the ebb tide he doubled the north point of the bay. In a half hour he would reach their first encampment.

Mrs. Clifton looked at Marc who was about to shout, "My father, my father is there," but with a supreme effort he held himself back.

The boat rapidly approached the shore. The waves under its stem were foaming and the wind tilted it. It was soon close enough for Robert to call out:

"Look, there is an animal on board."

"Yes, a dog," Marc replied, saying this in spite of himself.

His mother went to his side.

"Ah! If only it was our Fido," little Belle said.

A few moments later, as if he were answering his sister, Robert said:

"But it is Fido! I recognize him, mother! It's Fido."

"Fido," Mrs. Clifton murmured.

"Yes, mother!" the lad repeated, "Fido. Our brave dog. But how did he get there with Flip? Fido! Fido!" he shouted.

There heard a bark.

"He recognizes me! He recognizes me!" Robert repeated. "Fido! Fido!"

At this moment the boat reached the narrow channel between the islet and the shore. The tide pushed it forward at great speed. It came abreast the start of the cliff. It doubled the point thanks to a skilful movement of the helm.

At this moment the dog threw himself into the water and swam toward the group of children. He swam obliquely to the current that threatened to pull him under. He soon reached the sand and ran to the children who gave him many a caress.

But Marc ran to the boat. Mrs. Clifton, pale as death, followed him.

The boat avoided an obstacle and gently touched shore. Flip was at the helm. A man lying next to him lifted himself and Mrs. Clifton fainted into the hands of the husband who had given her so many tears!

# Chapter XV

**A**t last! They were reunited. They forgot about their deprivations, their miserable present, the menacing future that awaited them, the terrible ordeals struck by fate time after time. They forgot themselves in this common embracement that united them to Harry Clifton. What tears of joy! Mrs. Clifton recovered. She sank to her knees near the boat and thanked God.

According to Belle's almanac, today was Sunday, May 1, a day for thanksgiving. The entire family passed it at the patient's bedside. Harry Clifton felt better. The attention that Flip had given him, this bit of nourishment he had already been able to take, the hope, the joy, everything contributed to restore his lost strength. He was still very weak but alive, very much alive, as Flip had told young Marc.

Harry Clifton was not able to walk from the boat to the grotto. Flip and two of the children carried him on a stretcher of branches. On each side, Belle and Jack held their father's hand. Mrs. Clifton prepared a bed of grass and moss in the best corner of the grotto. Harry Clifton was placed there. Tired from the trip and the emotion, he soon fell asleep. Flip considered this a good thing.

"I am a bit of a doctor," he told Mrs. Clifton, "or at least I have often treated sick people. I know about this. This sleep is good, very good! As to the engineer's wound, It's a trifle. We will take care of it until he gets better. But I repeat, Madam, this wound is a joke. As for myself, I once had my head scratched between two vessels at the wharf in Liverpool. Does it show? No. And since this accident, I no longer have headaches.

You see, Mrs. Clifton, if one doesn't die from a headwound in three days, his recovery is assured."

Flip betrayed his pleasure by babbling on, all the while laughing and smiling. During Harry Clifton's sleep, he told the children and their mother all that occurred since the previous day, his exploration of the north shore, the crossing of the marsh, Fido's appearance, who deserved all the credit for the affair because Fido had recognized Flip but Flip, "imbecile, rattlehead," had not recognized Fido.

If the loyal dog was praised and caressed, it was painful to look at him. The day before Marc had killed a canard during a visit to the shores of the lake and he offered the canard to the intelligent Newfoundland animal. He made a meal of it, which prompted Jack to say:

"Good dog! That you are satisfied with raw meat!"

As to Mr. Clifton's story, how he escaped from the *Vancouver*, how he came here, Flip was still ignorant about it and he could say nothing.

"And that is fortunate," he added, "because we will give the brave gentleman the pleasure of telling us himself about his adventures."

However, they must think about Harry Clifton. If only, on his wakening, they could offer him a few cups of warm soup! They must not think of that. Instead of this comforting soup, Flip thought of preparing some fresh oysters, a real dish for an invalid, which a weak stomach could easily digest. Mrs. Clifton was put in charge of choosing the best of these mollusks from the oyster bed.

All this while, Flip searched the boat for anything Harry Clifton may have had with him, precious objects if ever they were. He found a knife with several blades and a saw, which could replace Flip's knife, and an ax the skilful sailor would appreciate and which would become his most useful tool. There was also a pistol, unfortunately unloaded, without a single grain of powder in it so they could make no fire from that. Of the three objects, it was the least useful, although Robert could amuse himself with it by bellicosely brandishing it.

They then waited for Harry Clifton to wake up. Around eleven o'clock, the engineer called for his wife and his children. Everyone ran to him. His tranquil sleep had strengthened him. The healing of the wound was already in an advanced stage and Mrs. Clifton and Flip soon dressed it.

Mrs. Clifton then offered her husband some oysters. They were so appetizing that he ate them with extreme pleasure. Poor woman. Her provision of meat and biscuit was exhausted and she trembled at the thought that her dear patient might ask for a little of this food that she no longer had. But this time, at least, the oysters were sufficient. His voice came back. He called everyone by name. A little color reappeared to his pale hollow cheeks. He was even able, with pauses between each phrase, to tell what had happened after the mutiny on the *Vancouver*.

After the death of Captain Harrison, the vessel turned south. The second in command had taken over. Clifton was a prisoner in his cabin and could speak to no one. He thought of his wife and his children abandoned on the ocean. What would become of them? As for himself, there was no doubt about his fate. These madmen would put him to death.

A few days passed and, as often happens when a vessel finds itself under these conditions, the Kanakas who were inspired to revolt against Captain Harrison by the second mate, in turn revolted against him. This wretch provoked them with his cruelty. The second mate was a rogue of the worst kind.

Three weeks after the initial revolt, the *Vancouver* turned back north. It was held in place by a calm wind. They sighted the northern shore of none other than this very land. However, they did not see the part already explored by Flip.

In the afternoon of April 24th, Harry Clifton, who was continually locked in his cabin, heard a commotion on the bridge mixed with shouting. He understood that there was a crisis. Perhaps this was a chance to break free. They would not be watching him so carefully and he might profit from it. He forced open the door to his cabin. He ran to the mess hall, grabbed a loaded pistol from the arms rack and a boarding ax. He then ran to the bridge. Fido was with him.

The revolt between the Kanakas and the crew was fearsome. When Clifton appeared on the bridge it became bloody. The howling crowd of Kanakas, armed with picks and axes, surrounded the crew. Soon the second mate was stained in blood and mortally wounded.

Clifton understood the new situation. The Kanakas would kill him in a moment. He saw a shore two miles windward. He resolved to risk his life to reach it. He ran to the bulwarks in order to throw himself into the sea.

But they saw Harry Clifton. Two of the mutineers ran toward him. He stopped one of them with a pistol shot. However, the other struck him on the head with a crow-bar which he could not avoid. He fell overboard. The cold water revived him. When he returned to the surface and opened his eyes, he saw that the *Vancouver* was already several cables in the distance. He heard a barking. It was Fido. The vigorous Newfoundlander swam to his side and he was able to hold on to the animal.

The tide carried him to land but it was a large distance to cover. Harry Clifton was wounded and exhausted. Twenty times he sank beneath the waters but twenty times his faithful companion held him above the waves. The current moved Clifton along and after a long battle he finally felt solid ground beneath his feet. With Fido's help, he struggled out of the wave's reach and dragged himself to the dunes. Here he would have died of hunger if Flip, guided by the dog, had not found him.

Harry Clifton ended his story and shook Flip's hand.

"When did you leave the *Vancouver* and its cargo of rascals?" the sailor asked him.

"The 23rd of April, my friend."

"Good!" Flip replied. "Since today is the first of May, it was eight days you were lying on the dunes awaiting death. And at first I was fearful. What a brute I am."

However, after he finished his story, after he received the caresses of his wife and children one more time, be asked for some warm soup.

Everyone looked at him. Mrs. Clifton grew pale. Must they tell the patient of their privations? Flip felt this was not the time to make this confession. Silently, he signaled Mrs. Clifton. With hesitation, he responded to the engineer.

"Good, sir," he said in a happy voice, "warm soup. Yes, very good, very good! Capybara soup. for example. We will make it for you. But at the moment the fire is extinct. While we were chatting I foolishly let the flame die out. But I will soon light it."

And Flip left the grotto followed by Mrs. Clifton.

"No, Madam," he said to her in a whisper. "No, we still must not tell him about it. Tomorrow! Later!"

"But what if he asks about the warm soup that you promised him?"

"Yes! I understand that! It is very embarrassing. But we must have more time. Perhaps he will forget about it. Hold on. Distract him. Tell him about what happened to us."

From *Le Phare du bout du monde* (*The Lighthouse at the End of the World*, 1905)

Mrs. Clifton and Flip returned to the grotto.

"Well, Mister engineer, how are you feeling," the sailor asked him. Better, no doubt. If you are strong enough to listen to us, Mrs. Clifton will tell you about our adventures. She saved the family. You will see that."

On a sign from her husband, Mrs. Clifton began her story. In detail she told of their separation from the *Vancouver* in the boat, the arrival at the mouth of the river, their first encampment under the overturned boat, the excursion into the forest, the exploration of the cliff and the shore, the discovery of the lake and the grotto, the hunting and the fishing. She did not forget to tell about the broken knife but she did not say a word about the storm and the extinguished fire. Then she spoke about their children, their devotion and their courage. They were worthy of their father. Finally, in tearful gratitude, she praised Flip and his sacrifices. The excellent man blushed, not knowing where to hide.

Harry Clifton rose up a bit, placed his two hands on Flip's shoulders, seating him near his bed.

"Flip," he said to him with a vivid emotion, "you saved my wife and children, you even saved me! Bless you, Flip!"

"Not at all, Mister engineer," replied the sailor, "it is nothing to speak of... it just turned out that way... You are a decent man..."

Then, whispering to Mrs. Clifton:

"Continue, Madam, continue. He is forgetting about the soup!"

He then spoke to Harry Clifton again.

"Besides," he replied, "much is still to be done. We are waiting for you. I will do nothing without your orders. I needed an ax and a knife to replace my broken knife and you were kind enough to provide me with one. Isn't that true, Mister Marc?"

"Yes, Flip," the young lad replied with a smile.

"Those are charming children you have there, Mister Clifton. A worthy, lovable family! Mister Robert is a little impatient but he will quiet down. Believe me, with these fine lads and with you, an engineer, we will do many things here."

"Especially if you help us, friend Flip," Mr. Clifton replied.

"Yes, father," Marc shouted. "Our friend Flip can do everything. He is a sailor, fisherman, hunter, carpenter, blacksmith..."

"Oh! Mister Marc!" Flip replied. "That is not an exaggeration. As a sailor I can do a little of everything but badly, very badly. I do not have ideas. I need supervision. But Mister Clifton has that, I... We will be very happy here!"

"Very happy," Harry Clifton said, looking at his wife.

"Yes, my dear Harry," Mrs. Clifton replied. "I have nothing to wish for since you were returned to me. Well, perhaps! But in any case, we have no parents or friends to depend on. We would return to our country as strangers! Yes! I agree with our friend Flip. We could live happily in this corner of the world counting on what the infallible Almighty has in store for us!"

Harry Clifton pressed his dear wife to his heart. She was so confidant and strong. His strength would return in this small world where he would focus all his affections.

"Yes," he said, "Yes! We can still be happy. But tell me, friend Flip, does this land seem to be a continent or an island?"

"I beg your pardon, sir," Flip said, preferring to carry on the conversation in this tone of voice, "but this is a question we still have not been able to resolve."

"It is important, however."

"Very important, in fact. But daylight will last longer now. As soon as your strength returns, Mister Clifton, we will explore our new domain and we will know if we have the right or not to qualify as islanders!"

"If this land is only an island," Harry Clifton replied, "we have little hope of ever leaving it, because ships hardly ever frequent this portion of the Pacific!"

"In fact, sir," the sailor replied, "in this situation we must rely only on ourselves and if we ever do leave it, it will only be because we ourselves have furnished the means of leaving it."

"By making a ship!" Robert shouted.

"Hey, hey!" Flip replied, rubbing his hands, "we have a boat, which is already something."

"My children," Harry Clifton said, "before looking for a way to leave the island, if it is one, we must first settle in. Later we will see what is best to do. But tell me, Flip, you have doubtless explored the immediate countryside. What do you think?"

"Much of it is good, Mister engineer. It is, without doubt, a charming land and especially very varied. In the north, where you were waiting for me, there is a vast marsh swarming with aquatic birds. This will be an excellent preserve for our young hunters.

"Yes, my boy, a marsh made just for you, but you need not get all soiled up there. In the south, sir, in an arid, savage region of rocks and dunes, there is a bank of oysters, good oysters like the ones you just ate, an inexhaustible bank. Then, beyond the shore, there are verdant prairies, magnificent forests, trees of every species, and coconut trees. I am not fooling you. We have real coconut trees. Mister Robert, if it will not trouble you, pick a coconut for your father, a coconut not too hard, you hear me, so it has the best milk!"

Robert left on the run. Harry Clifton, listening to the sailor's happy blabbing, did not think of asking about his warm soup. Flip, enchanted, continued with renewed ardor.

"Yes, mister engineer, these forests must be immense, and we have seen only a small part of it. Mister Robert has already killed a charming capybara! And then, but I really forgot, we also have a warren filled with excellent rabbits! We have a very agreeable islet that we have not yet had the time to visit! We have a lake, sir, not a pond, a real lake, with beautiful water and delicate fish that have no desire other than to be caught!"

Hearing this recital, Harry Clifton could not conceal a smile. Mrs. Clifton, with tearful eyes, looked at the good Flip and Belle and Jack could not take their eyes off him. Never had it occurred to them that their domain could provoke such enthusiastic descriptions.

"And the mountain," Jack said.

"Yes, the mountain," Flip continued. "The young man is right. I forgot about the mountain with its snow at the peak. A real peak, not a little sugar loaf. No, a high peak, six thousand feet high at least which we will climb one day! Truly, whether this land is a continent or an island, we could not have chosen a better one!"

At this moment, Robert returned, carrying a fresh coconut. Flip poured the milk into a bamboo cup and the patient drank this refreshing liquor with extreme pleasure.

For another hour Flip continued to charm his audience with a picture of the countryside, the incontestable advantages it presented, telling the engineer about the projects that could be easily completed, what you would do if you immigrated to your favorite land.

"We will be the Robinsons of the Pacific!" Marc said.

"Good!" said Jack. I have always dreamed of living on an island with the Swiss Family Robinson!"

"Well, Mister Jack, you have been given your wish!"

Flip forgot that in this imaginary tale the author placed all of industry and nature at the disposal of the castaways. He chose for them a particular island where there was no fear of the rigors of a winter climate. Each day, little by little, they found the vegetables and the animals they needed without looking for it. They already had arms, tools, powder, and clothes. They had a cow, sheep, a donkey, and pigs. Their stranded vessel furnished them with an oversupply of wood, iron, and grain of every kind. No! That situation could not be the same! The Swiss castaways were millionaires! Here were unfortunates, reduced to complete destitution, who must make everything they needed.

But Harry Clifton could not deceive himself. He kept thoughts to himself that differed with Flip's ideas. He confined himself to asking the good sailor if there was anything he really regretted.

"Nothing, Mister Clifton, nothing!" Flip replied. "I do not have a family. I was even an orphan, I believe, before coming into the world!"

With that, Flip began to talk again. He told Mr. and Mrs. Clifton that he was a Frenchman by birth, a Picardian from Marquenterre but really Americanized. He had travelled the entire world over land and sea. Having seen everything, nothing could astonish him. He had experienced all the accidents and adventures that could befall a human being. If, at any time, they wanted to sink into despair they must not count on him.

Hearing Flip speak this way with a sincere clear voice, seeing his reassuring gestures with his body full of health and energy, would bring a dying person back to life.

If Harry Clifton did not have the enchanted island of the Swiss Robinsons, he at least had the faithful devoted Flip. It would not be long before they would explore this unknown land and colonize it.

But at the moment, overcome by fatigue, he felt the need to sleep. Mrs. Clifton asked her children to let their father sleep.

They were leaving the grotto when Belle stopped short.

"Let's see, Mister Flip," she said. "We can no longer call you 'Papa Flip' since you found our father."

"Papa Flip," Harry Clifton murmured with a smile.

"Yes sir, pardon me," said the sailor. "This charming lady and Mister Jack are already in the habit of calling me papa, but now..."

"Well now," Jack replied, "papa Flip will become our uncle!"

"Yes! Uncle Robinson!" Belle said, clapping her hands.

Everyone agreed and gave "Uncle Robinson" three hurrahs.

# Chapter XVI

U ncle Robinson! This was the word of the day and the honor of thinking of it belonged to Jack and Belle. From now on this would be Flip's name. At first he hesitated to accept the name since he did not wish to be the humble servant of the family. But he understood that he would be neither master nor servant so he resigned himself. Besides, had he never changed his name? He was called Pierre Fanthome in Picard and Flip in America. Why should he not be Uncle Robinson on these lands of the Pacific Ocean?

Harry Clifton slept until the next day. But while the engineer was asleep, Uncle Robinson - or rather "Uncle" as his new nephews called him more often—Uncle was uneasy about when the engineer would wake up. In fact, the convalescent would ask for food and the question of soup would become a "burning" one!

Uncle chatted about it with Mrs. Clifton.

"What do you want, Madam," he repeated to her. "Sooner or later we must tell him about our situation. We recovered your husband and we will recover the fire in due course. How, I have no idea but we will recover it."

Mrs. Clifton shook her head in doubt and Uncle could not convince her otherwise.

The next day, May 2nd, Harry Clifton felt much better when he woke up. After embracing his wife and his children, after shaking Uncle Robinson's hand, he said that he was starving.

"Good sir, good," Uncle quickly replied with joy. "What would you like us to give you? Ask! Anything you want. We still have those fresh oysters."

"And you may say, Uncle, that they are excellent!" Harry Clifton said.

"We also have the coconut and its milk. It would be difficult to find a better food for a weak stomach."

"I agree, Uncle, I agree. However, without being a doctor, I imagine that a bit of well grilled venison would do me no harm."

"Is that what you think, sir," Uncle replied. "You must not be in a hurry to start eating such substantial food. You are in the same situation as those unfortunate castaways recovering from a shipwreck, dying of thirst and hunger. Do you think they should satisfy their appetite all at once?"

"Immediately, no" Clifton replied, "but the next day they should not restrain themselves, I suppose..."

"Sometimes, sir, sometimes," Flip said with assurance, "that should be eight days! Yes, Mr. Clifton, a full eight days. In 1855 I was shipwrecked. I had the good luck to save myself with a raft. Well, I wanted to eat quickly. I was dying of hunger. My stomach was..."

"Excellent?" Clifton asked.

"Excellent, I agree," Flip replied, "but in the end it took a turn for the worse."

It was hard not to smile at Uncle Robinson's logic.

"Well, Uncle," the engineer said, "I suppose I must still endure for today the diet you are prescribing for me. You will not be inconvenienced, I guess, if I have some warm soup?"

"Warm soup," Uncle Robinson shouted, leaning against the wall, "warm soup! Perfect, sir. As you wish! A broth, for example!"

"Yes."

"Good, well then, Mister Robert and I, we will go to thrash about the forest and kill a broth for you, a broth of the best quality, with large eyes like those of Mademoiselle Belle. Is that agreed?"

This morning, Harry Clifton was satisfied with some edible weeds, oysters and coconuts. Then Robert and Uncle Robinson went to the warren and brought back two rabbits captured with collars. Uncle showed the engineer the result of his hunt and they agreed that a warm rabbit boullion would help his recovery.

The children then occupied themselves gathering the fruits that formed their principal nourishment. Mrs. Clifton and Belle washed what little linen the colony had. All this while Uncle Robinson sat near the engineer's bed, talking with him.

Harry Clifton asked Uncle if he had ever thought about whether wild beasts roamed this part of the land. This could be a danger for people without defensive arms. Uncle had not dared to bring up this subject but he mentioned the footprints in the sand he saw during his first visit to the grotto three weeks earlier.

The engineer listened attentively. He suggested that they build a fence as soon as possible to protect the entrance to the grotto. He recommended that Uncle keep large fires burning during the night because wild beasts hardly ever cross a burning barrier.

Uncle Robinson promised he would not fail to do this adding that there would never be a lack of wood and that the colony possessed an inexhaustible supply.

The engineer then asked about the food supply and if there was any fear of a famine.

Uncle did not have to think about that. The fruits, eggs, fish and mollusks were there in abundance and their supply could easily be renewed once fishing lines and hunting tools were perfected.

Clifton then brought up the question of clothing. The children were rough on their clothes. How could they replace them?

Uncle Robinson asked that they divide the clothing question into two parts. They could do little about the underwear. As to the outerwear, that was another matter and they would look to the animals to solve that.

"You realize, Mr. Clifton, that while avoiding a visit from ferocious beasts, we can still profit from them by borrowing their fur."

"But they will not give them to us unless we beg them to do so."

"Then we will beg them to do so, sir, but do not be uneasy about that. First get better and everything will be fine."

During the day, Jack distinguished himself with a master stroke. With a coconut fiber and a piece of cloth he made a clever fishing line for catching frogs from the weeds of the lake. These batracians belong to a species improperly named brown toads; in reality they are and excellent to eat. Their light white meat contains much gelatin. What bouillon could be made for Harry Clifton! They could not make use of Jack's catch but Uncle Robinson praised him none the less for his skills.

The next day, Friday, after a rather fine night, the engineer felt much better. His wound had healed rapidly. However, on the advice of Uncle and Mrs. Clifton, he agreed to stay rested the entire day. He would take a walk in the neighborhood of the grotto the next day.

Uncle, with a stubbornness hard to explain, still avoided the question of the fire. But why? Sooner or later he would have to acknowledge it. Eventually Harry Clifton would find out. Didn't he deserve to be told about it? If his wife and his children were able to endure these troubles, couldn't he also endure them? Did Uncle Robinson hope that by some chance he could get a fire going again? No, but he could not make up his mind to speak about it. Mrs. Clifton herself urged him to remain silent. The dear wife, seeing that her husband was still weak, hesitated to cause him additional pain.

Be it as it may, Uncle Robinson no longer knew how to avoid Harry Clifton's requests. It was evident that when he would bring him his usual oysters and coconuts, Clifton would ask for the bouillon he was promised. Uncle did not know what to do.

Very fortunately, a change in weather saved him from the embarrassment. It was cloudy during the night and toward morning they had a violent rainstorm. Trees bent under the wind and the sand on the shore flew about like hail.

"Ah! This is a good rain, a good rain," Uncle shouted.

"This is a bad rain!" Marc said to him, since he had planned on going to the shore for some oysters.

"Very good, I tell you Mr. Marc. This will save us!"

Marc could not understand why Uncle was so happy but he got his explanation when he entered the grotto. He heard Uncle speaking to Mr. Clifton in a frustrated tone of voice.

"Ah! Mr. engineer, what weather, what wind, what rain. It wasn't possible to keep our fire lit. It was extinguished."

"Well, my friend," Clifton replied, "that is not a big misfortune. We will light it again when the storm is over."

"No doubt, sir, no doubt, we will light it again and this does not trouble me. This setback distresses me for your sake."

"For me?" the engineer replied.

"Yes! I was about to make you an excellent frog bouillon when all my cinders blew away."

"I can do without the bouillon."

"It is all my fault," said Uncle, exaggerating his white lie. It is my fault. Why didn't I make that unfortunate bouillon while I still had

From *Seconde patrie* (*Second Homeland*, 1900)

my fire? What a beautiful fire it was! Then you would have had this excellent beverage so good for your health."

"Don't be sad, Uncle Robinson. I can wait for another day. But how will my wife and children prepare their meals?"

"Well, sir. Don't we have our reserve of biscuit and salted meat?"

The reserve! The worthy sailor knew only too well that Mrs. Clifton had given him the last piece of meat when he went on his last excursion along the north shore.

"You realize, Uncle," Harry Clifton then said to him, "that we must find another place to install our fire. We cannot leave it where every gust of wind can blow it out."

"Agreed, Mr. Clifton. But how can we drill a chimney through this thick wall of granite? I have examined the surface. Not a hole or a crack anywhere. Take my word for it. Some day we will build a house, a real house!"

"A stone house?"

"No, a wooden house, a house with beams and girders. Now that we have your hatchet, this will not be difficult. You will see how yours truly handles this tool. I worked for six months in Buffalo as a carpenter."

"Good, my friend," the engineer replied. "we will watch you do your thing. I only ask to work under your direction."

"You! An engineer!" Uncle Robinson shouted. "But the plans. Who will prepare the plans if not you? We must have a comfortable home with windows, doors, rooms, salons, chimneys, chimneys everywhere! Don't forget the chimneys! And what a pleasure it will be to return from a long trip to see a blue smoke rising to the sky and to say to oneself that there is a nice warm fire waiting for us down there with good friends ready to feast us."

In speaking like this, the tireless sailor gave the entire family hope and courage. It rained into the night. It was impossible to venture outside. But there was work for everyone inside the grotto. Uncle Robinson finished a set of bamboo cups using the saw from Harry Clifton's knife. He even made some plates more useful than the shells they were using until this time. He also made a knife for himself, or at least he rounded off the rough edges of what had remained of his blade, rubbing it on a stone. The children, in turn, were not idle. They prepared the coconuts and the pine kernels. A few pints of fermented coconut milk were placed inside gourds. This would turn into an alcoholic liqueur. For his part, Robert cleaned his father's pistol which was rusted over with the salty water. He expected that it would come in handy. Mrs. Clifton washed her children's clothes.

The next day, Saturday May 3rd, the sky was serene again, promising a magnificent day. The wind had passed away to the northeast, and the sun was shining with a brilliance. Harry Clifton was again in a hurry to leave and explore the neighborhood. He wanted to bathe in the sun expecting it to give him a complete return to health. He therefore asked Uncle if he could lean on his arms. Having no plausible reason for refusing, Uncle resigned himself. He offered his arms and left the grotto as if he was the victim of a torture march.

First Harry Clifton gave a deep sigh of satisfaction. The air was fresh and invigorating. He inhaled it as if it was a tonic. He had never felt so warm! He looked at the sparkling sea. He saw the islet, the narrow channel, the meandering of the coastline and the natural harbor. Then he made an about face. He saw the first level of the cliff with its verdant curtain of trees and the luxurious prairie, the blue lake framed in a thick border of forests and the high peak overlooking this ensemble. This beautiful scenery pleased him. He foresaw good things from this charming country. The engineer hatched up twenty projects that he wanted to execute without delay.

Harry Clifton, sometimes leaning on his wife's arms, sometimes on those of Uncle Robinson, returned to the grotto. He examined the cliff and reached the location where the blackened rock indicated that this was the place where the fire had been burning.

"Was the fire here?" he asked. "Of course. Now I understand how the eddies of wind whirling around the cliff easily put out the fire. We will look for a better place. Come children, Marc and Robert. Bring one or two armfuls of dry wood. There must be no lack of fuel. Let's make a beautiful fire."

On hearing these words, everyone stared at the father without a word. Uncle lowered his eyes. He had a guilty look.

"Well, children?" Harry Clifton repeated. "Did you hear me?"

Someone had to speak up. Mrs. Clifton realized that it was her place to do so.

"My friend," she said, taking her husband's hand. "I have a confession to make."

"Which is, my dear Elisa?"

"Harry," Mrs. Clifton said in a solemn voice, "we have no fire."

"No fire!" Clifton shouted.

"And no way to light one!"

Harry Clifton seated himself at the edge of a rock without saying a word. Mrs. Clifton told him about what had happened after they landed, the incident of the single match, how the fire was carried up to the grotto, and under what conditions, in spite of the surveillance, it had been blown out by the windstorm. The mother did not mention Marc but he came over to Harry Clifton.

"And it happened while I was watching it," he said.

Clifton took Marc's hand and pressed it to his chest.

"Don't you even have a little piece of amadou?" he asked him.

"No, my friend," Mrs. Clifton replied.

Uncle then intervened.

"But all hope is not lost!" he said. "Isn't it possible that we could find a way to make a fire. Do you know what I am counting on, Mister Clifton?"

"No, my friend."

"On nature, sir, on nature itself to give it back to us one day."

"And how?"

"With a thunderbolt! A tree set afire and our hearth will be back."

"Yes," the engineer replied. "Waiting for your fire from a thunderbolt is very problematic and it will always be at the mercy of the first squall. But have you tried to get a fire by rubbing two pieces of wood?"

"Yes," said Robert, "but we were not successful."

"If we only had a lens!" Marc added.

"Perhaps we could replace the lens," Harry Clifton said, "with the glass from two watches with water introduced between them."

"Quite right, Mr. Clifton," Uncle said. "But if you have a watch, we don't have any."

"Or perhaps," Clifton said, "we could bring water to the boiling point by imparting a rapid movement to it in a closed vase!"

"An excellent way to make a broth but not a roast. You see, Mr. Clifton, all these means are not practical and my only hope is to find some mushroom species to replace the amadou."

"But burnt linen can serve as amadou."

"I know that," Flip replied, "but I say to Mr. Clifton that to get burnt linen we first need to have a fire and to have a fire…"

"We need something easier than all that!" Clifton replied.

"Which is?" Uncle Robinson shouted, opening his eyes wide.

"That we use the amadou I have in my pocket!" Clifton replied with a smile.

The children shouted hurrah! Uncle screamed. Would this man that nothing could surprise go mad. He danced a jig better than any

Scotsman. Then, taking Belle and Jack by the hand, he danced round about with them, while singing:

> He had amadou,
> And a fire for you
> All along he knew,
> He had amadou.

# Chapter XVII

When the worthy sailor's madness had subsided, one could see him tapping his head thinking about his disgraceful behavior. In fact, his trickery had cost them three days when the patient had in his own pocket... Perhaps Harry Clifton had prolonged the situation a bit by not revealing the amadou immediately after Mrs. Clifton spoke. Who could blame him for that?

When the small colony had calmed down, Uncle set about to light the fire. Nothing was easier. The broken blade would act as a lighter and with the flint and a piece of amadou, they had everything they needed.

The engineer's amadou was the size of a playing card. It was dry. Uncle tore off a piece of it and carefully put the rest away. He then prepared an exterior hearth with dead leaves, small pieces of wood and dry moss which would easily catch fire. That done, he was about to make the sparks fly when Robert said to him:

"Uncle Robinson!"

"Yes, Mr. Robert?"

"Couldn't my pistol be of help to you?"

"How?"

"Instead of powder, put a little piece of amadou in the chamber and fire. It will produce a flame."

"That's an idea, my boy, and by golly, that's just what we'll do."

Uncle took the pistol, put a small piece of amadou in the chamber and armed it.

"Let me fire it," Robert said.

The sailor gave the weapon to the boy. He fired it and the sparks ignited the amadou. Uncle turned the flame into the dry leaves and this produced a light smoke. Uncle blew into it, first like a whisper, then like a blast of air for a forge. The dry wood sparkled and a beautiful flame rose into the air. Cries of joy saluted its appearance.

A pot with fresh water was soon suspended over the fire and Mrs. Clifton put in some of the frog legs that the sailor had skinned with his usual skill.

At noontime the stew was simmering with an enticing odor. Uncle roasted a rabbit. Mussels and pigeon eggs completed the meal. Nothing was raw. Even the pine almonds were well done. The frog bouillon, even without vegetables, was praised. Harry Clifton saw to it that everyone had enough to eat. Uncle Robinson had to taste some of it although he tried to excuse himself. He had eaten salangane in China and grilled grasshoppers in Zanzibar, "that is to say perhaps the best the world had to offer," but he had to confess nothing was better than frog bouillon.[1] In consequence, Jack was put in charge of making the fishing devices for catching the batrachians.

Mr. Clifton felt much stronger. He wanted to extend the promenade with his wife and children up to the lake. But Mrs. Clifton wanted to take care of some domestic details. So the engineer, his three sons and the sailor walked along the cliff road. Robert and Jack carried their fishing gear. They passed the curtain of fine trees. When they reached the edge of the lake, the father seated himself on a broken tree trunk and admired the beautiful countryside; the forests, the mountains, the shape of the dunes, the magnificent lake of clear water, a lake of poetic melancholy like the Champlain and Ontario lakes described by Cooper.

Uncle Robinson told Harry Clifton about the excursions he and the children had already made into the surrounding countryside, the discovery of the warren in the south and the exploration of the river with its bend.

"We will visit our domain together, Mr. Harry," he said. "You will see the resources it has. We will run over to our islet and if I am not mistaken, it is only a refuge for a colony of web-footed birds. And the marsh, the large marsh I crossed in going to meet up with you, what a reserve of aquatic game, and in the forests, what quadrupeds only waiting for a skilful blow to land on our table! So then, to the north

---

1. Salangane are martins who build their nest with edible algae.

we have the birds in the marsh, to the south the rabbits of the warren, to the east the feather game and to the west the penguins, and heaven knows what else. You can see that we lack nothing."

"How will we kill this game?" Harry Clifton asked.

"We will make bows, Mr. Clifton. There is no lack of wood. As to the strings, the quadrupeds will furnish us that."

"Good," Clifton replied, "but before anything else, we must build a poultry yard with an enclosure and try to domesticate several couples of these animals that are still in the wild state."

"An excellent idea, sir," Uncle replied, "and an easy thing to do, and after we domesticate these animals, perhaps we can try to domesticate some garden vegetables. Mrs. Clifton will not complain about that."

"In fact, my worthy friend," the engineer said with a smile, "with a man such as you, nothing is impossible. Do you know, Uncle Robinson, - I really like that name - do you know that a house built midway between the lake and the sea would be in a charming place?"

"I have already given that some thought. It is as if it has already been done. Do you see down there, a little to the right, that cluster of nettle trees? It seems that nature put it there just for us. They protect the trees that will form the corners of the house and the partition walls. We can cut down the others. We will put in place thick traverse joists and leave room for doors and windows. We will have a thatched roof over girders and the house will have a fine look."

"It will also be easy to profit from the slope of the ground to draw the water from the lake into this house," the engineer added.

"We will do that, sir, we will do that!" Uncle shouted with enthusiasm. It will be superb! Ah, what other things we must do! Where the river leaves the lake, we must throw over a bridge there, to make it easy to reach the right bank."

"Yes," Clifton replied, "a bridge with a wheel, a sort of drawbridge, because if I remember correctly from the description you gave me, all of the land between the sea, the cliff and the lake is bordered by the river."

"Yes sir."

"To the north," the engineer replied, "from the mouth of the river to where it leaves the lake, we have a barrier that animals cannot cross. The lake, from the lower part of the river to the upper part, protects the northeastern section of the land. Wild animals could only come to the grotto from the south after having gone around the shores of the lake.

Well then, Uncle, suppose we could shut off the southern approach, either with a fence or with a large ditch fed by the very waters of the lake, a distance of a mile from the western corner of the lake to the sea, wouldn't we have enclosed all sides? We would then have created a vast parkland which our domesticated animals could not leave and which wild animals could not enter."

"Ah! Mister engineer," Uncle shouted, "if you gave me a piece of land on the borders of the Mohawk I could not make a park like that out of it. Let's get to work."

"Everything in due time, Uncle Robinson," Clifton replied, stopping the sailor who already had his hatchet in hand. "Before we

From *L'Île mystérieuse* (*The Mysterious Island*, 1874)

close up the park, even before we build the house, let's first begin by protecting the grotto we are now living in. Let's defend the entrance with a fence."

"Sir," the sailor replied, "I am always ready. If you would like to stay here at the lake with Mister Robert and Mister Jack who will be fishing for some trout, Mister Marc and I will go to the forest to chop down some trees."

The proposition was accepted. Uncle and his "nephew" Marc went to the north shore of the lake toward the woods. During this while, the two brothers amused themselves with fishing. Jack went a little further down and caught some more frogs. The father and his second son were busy throwing out the lines and were rather happy to bring in a half dozen fine trout. But more than once Mr. Clifton had to keep Robert's impatience in check.

While the sailor and Marc were gone and Robert was busy with his fishing tackle, the engineer gave some thought to the situation fate had created for him. He reviewed in his mind the important events that changed his existence so completely. He was not concerned about keeping his family in good health under actual conditions, but he wanted to know if there was any hope of ever seeing his country again. To know this he would first have to determine the position of this land in the Pacific. With that done, it would help in resolving the important question: Is this land a continent or an island?

Determining the position of this land without astronomical instruments was almost impossible. How could he measure the longitude without a chronometer and the latitude without a sextant? Estimating the route followed by the *Vancouver* from the final observations made by Captain Harrisson offered only inaccurate results. The engineer could not rely on these approximations. The vessel had been thrown off to the north outside its planned route but to what parallel could not be easily determined.

The second question was easier to resolve. In fact, there were two ways for Mr. Clifton to determine whether he had set foot on an island or a continent; climb the central peak or travel in a boat.

The peak had an elevation of five or six thousand feet above sea level. Then if the land was an island of average size, measuring forty or fifty leagues in circumference, an observer at the summit could see the sky touching the ocean all around him. But could they climb the peak? Could they cross the forest area and the succession of buttresses supporting the mountain's base?

The other way was more practical. It was sufficient to sail along the shore to determine its shape. Uncle was a good sailor and the boat would not draw much water. It could follow the meandering of the shore during the long days in June or July and they would soon know the nature of the land.

If it was a continent then getting home was possible. Their stay would be temporary.

If it was an island, the Clifton family was imprisoned at the mercy of the chance that some vessel would wander into these waters. In that case they must plan on definitely settling in. Besides, Harry Clifton was an energetic and courageous man who was not afraid of isolation. Only he wanted to know what to expect and he decided to undertake a reconnaissance as circumstances would permit.

While engaged in thought, the engineer was looking at the lake and he was rather surprised to see the water bubbling some hundred meters from the shore. What could produce this phenomenon? Was it caused by subterranean forces, which would explain the volcanic character of the land? Was it only a reptile that made the lake its regular home? Clifton did not know what to think. The bubbling soon stopped but the engineer decided to keep an eye in the future on these somewhat suspicious waters.

The day advanced and the sun was already low on the horizon when Mr. Clifton thought he saw, near the northern shore of the lake, a mass of considerable size moving on the surface. Did this object have something to do with the bubbling he had seen before? It was only natural that Clifton should ask himself this. As to the object itself, there was no doubt it must stir up the waters in moving along the northern shore.

Harry Clifton called his two children, Robert and Jack. He pointed out the moving mass and asked what it could be. One said a marine monster, the other an enormous piece of drifting wood. During this time, the mass came closer and they soon saw that it was a raft of wood steered by some men.

Suddenly Robert shouted out:

"But they are our own people! That's Marc and Uncle Robinson!"

The lad was not mistaken. His brother and the sailor had made a raft with pieces from the trees they had chopped down and they were directing it to the very corner of the lake that was closest to the grotto. In a half hour they would reach them.

"Go, Jack," Mr. Clifton said. "Tell your mother that we will be on our way..."

Jack looked at the cliff. It seemed that distance he had to walk was very long. And how could he cross the curtain of tall trees! Finally, he hesitated.

"Are you afraid," Robert asked, mocking him.

"Oh! Jack," his father said.

"Well then," said Robert. "I will go."

"No," his father said. "Marc and Uncle will need your help."

Jack looked around without a word.

"My child," his father said to him, getting down on knees, "there is nothing to be afraid of. You will soon be eight years old. You are already a little man. Think only that we are asking you to help us with our limited forces. There is nothing to be afraid of."

"I will go, father," the lad replied, suppressing a sigh.

He then left with determination, carrying his frogs.

"You must not laugh at Jack," Mr. Clifton said to Robert. On the contrary, you must encourage him. He went in spite of himself. That is good."

Harry Clifton and his son went to the point where the floating raft would come ashore.

Uncle and Marc skilfully directed the raft with long poles and soon reached land.

"Everything went well! Everything went well!" Uncle shouted.

"That was a good idea you had there of constructing a raft," said the engineer.

"That was Mister Marc's idea," Uncle answered. "Before long, your eldest son will become an adept woodcutter. He thought of this way of transportation. It drifts our material and ourselves!"

The floating raft was built with some thirty spruce trees each measuring about twenty or thirty inches in diameter at the base. Strong creepers tied them together. Uncle and the two boys went to work and before nightfall every trunk was unloaded.

"There will be plenty of work for tomorrow," Uncle said.

"Yes," Clifton said, "tomorrow we will bring this wood to the grotto."

"With your permission, Mister engineer," the sailor said, "we will cut up the wood here. It will make it easier to carry."

"You're right, Uncle Robinson. Now let's return to the grotto where dinner is waiting for us."

Uncle showed Clifton an animal a little larger than a hare belonging to the order of rodents. Its yellow fur was mixed with greenish spots. It barely had a tail.

"This animal," Clifton said, "belongs to the agouti genre. But it is a little larger than the agouti of the tropical countries. It is more like the American rabbit. This must be one of the long eared variety found in the temperate parts of the American continent. I am not mistaken. Look at the five molars on each side of the jaw. That is the distinguishing feature of agoutis."

"And how is it for eating?" Uncle Robinson asked.

"It is edible and easy to digest."

Marc suspended the agouti at the end of his stick. Uncle helped Clifton and they reached the grotto at about six o'clock. Mother was expecting her guests and had prepared an excellent meal. Evening came on and the entire family took a stroll on the beach. Clifton looked at the outline of the islet and the direction of the currents in the channel. He told Uncle that it would be easy to build a small port here by constructing a jetty in the channel. This project was left for some later time. But there was more pressing work for the small colony, in particular the construction of the fence. They even decided not to attempt any new excursions until this enclosure was completed.

The family then returned to the grotto, Mrs. Clifton arm in arm with her husband, Uncle chatting with Marc and Robert, Jack and Belle picking up shells and pebbles. They passed the oyster bank and added to their reserve. It looked like these gallant citizens were taking a walk in their own private park. Then during the night, Marc and Uncle Robinson carefully watched the fire, a task which made it urgent for them to find a flammable mushroom.

The next day Clifton and Uncle traced a line in front of the grotto where the posts of the fence would be placed. The first of these would be installed against the very wall of the cliff. This would give them a semi-circular area which could be used for various domestic purposes. After the line was drawn, Uncle cut the trench, an operation that was easily completed in the sandy soil. The work was finished by noon.

After lunch, Clifton, Marc and the sailor went to the edge of the lake where they had left the wood. There they cut them up into convenient weights and lengths.

The sailor was not embarrassed when they spoke of his skill in handling the hatchet. It was something to see how he rounded the foot of the tree like a real carpenter and cut off enormous chips to square it. The rest of the day and the next day were employed with this work. On Tuesday morning they began to lay down the posts. They were solidly dug into the soil and joined together with other wood transversely attached. At the foot of the fence, Clifton planted a sort of agave whose leaves would grow at the base of the cliff. This agave, a species of American aloe, would soon form hard spiny leaves making for an impenetrable hedge.

The work on the fence was finished on May 6th. The grotto was well defended. Harry Clifton could only be pleased with his idea because the next day a group of jackals came to roam around the encampment. They made a deafening racket. The fire, glowing in the dark, kept them at a distance. Several animals however came right up to the fence. But Uncle threw over some burning branches and they fled in a howl.

# Chapter XVIII

With these works completed, they had to occupy themselves with renewing all kinds of reserves. It goes without saying that Mr. Clifton had completely recovered his strength. His wound had healed completely and he no longer suffered from it. All his energy and ingenuity would now be devoted to the well being of his small colony.

It was Tuesday, the 7th of May. After the morning meal the children went fishing, gathered eggs from the nests and explored the shore and the cliff. Harry Clifton and Uncle Robinson took the boat to the oyster bank. The sea was calm. The gentle wind blew toward land. They sailed there without any incident. Clifton carefully observed this part of the coast. He was struck by its savage appearance. The soil was convulsed with enormous rocks scattered about. This formation was the result of plutonic activity. The engineer, very versed in the natural sciences, could not be mistaken about that.

When Uncle and he reached the bank of mollusks, they began to harvest them and soon the boat was fully loaded. This reserve of oysters was truly inexhaustible.

After getting underway, Uncle, recalling the incident of the tortoise and no longer having any reason to hoard the interesting batracians, proposed to Clifton that they rummage among the rocks. So they landed on the shore with the aim of going on a hunt. The soil showed little mounds which attracted Clifton's attention. Pressing down on these little hillocks, they found there a certain quantity of perfectly spherical eggs in a hard white shell. These were tortoise eggs whose white has the property of not coagulating when heated like the white of bird's eggs. The marine tortoises evidently preferred this beach. They came from the open sea to lay their eggs leaving to the sun the task of hatching them. There were countless eggs here which should not surprise anyone since these animals can each lay up to two hundred fifty eggs annually.

"It is a real egg field," shouted Uncle. "They are already hard and we have only to pick them up."

"Let us not take any more than we need, my worthy fellow," Clifton replied. "Once these eggs are taken from the ground, they will spoil. It would be better to let them hatch so they could produce new tortoises who could lay more eggs for us."

Uncle only took about a dozen eggs. Clifton and he then returned to the boat. The sail was hoisted and a half hour later the boat landed at the foot of the cliff. The oysters were deposited in the park and the eggs were brought to mother who incorporated them into the midday meal.

After lunch, Uncle discussed the question of arms with Mr. Clifton. They could not continue to hunt with sticks and stones. It was primitive, hardly a way to hunt and surely no way to protect themselves. In the place of firing arms, well made bows and arrows would be formidable weapons. Uncle resolved to make some.

Before anything else, it was important to find the right wood. Fortunately, Harry Clifton had discovered among a cluster of coconut palms, a certain species of wood known under the name of crejimba, a wood used to make the bows and arrows of the South American Indians. Father and children gathered a few branches of this crejimba and carried them to the grotto. In a few hours work, Uncle Robinson made three large bows with a smooth curvature. They would have elasticity and yet be light. The very resistant cord was made from coconut fiber. As to the arrows, Uncle was content to cut some small bamboos. The nodes were carefully leveled and he armed the larger end with the quills from a porcupine. Moreover, to stabilize their flight, he attached bird feathers to the smaller end. If skillfully used, these bows and arrows would be terrible weapons.

We can understand why the children wanted to try out their new weapons the same day. They were satisfied with the height their arrows reached up into the air. With experience they would put them to good use either for defensive or for offensive purposes. After experimenting with the range of these arrows, Mr. Clifton wanted to find out their power of penetration. He used the trunk of a coconut tree as his target. Several arrows were fired implanting themselves deeply into the wood. With these experiments over, father instructed his children not to lose their arrows and never to use them without necessity because making them consumed too much valuable time.

Night fell. Everyone entered the fenced in courtyard in front of the grotto. By the engineer's watch it was about eight thirty. This excellent instrument, enclosed in a double golden box, had not been damaged while immersed in the sea water, but it had to be rewound

From *Deux ans de vacances* (*Two Year Holiday*, 1888)

since its movement had stopped while Clifton was injured. To give it the correct time, he would have to make an accurate observation of the sun's height.

Nights were still disturbed by the howling of the jackals mingling with other cries that Mrs. Clifton had already heard. Evidently, apes were roaming around. A fence would be no barrier to these agile animals, but apes are less to be feared than other wild beasts. Nevertheless, Harry Clifton decided to find out what species of apes these were during his next excursion.

The next day, Wednesday the 8th of May, was employed with various activities. They renewed their supply of wood and paid a visit to the warren where a few rabbits were skillfully attacked with the bows and arrows. That same day, Mrs. Clifton asked for a good supply of salt. She intended to salt the meat from the two capybaras. Marc and his father went to gather the salt deposited by the sea into rock crevices. They brought back several pounds of this useful substance, the only mineral used in food. Mrs. Clifton thanked her husband and asked him if it would be possible to find some kind of soap to wash clothes. Clifton told her that certain vegetables could replace the soaps from the best soap makers and that he was sure to find them in these inexhaustible forests. However, it was agreed that they would take the greatest possible care of their clothing. Without imitating the ways of the savages, they could dress lightly during the warm season and economize on their clothing until such time as Uncle Robinson would find a way to replace them.

On this very day, a new plate appeared on the table at dinner time. It was a plate of excellent crayfish which swarmed in the upper part of the river. For bait, it was enough for Uncle to throw some branches into the current on which he had placed pieces of meat. When he returned a few hours later, all the branches were covered with these crustaceans. The shells of these crayfish had a fine cobalt blue color. They were grilled and were delicious to eat.

To occupy himself during the evening, Uncle Robinson made some more bamboo vases of different sizes. Ah! if only he could fire them. But their pot was always the only utensil they could use for preparing the food. If only Mrs. Clifton had a saucepan. Uncle responded to her request by telling her that a clay pot would suffice for their needs. He was put in charge of making one if he could find the right clay.

They then made plans for the next day's activities. While waiting for the long excursion that Clifton wanted to attempt into the inland, they resolved to pay a visit to the islet either as fisherman or as hunters. The children did not expect to return empty handed.

That evening the family had a small scare. When it was time to go back into the grotto, Mrs. Clifton noticed that little Jack had not answered her call. They looked for him in vain. They called again. There was no response.

We can imagine everyone's terror on not finding the child. No one could say exactly when he had disappeared. It was a dark night since there was a new moon. Father, brothers and Uncle soon dispersed in all directions, one to the shore, another to the lake, everyone shouting.

Uncle Robinson was the first to find out what had happened to Jack. In the darkest part, under a cluster of nettle trees, he spotted the little gentleman standing still with his arms crossed.

"Well, Mister Jack, is that you?" he shouted at him.

"Yes, Uncle," Jack replied in a disguised voice, "and I am afraid."

"And what are you doing there?"

"I am acting like a brave man."

Ah! What a dear child. Uncle took him in his arms and carried him to his mother with all possible speed. When they were told about the little man's response, how he was only trying to be brave, who could scold him? Everyone embraced and caressed him. The four night watches over the fire were scheduled and they went to sleep.

The next day, the 9th of May, a Thursday, preparations were made for the planned excursion. Harry Clifton, his three sons and Uncle then embarked in the boat in order to first go around the islet. They began the exploration by going through the channel. The side of the islet facing the mainland showed a steep bank of boulders but when they doubled the northern point, the engineer discovered that the western side was covered with rocks. The islet measured about a mile and a half in length. Its largest width was at most a quarter of a mile in the southern part. The islet would do well for a hunter's sack.

The explorers set foot on the southern tip of the islet. Innumerable groups of birds belonging to the sea gull genre took flight. They were the species of gull that make their nests in the sand or in the crevices of rocks. Clifton especially recognized the skua gulls with the pointed

From *L'Île mystérieuse* (*The Mysterious Island*, 1874)

tails, which are vulgarly given the name of stercoraries. The birds spread their wings, took to the open sea and disappeared.

"Ah!" Clifton said, "these birds evidently fear the presence of man."

"They assume that we are better armed than we really are," Uncle replied, "but there are other here who have not flown away and for good reason."

Uncle was referring to a species of heavy birds, divers the size of geese, unable to fly because their wings had no feathers.

"What clumsy awkward birds!" Robert shouted.

"They are great auks," Clifton replied, "fat and oily, 'penguis' in Latin, and they deserve their name."

"Good," said Marc, "they will experience the power of our arrows."

"There is no need to dull our porcupine quills," Uncle replied. "These birds are stupid animals and we can easily attack them with our sticks."

"But they are not edible," their father said.

"Agreed," Uncle replied, "but they are full of fat which we can use. We must not disregard that."

At these words, every stick was raised. It was not a hunt but a massacre. Some twenty birds allowed themselves to be killed without trying to escape. They were carried to the boat.

Some hundred feet further along, the hunters met with another kind of divers just as stupid, but at least their flesh was edible. They were penguins whose wings were reduced to the state of flat stumps formed like paddles with scales. It was easy to kill this game but they only killed enough for immediate use. These penguins have a deafening cry like the braying of a donkey. But this hunt, or rather this slaughter, which required neither skill nor courage, disgusted the children. They then resumed the exploration of the islet.

The small group continued to advance toward the northern point on sandy soil covered with innumerable depressions in which the penguins nested. Suddenly Uncle Robinson motioned to his companions to remain still. Toward the extremity of the islet he pointed to large black specks swimming in the waves. They were the heads of rocks in motion.

"So what are they?" Marc asked.

"They are," Uncle replied, "worthy amphibians who will give us jackets and overcoats."

"Yes." Mr. Clifton said. "It is a herd of seals."

"Without doubt," Uncle replied, "and we must catch them at any price. But cunningly, because we will only get near them with guile."

First they must allow the animals to come ashore. In fact, with their narrow pelvises, short compact chest hair and streamlined shape, these seals are excellent swimmers. However, they are clumsy on land. With their short webbed feet, real oars, they can only crawl along.

Uncle knew their habits. He knew that once on land, they would stretch out under the sun's warmth and go to sleep immediately. Everyone waited patiently, even impatient Robert, and in a quarter of an hour some half dozen of these marine mammals were in a deep sleep.

Uncle Robinson decided to glide with Marc in back of a small promontory toward the north of the island so as to position themselves between the seals and the sea. All this while, the father and the two other boys would stay hidden until they heard Uncle shouting. Uncle would attack the seals with his ax. Equipped with only sticks, the others would try to cut off their retreat.

Uncle and the lad went first and disappeared behind the promontory. Harry Clifton, Robert and Jack silently crept along awkwardly toward the shore.

Suddenly the tall sailor jumped up. He shouted. Clifton and the two boys threw themselves between the seals and the sea. Uncle struck two of the seals on the head with his ax and they fell dead on the sand. The others tried to reach open water but Clifton fearlessly blocked them and two more seals fell under Uncle's ax. The remaining seals reached the sea but not without throwing Robert to the ground. He let out a frightful yell out of fear but he got up safe and sound.

"A good hunt!" Uncle shouted, "for the pantry and for the wardrobe."

These seals were relatively small. They were not more than a meter and a half in length. Their head resembles a dog's head. Uncle and Marc found the boat and loaded the seals. The boat crossed the channel and landed gently at the foot of the cliff.

Preparing the seal skins was a rather difficult operation. However, Uncle went to work in the following days and he worked skillfully at it. The skins would be used to make some of the winter clothes. He had more ideas. He thought of getting a bear coat for Clifton to help pass the winter. He never saw any bears but he did not despair of meeting one. He told no one about this. He wanted to act in secret and surprise the engineer Clifton.

⊙

# Chapter XIX

.

During the following two weeks Clifton was not able to undertake his important excursion. Various domestic occupations required the services of everyone in the grotto. The question of clothing was first among others. They would need animal skins to take the place of fabrics. So they conducted additional seal hunts. Uncle was able to kill another half dozen, but soon these amphibians, becoming very defiant, abandoned the islet and they had to give that up.

Fortunately the seals were replaced by another group of animals. A dozen of them fell under the children's arrows during the 18th and 19th of May. These were foxes of a long eared species, with a gray yellow coat of fur, a little larger than the ordinary fox. This encounter was advantageous to the pantry reserve. Mrs. Clifton was satisfied. Uncle was enchanted. It seemed there was no longer anything left to wish for in this world. However, when Clifton asked him if he wanted anything else:

"Yes," he replied. But he would not say what it was.

When these indoor tasks were completed, Mr. Clifton was completely occupied with exploring the land, to finally know if fate had thrown them on an island or on a continent. They decided then to undertake an expedition to the interior with the double goal of determining the layout of the land and to examine its natural riches. On this subject, Uncle Robinson had an excellent idea.

"We would like," he said, "to go inland. Well then, why not profit from the watercourse that nature has given us? Let's go up the river in our boat. We'll go as far as it's navigable and when it can no longer transport us we'll go on foot. Then we can make use of the boat on our return."

This plan was adopted. There remained only one important question to resolve. Who should take part in the expedition? Leaving Mrs. Clifton alone in the grotto was opposed by her husband even though she was willing to pass a night or two alone with her young daughter. Marc knew that he would be sorry to be left out of the expedition but he generously offered to remain at the grotto. They could see what the sacrifice would cost the lad.

"But," said Uncle Robinson, "why can't the entire family come along? The first days of June are fine days and the nights are already very short. A night passed in the woods, what is that? Nothing. I propose that everyone come along. If nothing gets in our way we can leave Monday morning and return by Tuesday evening. Besides, we can go most of the way by boat with little or no fatigue."

Needless to say, this was everyone's preference, young or old. They began their preparations. Roasted meat, hard eggs, grilled fish and fruit were put in reserve for the expedition. Uncle made new arrows and sticks were hardened in fire. In Clifton's hands, the ax could be used for attack or defense as needed. They settled the question of fire this way: The piece of amadou was torn in two, with half to stay at the grotto to rekindle the fire on their return. The other half would be carried with them to be used as needed. It goes without saying that finding the proper substance to replace the amadou was the most important goal of this and future expeditions.

The evening prior to the departure - it was a Sunday - was devoted to rest and sanctified by prayer. Mr. and Mrs. Clifton spoke to their children about ethics and Uncle Robinson told them about the principles of natural philosophy he followed. Everyone rose the next day, the 31st of May, at daybreak. The day promised to be an excellent one. They readied the boat. Uncle needed the sail to profit from the favorable breezes, two oars to maneuver against the wind and a long rope of coconut fibers for hauling it along land.

The boat was launched. At six in the morning, everyone took his proper place. Marc and Robert were up front, Jack and Belle near their mother in the center, and Uncle and Clifton at the bow. Uncle was at the helm and Clifton in charge of the sail.

The wind blew from the open sea. It rippled along the surface of the water. Shouts of joy filled the air. The sail was hoisted and the boat moved gently through the channel between the islet and the mainland.

The tide began to rise which was a favorable circumstance because for a few hours it would move the boat to the upper reaches of the river.

In a short while, aided by wind and tide, they reached the northern extremity of islet near the entrance to the river. Clifton turned the sail and they ascended the water course with the wind to their rear. No longer in the cliff's shadow, they were now in the sunshine. Fido barked with joy and Jack joined in.

The children recognized their first encampment when they passed it. Mrs. Clifton showed her husband where they had turned the boat over to serve as a tent. But the tide moved them along rapidly and the first encampment was soon left behind.

Moving between green banks, the craft soon reached the place where the forest formed a sharp angle with the river. The voyagers then went under a dome of vegetation. A few of the larger trees intermingled their branches to the level of the water. Without wind, the sail was useless. Uncle asked Marc and Robert to haul it down and the two boys did it skilfully. The oars were put in place in case they were needed but the tide was strong enough to move the boat at a good speed. However, the helm no longer responded because the speed of the boat and the current were equal. Uncle then used an oar at the rear to keep the boat in the center.

"These banks are truly charming," Clifton said, looking at this winding river hidden under the vegetation.

"Yes," mother replied. "With a little water and a few trees, nature achieves these beautiful reflections."

"You will see more of these, Madam," said Uncle Robinson. "I repeat that fate has cast us on an enchanted land."

"Then you have already explored this waterway," Mrs. Clifton asked.

"Without doubt," Robert replied. "Uncle and I have ascended the right bank through the creepers and the brushwood."

"What fine trees!" Clifton said.

"Yes," Uncle said. "We will never lack for trees, whatever use we put them to."

In fact, on the left bank of the river there rose magnificent specimens of ulmaceous plants, those precious French elms so sought after by builders, which have the property of bearing up well in water for a long time. Then there were numerous groups belonging to the same family, nettle trees among others, whose almond produces a very useful oil. Further on, the engineer noted some lardizabalaceae whose flexible boughs, soaked in water, make an excellent cord, and two or three ebony trunks of a beautiful black color, divided into capricious veins.[1] Clifton also recognized a North American species, the dios piros virginiana (divine Virginia pear tree) encountered up to the latitude of New York.

Among the most beautiful trees were the giants of the liliaceous species. Humboldt had seen specimens of these in the Canaries.

"Ah! What fine trees!" Robert and Marc shouted.

"These are the dragon trees," Mr. Clifton replied, "and it will surprise you to know that these trees are only ambitious leeks."

"Is it possible?" Marc replied.

"At the least," said Clifton, "they belong to the same liliaceous family as the onion, the shallot, the chive and the asparagus. The humble members of this family could be more useful to us than these gigantic trees. I will add that the liliaceous species includes the tulip, the aloes, the hyacinths, the lilies, the tuberose and this phormium tenax, the linseed of New Zealand that your mother could make good use of."

"Father," Marc asked, "how can the naturalists group into the same family the dragon trees which are a hundred feet tall and the onions which are two inches in width?"

"Because the typical characteristics of these vegetables are the same, my dear child. It's the same with the animals and it will surprise you to know that foxes and ray fish are in the same category. It therefore follows that this liliaceous family is a considerable one, containing at least twelve hundred species scattered over the surface of the globe, but especially in the temperate zones."

"Good!" Uncle shouted, "I will not despair of one day finding other specimens of these liliaceous plants that you regret not having, Mrs. Clifton. Besides, let us not speak ill of the dragon trees. If I remember correctly, in the Sandwich Islands people eat their ligneous roots which they call the roots of Ti. When cultivated, they are excellent. I have eaten some of it. Ground and subject to a certain fermentation, it makes a very agreeable liquor."

"True," replied the engineer, "but those roots come from the purple dragon tree which we may meet up with perhaps. As for these, they only yield a blood-dragon which is a resin than can be used to advantage in treating a hemorrhage. Bethencourt collected it during the conquest of the Canaries."

---

1.    A family of vines found in China, Japan and Chile.

From *Les Naufragés* du Jonathan (*The Survivors of* the Jonathan, 1909)

The boat left at six in the morning. An hour later, with the help of the tide, it reached the lake. It was a joy for the children to travel on this vast plane of water where formerly they could only move along its shores. From this position they could once again see the western cliff, the curtain of large trees, the yellow carpet of dunes and the sparkling sea. They then crossed the northern part of the lake in order to reach the mouth of the upper river. There was a fine wind no longer hindered by the screen of trees. Uncle hoisted the sail and the light vessel moved rapidly toward the west. Remembering the inexplicable bubbling he had seen at the time of his first visit to the lake, Harry Clifton carefully observed these somewhat suspicious waters. But the children could only admire the scenery. Little Jack dipped his hand in the water outside the boat and amused himself by tracing a small wake while twittering.

At Marc's request they went to explore a tiny islet that emerged some three hundred meters from the shore. The boat reached it in a few moments. It was a solid rock measuring some hundred square meters in area, covered with aquatic grass. The birds from the lake favored it. It was like an enormous nest where the winged community lived in harmony. Fido barked and wanted to jump ashore but Mr. Clifton held him back. This islet was a reservation for aquatic game. They must not casually disturb this bird retreat and give them the idea of nesting elsewhere.

With this exploration completed, Uncle Robinson directed the boat toward the mouth of the upper waterway. At this point they not only had to lower the sail but also remove the mast. They could not advance under this arc of low thick vegetation. Since the tide was not felt in this upper part of the river, Uncle and Marc took to the oars leaving the engineer to attend to the helm.

"We are now in an undiscovered area!" Clifton said.

"Yes," Uncle replied. "We never went this far. We waited for you before making this excursion. Where this river goes I cannot say but it would not surprise me if goes a long way into the interior. As you will see, this is a large land."

In fact the width of the new river was over eighty feet and the channel did not seem to narrow. Very fortunately the current was not strong and the light boat, driven with the oars, easily moved along sometimes near one bank, sometimes near the other.

They went along in this way for about two hours. Even though the sun was high in its course, it barely showed through the thick foliage. A few times the explorers set foot on one of the banks. During these halts, they made a few useful discoveries in the vegetable kingdom. The chenopod family was represented principally by a sort of wild spinach which had crossbred spontaneously. Mrs. Clifton gathered some of it and promised to transplant them later. She also found many specimens of wild mustard plants with high hopes of transplanting them. In the cabbage family, they found cress, horse radish, turnips and small slightly rough hairy stems, a meter high, which produced an almost brown grain. Clifton easily recognized the charlock from which mustard is made.

These precious vegetables were stored in the boat and the voyage was resumed. It was truly a charming trip. The trees served as a refuge for a large number of birds. Marc and Robert got hold of two or three couples of gallinaceae in their nests. They were birds with long slender beaks, long necks, short wings and without an apparent tail. They were tinamous. It was decided that they would keep a male and female alive to populate a future poultry yard. With bows and arrows the young hunters also killed a few touraco lories, a sort of parrot the size of a pigeon, all daubed in green with a part of its wing of a crimson color and a narrow festooned crest with a white border, charming birds especially excellent from a culinary point of view because its meat is very tasty.

During one of these stops, they made another very important discovery thanks to little Jack who could hardly stay confined on the boat. The young man went to frolic in a sort of clearing. When he returned his clothes were completely soiled with a yellowish soil which earned him a scolding from his mother. Jack was totally disgraced.

"Take a look, Madame Clifton," Uncle Robinson said. "Don't scold him. It is fortunate that the child amused himself."

"That he messed himself up?" the mother replied.

"But how could he amuse himself without getting all messed up?" Uncle asked.

"Ah! Worthy Uncle!" Mrs. Clifton replied. "I would like to know what his father thinks about this."

"This once," Clifton said, "I think that Jack should not be scolded. On the contrary, we should congratulate him for have messed around with this yellowish soil."

"And why?"

"Because this yellowish soil is clay, a loamy soil which can be made into crude but useful pottery."

"Pottery!" Mrs. Clifton shouted.

"Yes, and I have no doubt that Uncle Robinson is as good a potter as he is a carpenter, a woodsman and a tanner."

"Just say sailor," Uncle replied, "and that does it."

Little Jack led Clifton and Uncle to the clearing. The engineer recognized that the soil was formed of a clay earth called figuline clay which is used mostly for making ordinary earthenware. He could not be mistaken about this and besides, having placed a bit of this substance on his tongue, he sensed the extreme avidity that the argile exhibits toward liquids. So then, this precious material, spread over the surface of the globe, was freely offered to the small colony. They would use this argile as a paste base.

"An excellent discovery!" Mr. Clifton shouted. "For a moment I thought it was kaolin so that we could make porcelain. But now, by pounding this clay soil and washing out its larger particles, we will get our earthenware."

"We will be happy with simple pottery," Uncle replied. "I am certain that Madame Clifton would pay dearly for an earthen bowl."

They placed a good quantity of this plastic soil in the boat to replace the ballast of rocks. When Uncle returned to the grotto, he would lose no time in making pots, dishes and plates to the great satisfaction of the household.

They embarked again and the boat, propelled by the oars, tranquilly ascended the river course. It had now become winding and sensibly narrower. They could now believe that its source was not far off. The river's depth had also diminished. On taking a sounding, Uncle realized that the boat had no more than two or three feet of water under the keel. Clifton estimated that they had now gone about two leagues from the upper entrance into the lake.

The narrow valley the explorers then crossed was less wooded. Instead of a thick forest, the trees were scattered in clusters. Large rocks jutted out on the banks. The soil here was different. This was the beginning of the mountain system to culminate at the central peak.

At about half past eleven, it was impossible to go further. There was little water under the boat. Black rocks, not grass, lined the riverbanks. Soon they heard the noise of a waterfall not far off.

In fact, after turning a sharp corner, they came in sight of the cascade. It was a charming place. The stream plunged some thirty feet to the bottom of a picturesque gorge filled with mossy rocks. The volume of water was not considerable but the sharp rocks scattered it about. Its jets intersected each other and collected into certain natural hollows. They stopped to admire this wonderful spectacle.

"Oh! What a wonderful fall!" Jack shouted.

"Father, father," Belle said in her turn, "let's get closer."

But the girl's wish was not to be satisfied. The boat scraped bottom with each stroke of the oar. They had to make for the left bank some fifty feet from the falls. Everyone left the boat and the two youngsters began to frolic about the bank.

"What will we do now?" Marc asked.

"Let's go to the base of the mountain," Robert replied impatiently, pointing to the peak to the north.

"Children," Mrs. Clifton said. "Before we go on any new excursions, I have a suggestion to make."

"What, mother!" Marc asked.

"Let's eat."

The suggestion was accepted without any quarrel. They removed their provisions from the boat. To the cold meat they added some lories and tinamous meat. A wood fire was lit. The small game was placed on a spit and was soon roasting over a sparkling flame.

The meal was soon finished. They had to push forward in haste. Clifton and Uncle took a careful look at the surroundings so as not to miss it on their return. Besides, they could not fail to discover again this watercourse that had made such an impression.

# Chapter XX

The family went on its way. Uncle and his two friends, Marc and Robert, carried their bows and arrows and surveyed this new land. Mr. and Mrs. Clifton came behind them with Jack and Belle frolicking about, running and tiring themselves uselessly whatever one could tell them.

The ground was uneven evidently convulsed by plutonic forces. They noticed many basalt debris and pumice rocks. They saw more and more evidence of the volcanic nature of this region. However, the travelers still had not passed the zone of trees leading to the snowy peak. These conifers, like all those growing at this height, were pines and spruce, which little by little became more scarce.

During the last part of the climb, Uncle drew Harry Clifton's attention to the large footprints encrusted in the ground indicating the presence of large animals. What animals these were, they could not say. It would be prudent to keep on guard and the children were cautioned not to wander off.

Mr. Clifton and Uncle were chatting and these footprints gave rise to a rather plausible idea in the engineer's mind.

"These animals," he said to Uncle, "are evidently powerful and numerous. I am led to believe that fate has thrown us on a continent rather than on an island, at least an island of considerable size. But I do not recall any islands in this part of the Pacific where the *Vancouver* has abandoned us. Yes, we are on a continent probably somewhere on a part of the American shoreline between the fortieth and fiftieth north latitudes."

"Let's climb further," Uncle replied, "and we will perhaps know what we have to deal with when we pass the tree zone."

"But, my worthy friend," said Clifton, "so far we have only seen the shoreline of this land, until we get to the top."

"That will be a nasty business," Uncle replied. "If the summit is not accessible, we may have to go around it at its base to find out if we are islanders or, how shall I say it, continenters."

"Well, let's press on!"

From *Seconde patrie* (*Second Homeland*, 1900)

"I suggest," Uncle said, "that we be content for today to reach the end of the tree zone. There we can camp for the night which will be a fine one. I will be in charge of organizing a camp and tomorrow, at dawn, we will try to climb to the top."

It was then three o'clock. They continued their climb. If the ferocious animals, judging from their footprints, were no longer here, no one thought of complaining. There was no lack of food and Fido put to flight several food worthy species difficult to recognize. However, Marc and Robert's arrows soon felled a gallinule couple of the pheasant family. The birds had a fleshy wattle hanging from their throats and two slender cylindrical horns set behind their eyes. These fine birds were the size of a rooster. The female was brown but the male sparkled with a red plumage dotted with white teardrop shapes. Mr. Clifton gave the gallinule birds their real name calling them tragopans. Mrs. Clifton was sorry they had not been caught alive. These pheasants would have adorned the poultry yard but they had to be content with making a roast of them at the next stop.

Another animal, a large one, was soon spotted among the basalt rocks. They could not capture it but Clifton was glad to know they were here. It was one of the large sheep that live in the mountains of Corsica, Crete and Sardinia. These were a distinct species going under the name of moufflon. Clifton easily recognized their strong horns curving rearward and flat at the tip with woolen fleece hidden under long silky buff colored hair. This fine animal stood still near the trunk of a fallen tree. Clifton and Uncle came closer. The moufflon looked at them with astonishment as if he was seeing human bipeds for the first time and then, his fears becoming aroused, he disappeared across the clearing and the rocks beyond the reach of Uncle's arrows.

"Au revoir!" Uncle shouted at him, in a comic tone of frustration. "The wretched animal! It is not the legs but the fleece I am sorry about! He took a jacket away from us but we will get it back!"

"At least we will try," Clifton replied, "and if we succeed in domesticating a few couples of these animals, as Uncle says, we will no longer lack for legs and jackets."

At six in the evening, the small troop reached the tree limit. They decided to stop, prepare the evening meal and camp for the night. Their only thought was to find a convenient place for sleeping. Marc and Robert went off in one direction and Clifton and Uncle to the other. Mrs. Clifton, Jack and Belle were sheltered under a large pine tree.

Marc and Robert were gone for barely a few minutes when their mother saw them returning in a fright. Mrs. Clifton went to them.

"What is it, my children?" she asked them.

"Smoke," Robert said. "We saw smoke rising from the rocks."

"Are there people here?" Mrs. Clifton asked.

She seized her children.

"But what kind of people, savages, cannibals?"

The children looked at their mother without answering.

At this moment, Uncle and the engineer reappeared. Marc told them what happened. Everyone was quiet for a few moments.

"Let's act prudently," Uncle Robinson finally said. "It is evident that there are human creatures near us. We do not know who we have to deal with. I truly fear them more than I want them. Stay near Mrs. Clifton, Mister engineer. Mister Marc, Fido and I will do a reconnaissance."

Uncle, the young lad and the faithful dog left without delay. Marc's heart was pounding. Uncle, his lips tight and eyes wide open, advanced carefully. After a few minutes moving in a northeast direction, Marc suddenly stopped and showed his companion a smoke rising into the air at the border of the last trees. No wisp of wind blew and the smoke rose to a great height.

Uncle stopped. Fido wanted to spring forward but Marc restrained him. The sailor made a sign to the lad to wait for him and he glided like a serpent among the rocks and disappeared.

Marc stood still with emotion, waiting for his return. Suddenly he heard a shout echoing from the rocks. Marc jumped forward ready to help his companion but the shouting was followed by a hearty laughter and Uncle soon reappeared.

"This fire," he shouted, swinging his large arms, "or rather this smoke..."

"Well, it is made by nature! It is a sulfur source that will allow us to effectively treat our laryngitis."

Uncle and Marc returned to where Clifton was waiting for them and Uncle told him about the situation all the while laughing.

Father, mother and children wanted to go there to see the gushing source a little beyond the tree line. The soil was mostly volcanic. From a distance, Clifton recognized the sulfuric acid odor of the gushing gases combining with the atmospheric oxygen. These sulfuric waters flowed abundantly among the rocks. The engineer dipped his hand into it and found it oily to the touch and that its temperature was about thirty seven degrees (Celsius). It tasted somewhat sweet. This source, like those in Luchon or Cauterets, have been effectively used for the treatment of respiratory ailments and, thanks to the heat, even for lymphatic constitutions.

Marc then asked his father how he was able to estimate the thirty seven degree temperature of this source without a thermometer. Mr. Clifton told him that when he immersed his hand into the water he felt no sensation of cold or hot; consequently he concluded that they were at the same temperature as the human body which is about thirty seven degrees.

With these observations made, they decided to camp here between two large basaltic rocks under the protection of the last trees. The children gathered some dry wood, enough to keep the fire going all night. A howling in the distance made precautions necessary. Ferocious animals would not cross a barrier of flames.

These preparations were quickly completed. Mother, helped by Jack and Belle, were occupied with making supper. The two pheasants were roasted. With the meal over, the children lay down on their beds of dry leaves. They were exhausted and were not long in falling asleep. During this time, Clifton and Uncle Robinson made a reconnaissance around the camp. They even went as far as a small bamboo woods growing on the initial slopes of the mountain. Here they distinctly heard the howling of ferocious beasts.

In order to better defend the approaches to his camp, Clifton then thought of using an idea recommended by Marco Polo, one used by the Tartars during the long nights to protect against dangerous animals. Uncle and he cut a quantity of bamboos which they carried to the camp. From time to time they threw a few pieces of this vegetation onto the incandescent cinders. A fireworks ensued that cannot be imagined by those who have never heard it. Marc and Robert were awakened by the noise. They were amused by the detonations, violent enough to frighten the nocturnal prowlers. In fact, the night passed without troubling the sleep of the Clifton family in any way.

The next day, the first of June, everyone was on foot at an early hour, ready to make the climb. They left at six o'clock after a quick meal. The tree zone was soon crossed and the small troop ventured onto the initial slopes leading to the peak. There was no doubt that the peak was a volcanic one. In fact, the slopes were covered with cinders and slag with lava flows appearing among them. Clifton saw materials indicating previous volcanic eruptions. They were pozzuolanas in small irregular shapes and highly torrefied white cinders made by an infinity of small feldspar crystals.

They climbed rapidly over the steep slopes made of capriciously ridged lava. Small solfatara sometimes blocked their path and they had to go around them. It was a pleasure for Clifton to talk about the abundance of sulfur all around in the form of encrusted crystals.

"Good!" Clifton shouted. "Children, here is a substance that comes to us just in time."

"To make candles?" Robert asked.

"No," the father replied, "to make powder, because however carefully we look, we will not be able to find saltpeter."

"Is it true, father?" Marc asked. "You can make powder?"

"I cannot promise you powder of the first quality but a substance that will give us good service."

"Then we will no longer lack for anything," Mrs. Clifton said.

"For example, my dear Elisa?" the engineer asked.

"Firing arms, my friend"

"Well, don't we have Robert's pistol?"

"Oh yes," shouted the noisy lad, shouting as loud as a gun.

"Calm down, Robert," Mr. Clifton said, "and let's continue our climb. We'll gather in some sulfer on our way down."

They continued on their way. Already, their view embraced a vast semi-circular horizon beyond the eastern part of the shore. The shoreline seemed to turn sharply to the north and to the south; in the north, beyond the large marsh not far from where Clifton had been found; in the south, beyond the promontory to the rear of the oyster bed. From this elevated point the travelers distinctly saw the vast bay where the river emptied, the winding course of its flow across the clearings, the foliage of the forest and the lake which appeared like a vast floor. To the north, the shore seemed to follow a west to east line. It was indented forming a wide bay ending in the east by a rounded cape. They could not see beyond because the mountain hid their view. In the south, on the contrary, the land was as straight as if it had been traced with a drawing pen. All of this shore, from the cape to the promontory, measured about six leagues. However, behind the peak they did not know whether there was a continent of some sort or an ocean beating against a still invisible shore. As to the land situated at the base of the peak and irrigated by the two branches of the river, it seemed to be very fertile. The southern region was ridged with savage looking dunes and the northern region looked like an immense marsh.

The family stopped to better observe this land and the ocean.

"Well, what do you think, Mr. engineer," Uncle said. "What is your opinion? Are we on an island or are we on a continent?"

"I do not know what to say, my worthy companion," Clifton replied. "I cannot see through the mountain that hides the east. We are not more than three hundred feet above sea level. Let us climb further to the plateau on which the peak rests. Perhaps we will then be able to go around it and see the eastern shore."

"I'm afraid," Uncle said, "that Mrs. Clifton and her two youngsters will find this second part of the climb a bit tiring."

"But here," the mother replied, "there is nothing to fear from an attack and I can wait with Jack and Belle for your return."

"In fact, my dear friend," Clifton replied, "I believe that we need fear neither people nor animals here."

"Besides, don't I have Jack to protect me?" Mrs. Clifton said with a smile.

"And he will defend you like a hero," Uncle said. "He is a little lion, afraid of nothing, but if you wish, Madame, I can stay here with you."

"No, my friend, no. Go with my husband and children. I would rather you did. Jack, Belle and I will wait here and rest."

That settled, Mr. Clifton, Uncle, Marc and Robert continued their climb and soon, with the distortion of distances peculiar to mountainous regions, mother and children appeared as three barely distinguishable points.

The path was no longer easy. The slopes were steep and their feet slipped on the streaks of lava but they climbed quickly toward the upper plateau. As to reaching the summit of the volcano, they would have to give that up if the slopes were steeper here than those on the western side.

Finally, after a painful hour's climb with very dangerous slips, Uncle, father and the two boys reached what may be called the base of the peak. It was an irregular narrow plateau but sufficiently practical. Situated at nine hundred or thousand meters above sea level, it rose gradually to the north by an oblique curve. The peak dominated it by seven or eight hundred meters. This grand slab of snow sparkled under the sun's rays.

In spite of the climbers' fatigue, there was no question of resting for a moment. They hurried to turn the mountain. Their view of the north gradually enlarged.

After an hour's march, the northern part of the peak had been turned. There was no land beyond. But father, Uncle and the boys moved forward, speaking little and all a prey to the same emotion. Marc and Robert, tireless, were in front. Finally, at about eleven o'clock, the sun's position indicated to Clifton that they had reached the opposite side.

The travelers saw nothing but an immense sea to the limits of the horizon. They watched in silence this ocean that imprisoned them. There could be no communication with other people, no help from them. They were isolated on a land lost in the Pacific Ocean.

According to the engineer's estimate, the island's circumference measured about twenty to twenty five leagues, an island larger than Elba, with a perimeter twice that of Saint Helena. This island was relatively small and Clifton did not know how to explain the presence of these large animals, whose traces they had seen, on a land so restricted. Perhaps its volcanic nature could explain some of these things. Was it possible that the island had once been part of a larger one now sunk under the waves or that it had drifted away from a continent? Clifton promised himself that he would verify these hypotheses when he would make a tour of the island. In the presence of this ocean without limits, the boys understood the gravity of their situation and they remained silent.

They did not want to question their father. He gave the signal to depart. The descent was rapid. In less than a half hour they rejoined Mrs. Clifton waiting for them, absorbed in thought.

When she saw her husband and her children she rose and went to them.

"Well," she said.

"An island," the engineer replied.

"The will of God be done," the mother murmured.

⊙

# Chapter XXI

While the voyagers were away, Mrs. Clifton had prepared a meal with the remainder of the game killed the previous day. At twelve thirty everyone began to descend the slopes of the mountain. The tree zone was crossed at right angles and they reached the river in the upper part of its course, that is to say above the cascade. At this point it formed a real rapid and its current foamed on the heads of black rocks. The site was extremely savage. After crossing an inextricable jumble of trees, creepers and brambles, they reached the boat. There they placed the provisions, plants and various things collected during the exploration. The boat moved rapidly down the waterway. At three o'clock they reached the entrance to the lake. The sail was hoisted and the boat, running on a close hauled tack, arrived at the lower rivercourse. At six in the evening everyone was back at the grotto. The first word from Uncle was an exclamation. The palisade enclosure bore evident traces of damage. Someone had tried to force it and uproot some posts which fortunately held secure.

"It was those nasty monkeys," Uncle said, "who paid us a visit during our absence. They are dangerous neighbors, Mister Clifton, and we must do something about it."

After this fatiguing day, the travelers had an irresistible need to go to sleep. Everyone went to his sleeping place. The fire had not been lit so there was no need to watch it but the night passed pleasantly. The next day, Wednesday June 2nd, Uncle Robinson and the engineer were the first to wake up.

"Well then, Mister Clifton!" Uncle shouted with joy.

"Well then, my worthy friend!" the engineer replied with resignation. "Since we are islanders, let's act like islanders and organize ourselves as if we will always be here."

"Well spoken, Mister Clifton," Uncle replied with confidence. "I say again that we are well off. We will make a Garden of Eden with our island. I say our island because it really is ours. Notice that if we have nothing to expect from other people, we no longer need be afraid of them. That must be taken into consideration. Has Mrs. Clifton adjusted to the new situation?"

"Yes, Uncle. She is a courageous woman and her trust in God will not fail her."

"He will not abandon her," Uncle said. "As to the children, Mr. Clifton, I am certain that they are enchanted to be here."

"Then, Uncle Robinson, there is nothing you regret?"

"Nothing, or rather yes, only one thing."

"What is that?"

"Must I say it?"

"Yes, Uncle."

"Well then, tobacco. Yes, tobacco. I would give one of my ears to be able to smoke a pipe."

Clifton could not hold back a smile while listening to the sailor express his regret. Not being a smoker himself, he could not understand the addiction created by this habit. Nevertheless, he resolved to try to satisfy Uncle Robinson some day.

Mrs. Clifton had asked for the establishment of a poultry yard. Her husband believed that he should begin his permanent installations on the island with this building. Near the palisade enclosure, at the right, he built a second enclosure with an area of hundred square meters. The two enclosures were in contact with each other through an interior door. The work was completed in two days. Two small huts made of branches were divided into compartments only waiting for the arrival of their guests. The first of these was the tinamou couple that had been taken alive during the preceding excursion. Mrs. Clifton cut their wings. Their domestication was easy. For companions they gave them a few ducks that frequented the shores of the lake who were content with the water in the bamboo vases that was renewed every day. These ducks belonged to this Chinese species whose wings open like a fan and who rival the gilded pheasants with the brilliance and brightness of their plumage.

During the weekend, hunts were organized for the purpose of populating the poultry yard. The children captured a gallinaceous couple with rounded tails made of long feathers. They could be mistaken for turkeys. They were alectors who were not long in becoming tame. All of this miniature world, after several disputes, ended by coming to terms and soon increasing in reassuring proportions.

Clifton, wanting to complete his plan, built a pigeon house in a friable part of rock. Some dozen pigeons were lodged there whose eggs furnished the family with important nourishment. These pigeons easily became accustomed to return to their new dwelling each evening. Besides, they showed more of a tendency to become domesticated than their congeners, the wood pigeons, who would only reproduce in the wild state.

During the first fortnight of June, Uncle Robinson made some marvels in the art of ceramics. We will remember that the boat had carried a certain quantity of argile useful for making large pottery. Not having a wheel, Uncle was content to make his pots by hand. They came out somewhat awkward, somewhat deformed, but they still were pots. During the baking of these utensils, not knowing how to regulate his fire, a certain number broke, but very fortunately there was no lack of argile and after a few fruitless attempts, he could give the family some half dozen pots or dishes that could give acceptable service. One of them was an enormous pot worthy of the name boiling pot.

Since Uncle was occupied with making these household articles, Clifton, sometimes with Marc, sometimes with Robert, made some excursions within a radius of a league around the grotto, and so he visited the marsh full of game, the warren that seemed to be inexhaustible, and the oyster bed whose precious products were carried to the oyster park. He was always on the lookout for some cryptogamous useful for replacing the amadou, but he still could not find it.[1] It was at this time that by chance he was able to satisfy one of Mrs. Clifton's strong wishes. Mrs. Clifton was always asking for some soap for washing the clothes. Clifton had intended to make some by treating animal fat, oil or grease, with soda made from the incineration of marine plants but the operation was a long one and he was able to avoid doing it thanks to finding a certain tree of the pine family. It was the savonnier whose

---

1. The cryptogamous are plants whose reproductive organs are barely visible like the ferns and the mosses.

From *Seconde patrie* (*Second Homeland*, 1900)

fruits work up an abundant lather in water to replace ordinary soap. The engineer knew that these fruits could wash sixty times as much linen by weight as soap could. Mother used them immediately with success.

Harry Clifton also wanted to get, if not cane sugar which can only be found in the tropics, at least some analogous substance from a maple tree or any sacchariferous tree.[2] He was constantly looking for it in the wooded parts of the island.

It was during one of these excursions made in the company of Marc, that Clifton discovered a vegetable product that would give exquisite pleasure, because it would allow him to satisfy Uncle Robinson's only wish.

On the 22nd of June, Marc and he were exploring the right bank of the river in the wooded portion to the north. While crossing through some tall grass, Marc was surprised by the odor emanating from certain plants with straight cylindrical branchy stems in the upper part. These plants were very sticky and produced small clustered berries. Marc tore off one or two stems and returned to his father, asking him to identify the plant.

"And where did you find this plant?" father asked.

"There in the clearing," Marc replied, "where it grows abundantly. It seems to me that I know it but..."

"Well," Clifton said, "you made there, my child, a very precious discovery. There will no longer be anything lacking for Uncle's happiness."

"Then it is tobacco!" Marc shouted.

"Yes, Marc."

"And what happiness!" the lad shouted. "What joy for worthy Uncle! But we must not say anything to him, father. You will make a fine pipe for him and one fine day we will present him with a full pipe."

"Agreed, Marc."

"Will it be difficult to transform these leaves into smoking tobacco?"

"No, my child. Besides, if this tobacco is not of the first quality, it is nevertheless tobacco and Uncle will not ask more of it."

Clifton and his son gathered a good quantity of this plant and they brought it into the grotto "deceitfully" with as much precaution as if Uncle had been the most severe of customs inspectors. The next day,

---

2.   Which produces a sugary substance.

during the absence of the worthy sailor, the engineer, having detached the smallest leaves, left them to dry, intending to chop them later and to subject them to a certain torrefaction over some hot stones.

However, Mrs. Clifton was always occupied with the question of clothing. There were enough skins from the seals and blue foxes but the difficulty was to piece them together without a sewing needle.

On this subject, Uncle told how he had once swallowed the an entire box of needles "by accident" he added, but unfortunately these needles had exited his body little by little, which he now regretted. However, with long thorns and coconut thread, Mrs. Clifton, helped by little Belle, was able to make a few large coats. Uncle, who, like all sailors, knew how to sew, did not spare his help and his advice.

The month of June came to an end when all these activities were completed. The poultry yard prospered and the number of its hosts increased every day. Agoutis and capybara frequently fell under the boys' arrows. Mother quickly transformed them into smoked hams assuring provisions for the winter. They need not fear any famine. The engineer also thought of making an enclosure for wild quadrupeds, moufflons and others, to capture and domesticate them. He decided on a large expedition for this purpose to be held at the northern part of the island, fixing the date for it on July 15th. Clifton also wanted to see if the island contained any specimens of this artocarpus tree which would be useful. The breadfruit tree grows as high as this latitude. They had no bread in their diet and several times Master Jack begged for a piece.

However, the time was ripe for the colony to acquire wheat flour. Belle, turning her pocket inside out one day, saw a grain of wheat fall out, but only a single grain. The little lady ran into the grotto with joy. She showed he grain of wheat to everyone triumphantly.

"Good!" Robert shouted mockingly, "What shall we make with it?"

"Do not laugh, Robert," Clifton replied. "This grain of wheat is as precious to us as a nugget of gold."

"Without a doubt, without a doubt," Uncle replied.

"A single grain of wheat," father repeated, "produces an ear; an ear can yield up to eighty grains so our little Belle's grain contains a full harvest."

"But why did you find this grain in your pocket?" Mrs. Clifton asked her little girl.

"Because I sometimes gave some of it to the chickens on board the *Vancouver*."

"Well," the engineer said, "we will take care of your grain of wheat, we will plant it next season and one day you will have cakes to eat, my child."

Belle was enchanted with this promise and all afire as if she were Ceres herself, the goddess of the harvest.

The day fixed for the excursion to the northeast of the island arrived. It was agreed that this time Marc would stay with his mother, Jack and Belle. Clifton, Uncle and Robert would plan on going quickly and possibly returning as soon as possible that very evening. At four o'clock in the morning, the 15th of July, they were on their way. The boat took them on the river to the point where the cliff ended in the north. There they debarked and instead of turning the marsh by going toward the shore, they went directly northeast.

Already it was no longer the forest because the trees were grouped in isolated clusters, but it was still not a plain. Bushes grew here and there on uneven ground. Among the trees, Clifton recognized several new species, among others the citron trees in a wild state. Its fruits were not as valuable as those from Provence, but they contained a sufficient quantity of citric acid and they had the same sedative property. Uncle Robinson plucked some dozen of them which would be well received by Mrs. Clifton.

"Because," the worthy sailor added, "we must think of our pantry in everything that we do."

"Well then," Clifton replied, "if I am not mistaken, here is a plant that will delight her."

"What, these dwarf trees?" Robert shouted.

"Without a doubt," Clifton replied. "They belong to the ericine genre and contain an aromatic oil with a pleasing odor which is antispasmatic.[3] It is found in North America where it is vulgarly called palommier. You must know this plant, Uncle Robinson."

"I must know it but I don't know it."

"As palommier perhaps, but as mountain tea or Canadian tea?"

"Ah! Sir, you said it right!" Uncle replied. "I know this Canadian tea well. It is the tea of the emperor of China. Unfortunately it is sugar

---

3. Or ericacea plants, which comprise the heather, the strawberry trees, rhododendrons and azaleas.

that we still do not have but we will find that later. Let us collect this tea as if the beets were growing in our fields and as if our sugar mills were ready to go into operation."

They followed Uncle's advice. The tea joined the citrons in the bags of the voyage. Clifton and his two companions then continued with their journey to the northeast. The birds were numerous in this part of the island but they flew from tree to tree not allowing anyone near them. For the most part, they were finches of the order of sparrow, recognizable by the two short jaws of their beak. Besides, from an edible point of view, they were not worth an arrow. However, Robert skillfully killed a few gallinaceous from the tridactyl group which have long pointed wings.[4] The upper part of their bodies are an ashen yellow with black rays and bands. These tridactyls walk poorly but they fly very fast which however did not save them from Robert's arrows.

At about eleven o'clock in the morning, they halted near one of the sources of the river. Lunch consisted of a piece of cold capybara and rabbit mixed with aromatic herbs. The river source furnished fresh water. Uncle added some citron juice which softened the raw taste. They then continued on their way. Clifton was always thinking of his amadou and he was astonished that he still had not found this parasitic plant which counts more than ten thousand species and grows naturally everywhere on earth.

At this moment a rustling of wings was heard in a thicket. Robert leaped forward preceded by a growling Fido.

"Well done, Fido, well done!" Robert shouted.

This recommendation would not have been followed if Robert had not arrived promptly. Fido's victim was a magnificent wild cock that the lad could still take alive. Clifton was not mistaken about the origin of this gallinule. It evidently belonged to the domestic race of medium height of a variety called the Benthane cock. The feathers of its ankle make a sort of cuff. However, one feature of this animal caught Robert's attention.

"Look, a cock with a horn on its head."

"A horn!" Clifton shouted, examining the animal.

"In fact," Uncle replied, "a horn firmly implanted at the base of its comb. This cock would be fierce in combat. Well, Mr. Clifton, I who have seen everything have never seen a cock with horns!"

---

4.   Birds whose feet have three digits.

Harry Clifton did not know what to say. He looked at the bird in a strange way and all he could say was:

"Yes, it really is a Benthane cock!"

Uncle tied the bird's wings. He wanted to carry it alive to the poultry yard. The voyagers then continued their excursion turning a bit to the east to join the watercourse. However, neither mushrooms of the polypore genre nor morels that could take the place of amadou were found. Fortunately they did find a plant that could be used for this

From *L'Île mystérieuse* (*The Mysterious Island*, 1874)

purpose. The plant belonged to this large family of composite flowers. It was the artemise, vulgarly called armoise which counts among its principal species the wormwood, the citron tree, tarragon, alpine wormwood, etc. This species was Chinese armoise or omoxa armoise covered with a cotton down. It was frequently used by the doctors of the Heavenly (Chinese) Empire.

Clifton knew that the leaves and stems of this plant, covered with long silky hair would catch fire from a spark when they were thoroughly dried.

"At last, this is our amadou," Clifton shouted.

"Good!" Uncle replied with joy. "Our day has not been wasted. And all I can see is that Providence always gives us the best. That is all I can see. It must not do otherwise. We can depend on it."

They collected a certain quantity of the armoise and then went southwest. Two hours later they reached the right bank of the river and at six o'clock in the evening the family was reunited at the camp. For supper they had a spiny lobster caught by Marc among the rocks at the point. Clifton described all the details of their excursion. The Benthane cock was placed in the poultry yard where it was the finest ornament.

But when the meal was over there was a big surprise, even an emotional one, for Uncle Robinson. Belle came to him and gave him a glossy red lobster leg shell stuffed with tobacco. At the same time Jack presented him with a hot cinder.

"Tobacco!" Uncle shouted, "and you said nothing about it to me!"

In spite of himself, the worthy sailor blinked his wet eyes. The pipe was soon lit and a fine odor of tobacco filled the air.

"You saw it well, my worthy friend," Clifton then said, "that Providence which has already given us everything, reserved yet another surprise for you."

⊙

# Chapter XXII

U ncle Robinson was at the peak of happiness; a superb island, an adorable family and a pipe of tobacco! If some vessel had presented itself at this moment he would certainly have hesitated to abandon this corner of the earth.

And yet there still were some things that the colony needed. Harry Clifton had to know not only how to provide for the future but he also could not neglect his children's education. He had no book to put into their hands but he himself was a veritable living encyclopedia. He taught them relentlessly on every subject, drawing the best lessons from nature. Example immediately followed theory. The sciences, especially natural history, geography, then religion and ethics, were practiced every day. As to philosophy which gave one a sense of right and wrong, what better teacher could they have than Uncle Robinson who was better than any professor from Oxford or Cambridge? But nature was their best teacher and Uncle was the perfect disciple of that school. As to Mrs. Clifton, with her woman's tenderness and the dignity of a mother, her love bound the little world together. She was the soul of the colony.

We will remember that during the excursion to the mountain, the voyagers had been able to acquire a certain quantity of sulfur. The engineer intended to make some sort of gunpowder if by chance he could discover some saltpeter. Now, precisely on the 20th of July, while he was exploring some cavities in the northern part of the cliff, he found a sort of humid grotto whose walls were covered with deposits of sodium nitrate salts. Over the ages, this salt was deposited on the surface of the granite through capillary action.

Clifton told Uncle about his discovery and announced his intention to make powder.

"I cannot obtain a perfect powder," he added, "because I cannot separate the impurities from the saltpeter by refining so I will be forced to use it in its natural state, but it will still give good service to break up rocks and create explosions."

"Good, sir," Uncle replied. "We will be able to build a powder magazine near the grotto."

"Besides," Clifton added, "we can saltpeter the courtyard ground. Mixed with saltpeter and pounded in, it will become rainproof."

This was the major use for the saltpeter. The courtyard and even the very soil in the grotto was pounded in and took on the consistency of granite. Mother made it shine like a wooden floor.

The engineer went on to make the powder. The children followed all the details with interest. Even though the colony had only one pistol, they acted as if they had to provide an entire artillery regiment.

Saltpeter, sulfur and charcoal must be intimately mixed in order to develop the powerful gas forces needed in firearms or in mines. Clifton had saltpeter and sulfur. He needed charcoal. This was easy. Instead of chestnut or the poplar wood which is used to make war powder, the engineer used the elm whose charcoal is especially suited for mines. He chose a few young branches and used the bark to make cinders. He carbonized them in pits.

Needless to say, the engineer knew the proper proportions. In a hundred parts, the powder contains seventy five parts of saltpeter, twelve and a half parts of sulfur and twelve and a half parts of charcoal. These three substances were subjected to various grinding operations, moisturized and finally pounded with a wooden pestle in a thick clay bowl made by Uncle. Clifton obtained a sort of large pancake which could only be used if it was granulated.

This was a difficult but indispensable part of the operation. In fact, if the powder remains in a compact form, it will detonate but the detonation will not occur simultaneously throughout and no explosive effect will result. It will be a detonating mixture but not an explosive mixture.

The engineer tried to obtain any kind of granulation. The powder was reduced by pulverization and left to dry for two days. It was broken into pieces with the fragments placed in a flared clay vase. By means of a cord and a pulley from the boat, he was able to impart a rather rapid gyratory motion to it. After determined and fatiguing work, he obtained a powder in large, sharp, unpolished form, but it was granular at last. The explosive material in this form was exposed to the sun's heat and it dried completely.

The next day, Robert did not stop urging his father to experiment with the new product. The pistol was cleaned and made ready. The flint was put in place, and charged and primed. Robert wanted to be the first to fire it, but Uncle himself wanted to make the trial since he did not want to expose the boy in case the powder exploded prematurely. Besides, he took the necessary precautions so that he himself would not be injured.

The gun was fired. The ignition of the powder in the chamber did not proceed rapidly it must be said but it finally caught on and, half ignited, half detonated, it pushed out a stone cannon ball placed there by Uncle.

The hurrahs were louder than the detonation itself. It was the children shouting with joy. At last they had a gun. They had to let Marc and Robert each take a try at it and they were enchanted with the results. In sum, it seemed that the powder left much to be desired for use as gunpowder but it could, at least, be used in a mine.

During these various activities, Mrs. Clifton was occupied with overseeing the prospering poultry yard. The gallinules had been successfully domesticated so why not quadrupeds? Clifton decided to build a special enclosure of several acres which he chose to the north of the lake about a mile from the camp. It was a grassy prairie fed by the water from the river. The perimeter of the new enclosure was traced out by the engineer and Uncle was occupied with choosing, cutting down and squaring the trees destined to become the posts of the palisade. The work was hard but it was carried out without delay nevertheless because Uncle counted on populating it before the coming spring. We should understand that as a result of this activity, there were frequent visits to the forest. Uncle planned it so that the cutting of the necessary trees laid out a pathway to make for easier exploitation of the area.

During one of these excursions, the engineer discovered a precious tree of the cycadacea family, very common in Japan, whose presence seemed to prove that the island was not located as far north as they had assumed.[1]

---

1.   An exotic shrub, a sort of palm with a flour that has given it the name of bread tree.

On this day, after a excellent dinner in which neither fish nor meat were spared, Clifton said to his children:

"Well then, my children, what do you think of our life? Is there anything you lack?"

"No father," Marc, Robert and Jack replied with one voice.

"Not even food?"

"That would be difficult to name. We have so much game, fish, mollusks and fruit. Who needs anything else?"

"Ah, yes!" said little Jack.

"Which is?" father asked.

"Cakes."

"There is our gourmand," Clifton replied, "but the boy is right. However, we have no cakes because we have no bread."

"That is true," Flip said, "we forgot about bread. But don't be anxious about that, my lads. We will make that when Miss Belle's grain of wheat is planted."

"We will wait a long time for that," Clifton replied, "but this very afternoon I discovered a tree that produces an excellent flour."

"Is it sago!" Marc shouted. "Like in Swiss Family Robinson!"

"Sago," Uncle replied, "but it is an excellent food. I ate some of it on the Molucca Islands where one finds entire forests of sagoes with each trunk containing perhaps as much as four hundred kilograms of this tasty and nutritious paste. That is a precious discovery that you made there. Onward to the forest of the sagoes!"

Uncle got up and reached for his axe. Clifton stopped him.

"One moment, Uncle Robinson," he said. "Let us not speak of a sago forest. That tree is a product of tropical countries and our island is very certainly situated to the north of the tropics. No! We simply have here a vegetable belonging to the cycadacea family which produces a substance similar to sago."

"Well then, sir. We will treat it as if it is sago."

Clifton and Uncle, leaving the children at the grotto, soon took to the road to the forest and reached the river that they had to cross.

"Sir," Uncle said, stopping at the bank, "we must decide to build a bridge here because we must always bring the boat here which will be a waste of time."

"I agree," the engineer replied. "We will make a drawbridge to get us to the left bank. It will form our natural frontier on this side. Let us

From *Seconde patrie* (*Second Homeland*, 1900)

not forget that this river covers the north and protects us from wild animals."

"No doubt," Uncle replied, "but they can get through because a southern route is open to them."

"And who is to prevent us," Clifton said, "from blocking this passage be it with a long palisade or with a diversion of the waters from the lake. Who is to stop us?"

"It will not be me," Uncle Robinson replied, "but while waiting for our bridge to be built, I will cut down a trunk that will take us to the other side."

A few minutes later, Clifton and Uncle moved through the forest in a northeast direction. Fido, who was with them, drove many capybara and agouti out of the bushes. Uncle remarked that several groups of monkeys were scampering about the branches but so rapidly that they could not recognize the species they belonged to.

After walking for a half hour, the two companions reached the edge of the forest on a vast plain covered with clusters of trees resembling sago trees. These were the trees that had attracted Clifton's attention. These trees, belonging to the sago palm species, showed a single stem covered with a scaly bark which held striped leaves with small parallel veins. They were rather small making them more like bushes than trees.

"In their trunk," Clifton shouted, "these precious vegetables carry a nourishing flour that nature has given us fully ground."

"Mr. Clifton," Uncle replied, "nature does well in everything it does. What would become of a poor devil thrown on a deserted shore if nature did not come to help him? You see, I have always thought that there are islands for castaways, created especially for them, and most certainly this island is one of them. And now, to work!"

That said, Uncle and the engineer cut some palm branches and then, not wanting to carry excess wood, they decided to extract the flour on the spot.

The trunk of the palm was composed of a glandular texture. It enclosed a certain quantity of floury pith, traversed by ligneous bundles and separated by rings of the same substance arranged concentrically. This flour was mixed with a gummy sap with a disagreeable taste that would be easy to remove by pressure. This cellular substance formed a real flour of superior quality. A very small quantity was enough to nourish a man. Clifton told Uncle that the exportation of this precious vegetable was formerly prohibited by Japanese laws.

After a few hours work, the two companions extracted a large quantity of flour. With a full load they took the road back to the encampment. On returning to the forest, Clifton and Uncle Robinson found themselves among many groups of monkeys. This time they were able to observe them carefully. They were tall animals and could be regarded as among the highest order of the quadrupeds. The engineer could not be mistaken about that. That would make them either chimpanzees or orangs or gibbons, certainly belonging to the anthropoid apes, so called because of their resemblance to the human race.

These animals could become formidable adversaries because they were powerful and intelligent. Had these already seen men? What did they think of these bipeds? Whatever the case, they made contortions and grimaces while Clifton and Uncle passed by at a steady pace, not anxious for a battle with these fearful animals.

"Sir," Uncle said. "We could have quite a problem with these jolly fellows."

"In fact," Clifton replied, "it is certain they have seen us. It would be unfortunate if they followed us to the grotto."

"We need not fear that." Uncle said. "The river will soon stand in their way but let us move on."

The two companions moved on quickly without provoking the grimacing troop neither with a gesture nor by looking at them. The apes, about a dozen of them, continued to escort them. From time to time, one of them who seemed to be the leader of the band, came closer to Clifton or to Uncle, looked at them face to face and then returned to his companions.

Under these conditions, the engineer was able to observe him closely. This orang was six feet tall. He had an admirably proportioned body, a large chest, a head of average size with a facial angle of sixty five degrees, a rounded cranium, a prominent nose, a skin covered with a sleek, gentle and glossy hair, in short an accomplished type of anthropomorph. His eyes, a little smaller than human eyes, shown with a vivacious intelligence. His white teeth showed through his moustache and he had a small beard with a hazel color.

"My word, a fine lad," Uncle murmured.

However, Clinton and he moved on quickly. Little by little they saw with satisfaction that the group dispersed themselves in the woods. The escorting group were reduced to three or four apes and soon the large orang was the only one following them. This animal had attached himself to them with an incomprehensible stubbornness. They could not for a moment think of outdistancing him. With his long legs, he could move at top speed.

Clifton and Uncle finally reached the river at four o'clock. They easily found the place where they had moored the temporary raft. There they had to decide what to do about the ape.

The orang came right up to the bank. He looked at the two men unloading their provisions on the raft and he observed all their movements with interest. He walked along looking at the other side and seemed little disposed to abandon his travelling companions.

"This is the moment when we part company," Uncle said.

The cable was detached. Clifton and Uncle jumped on board and began to move away from shore. But in a flash the orang threw himself on board, landing at the edge of the raft at the risk of capsizing it. With his ax in hand, Uncle dashed toward the ape but the latter stayed put, staring at him and demonstrating no hostile intentions.

Uncle lowered his weapon. This was not the time to start a fight which would be a dangerous one under these conditions. Once on the other side, they would decide on the best course of action.

They crossed the river. Uncle and Clifton disembarked. The ape did likewise and followed them along the road to the grotto. They went around the north shore of the lake, passed the coconut trees and skirted the cliff with the ape close behind. They finally arrived at the palisade, opened the door and quickly closed it behind them.

Night came on, a night of thick clouds making for poor visibly. Was the ape still there? Yes, because several times throughout the night they heard a strange cry that disturbed the silence of the night.

# Chapter XXIII

During supper, Clifton told his wife and his children about the various incidents that marked this excursion. They agreed to postpone the question of the ape to the next day. They rose at an early hour. The children looked through the cracks in the palisade. Their exclamations caught the attention of Clifton and Uncle Robinson.

The orang was still there. Sometimes he leaned against the trunk of a tree with his arms crossed, so to say, and examined the palisade. Sometimes he went up to the door, shook it vigorously and, not being able to open it, he went back to his post of observation.

Everyone gathered behind the stakes to look at him.

"What a fine ape!" Jack shouted.

"Yes," Belle replied. "How nice he looks. He is not making too many faces at me and I am not afraid of him."

"But what are we going to do with him?" Mrs. Clifton asked. "He can't stay there forever watching our door."

"Could we adopt him?" Uncle suggested.

"Is that what you're thinking, my friend?" Mrs. Clifton replied.

"Honestly, madame," Uncle replied, "some apes are well behaved. This one could make an excellent servant. If I am not very much mistaken, he has every intention of attaching himself to us. The only difficulty is that we must find out more about him."

Uncle laughed all the while but he was not exaggerating in any way. The intelligence of these anthropomorphs is truly remarkable. Their facial angle is not significantly less than that of the Australians and of the Hottentots. Besides, the orang has neither the ferocity of the baboon, nor the thoughtlessness of the macaco, nor the filthy ways of the saguin, nor

227

the impatience of Barbary ape, nor the bad instincts of the cynocephalus, nor the bad temper of the cercopithic monkey. Harry Clifton knew some of these ingenious animals and he cited several examples of their quasi human intelligence. He told the children that they knew how to light a fire and to use it. Several apes had been usefully employed in homes. They served at the table, cleaned rooms, cared for clothes, drew water from wells, polished shoes, handled a knife, a spoon, a fork, cleaned dishes, drank wine and liquors, etc. Buffon possessed one of these apes who served him for a long time as a faithful and zealous servant.

"Very well," Uncle then replied. "Since that's the way things are, I do not see why this orang should not be given the title of servant to the colony. He seems to be young, his education will be easy and he certainly will become attached to his masters if we are good to him."

After thinking for a few moments, Harry Clifton turned to Uncle and said to him:

"Are you seriously thinking of adopting this animal?"

"Very seriously, sir. You can see that we will not be obliged to use force to domesticate him nor to pull his teeth as is done in similar circumstances. This orang is vigorous and can be a great help to us."

"Very well, let's try it then," Clifton replied, "and if later his presence becomes too troublesome we will see about getting rid of him."

That agreed, Clifton asked his children to go back to the grotto. Then Uncle and he left the palisade enclosure.

The orang had returned to the tree. He allowed his future masters to approach him and looked at them while gently moving his head. Uncle had taken some coconut nuts and offered them to the ape. The latter put them in his mouth and ate them with evident satisfaction. He certainly had a fine figure.

"Well, my boy," Uncle said to him in a playful tone. "How are you feeling?"

The orang replied with a slight grunt of good humor.

"Would you like to join the colony" Uncle asked, "and enter the service of Mr. and Mrs. Clifton?"

The ape uttered another grunt of consent.

"And you will be content with our food as your full wages?" Uncle added, offering the animal a handshake.

The latter responded with a similar gesture, offering the worthy sailor his hand and uttering a third grunt.

"His conversation is a bit monotonous," Clifton noted with a smile.

"Good, sir." Uncle replied. "The best servants are the ones that talk the least."

However, the ape rose and deliberately went to the grotto. He entered the palisaded enclosure. The older boys were at the door of the grotto and the youngsters were clutching at their mother opening their eyes wide at the gigantic animal. The latter seemed to be inspecting the place. He examined the poultry yard and threw a glance at the interior of the grotto. He then returned to Clifton whom he seemed to recognize as the chief of the family.

"Well, my friend," Uncle said. "The house suits you? Yes? Understood. To begin with we will give you no wages but later we will double it if we are satisfied with you."

And so, without further ado, the orang was installed in the Clifton house. It was agreed that they would build a wooden hut for him in the left corner of the yard. As for his name, Uncle asked that they use the name of many American negroes and he was baptized with the name of Jupiter or Jup for short.

Clifton had no reason to fault this new recruit. This orang was amazingly intelligent, exemplary in his gentleness and trained by Uncle for various tasks that he performed perfectly. Fifteen days after his admission into the family, he carried wood that he found in the forest, drew water from the lake in bamboo vases and swept the courtyard. He quickly climbed to the top of a coconut tree to pluck its fruits. Agile Robert could not think of competing with him. During the night he kept guard so keenly that Fido had to be jealous of him. Besides, the dog and the ape made a good team. As to the children, they quickly became accustomed to the ape's services. Jack teased him and never left his side. Friend Jup let him play his games.

However, the days flew by. The second half of September came by while these activities were still going on. In anticipation of the approaching winter, every kind of reserve was increased. Uncle Robinson built a large covered shed at a corner of the cliff to cut and store the wood. Regular hunts were organized to procure a large number of agoutis and capybara whose meat was salted and smoked. In addition, the poultry yard was populated with gallinules of all kinds to assure the colony fresh meat during the rainy season. They made a clean sweep of the rocks in the south, capturing sea tortoises whose carefully preserved flesh promised excellent soups in the future. Needless to say, the supply of sago was increased to be made into bread, biscuits or cakes, making it an excellent food. The question of food for the winter was very nearly resolved.

Mrs. Clifton was no longer concerned about the question of clothing. Thanks to Uncle's efforts, there was no lack of fur. There were warm leather clothes of all sizes. It was the same with the shoes. Uncle skillfully made wooden soled shoes, half wood and half leather, to be put to good use in rain or in snow. Some were made into high boots to be used for hunts in the marsh when the frost would harass the aquatic game at the north of the island. As to hats, bonnets or caps, they were made of sea otter skins bright as a button. They could not have done better neither in quality nor in quantity. The otters, in fact, seemed to seek refuge in this part of the Pacific and the children captured several of them by surprise among the rocks of the southwest of the island.

It must be said nevertheless that Uncle still had not been able to give Clifton a fine bear fur coat. There was no lack of traces of bears but until now these animals had not shown themselves. It was principally to the south of the lake on the road to the warren that a large number of their footprints were to be found. Evidently a few of these animals passed this way to drink from the lake. Uncle then decided to use the only way he could to bring about the capture of one of these plantigrades. He confided his plan to Marc. With his help he dug a pit some ten to twelve feet deep and covered the opening under a pile of branches. This was a primitive method but Uncle could do nothing else. He did not have any weapons to attack a bear face to face. He could only hope that by chance on a dark night one of these animals would fall into the pit. Each morning, under one pretext or another, Uncle or Marc visited the pit which unfortunately was always empty.

While all these various occupations were going on, Uncle did not neglect the education of his ape. Besides, he was aided by the animal's remarkable intelligence. The orang was used with daring and skill for the heavier work. They liked each other a great deal and an insignificant detail occurred which drew them closer. One day Uncle found Jup smoking his pipe, yes, his very lobster shell pipe. The tobacco seemed to give the orang unparalleled pleasure. Uncle, enchanted, told Mr. Clifton about it. The latter was not surprised at all about the news. He cited several examples of apes who were familiar with the use of tobacco. At the end of the day

Master Jup had his own pipe which hung in his cabin with a supply of tobacco. Master Jup filled it himself, lit it with a hot cinder and smoked with pleasure. In addition, Uncle offered him a small cup of fermented coconut juice each morning. Mrs. Clifton was afraid this would give him a drinking problem but Uncle invariably said to her:

"Be assured, Madame, this ape has received a good education and he will never become an addict."

There was fine weather for all of the month of September. No rain or heavy wind. There was a refreshing light breeze morning and evening. The leaves from the trees changed color with the beginning of autumn and fell to the ground little by little. The cold season had not yet been felt when one morning, it was the 29th of September, they heard little Jack shouting outside:

"Come Marc! Come Jack! There's snow outside. Let's have fun!"

They all got up. There was nothing on the ground between the grotto and the sea. Robert began to make fun of him but Jack pointed to the islet which was all covered with white.

"That's strange," Clifton said.

They could not explain the appearance of snow at this time of the year with a brilliant sun so high in the sky.

"Wonderful!" Uncle shouted. "We have a phenomenal island."

"We must see what it is," Clifton said.

"Let's take the boat and cross the channel," Marc replied.

To launch the boat into the sea was the matter of a moment. In a few strokes of the oars, they reached the islet but no sooner had they touched shore when the supposed layer of snow rose up and spread out over the islet, hiding the sun for a moment. This so called snow was a huge flock of white birds. They disappeared so quickly into the distance that Clifton could not identify them.

However, the rainy season was approaching. The days were getting shorter. It was the beginning of October. There were ten hours of daylight versus fourteen hours of darkness. It was too late to undertake a voyage around the island as Clifton had planned. They now had equinoctial winds and heavy squalls churning up the sea. The frail boat could be exposed to the rocks along the shore or to be lost at sea. They must put off the exploration for the next year.

The evenings were already long with sunset at five thirty. These evenings were spent together as a family with everyone chatting and

From *L'Île mystérieuse* (*The Mysterious Island*, 1874)

improving themselves. They made plans for the future. They were quite settled in and accustomed to their island.

Clifton had to find a way to light up these long winter evenings since they did want to go to bed at sunset. They asked Mrs. Clifton to carefully save any animal fat that could be used to make tallow. But this tallow was in a raw state. Having no sulfuric acid, they could not purify it nor remove its aqueous material. Nevertheless, such as it was, they used it that way. Using a thick wick made from coconut fibers, Clifton made tallow candles that sparkled at first while burning but finally they give something of a light at least around the table where the family gathered. Next year they would think of a better way to light the place using oil instead of fat, "until gas light is installed" Uncle would say, no longer doubting anything.

However, even though the island was perfect and had everything, he declared one evening that there was still something missing.

"What could that be," Mrs. Clifton asked.

"I'm not quite sure. It seems to me that our island does not exactly exist but that is a trivial matter."

"I understand you, Uncle," the engineer replied. "It is not an official place."

"Exactly."

"And what is missing is a name."

"A name, a name!" the children shouted with one voice. "Let's give the island a name."

"Yes," father replied, "and not only a name for the island but also names for the various parts of the island. That will simplify our instructions in the future."

"Yes," Uncle replied, "so when we go somewhere we will at least know where we are."

"Well, let's use our own names," impetuous Robert shouted. "I propose we call it the Robert Clifton Island."

"One moment, my boy," the engineer replied. "You must not think only of yourself. If we use names of people we hold dear for the capes, the promontories, the watercourses and the mountains of this island, let us also use names that recall for us events and situations. But let's proceed methodically. First a name for the island."

The discussion began. Several names were suggested but they could not come to an agreement.

"My word," Uncle said. "I think we can agree that in every civilized country it is the right of the discoverer to name his discovery and for this reason I propose to call this island Clifton Island."

"Agreed," the engineer replied vividly, "but then this honor must be reserved for the real discoverer of this island, to the savior of my wife and my children, to our devoted friend. From now on, this island is called Flip Island."

Hurrahs were shouted. The children crowded around Uncle Robinson. Mr. and Mrs. Clifton rose and extended their hands to him. The worthy sailor, very emotional, wanted to protest this honor but he had everyone against him and in spite of his modesty, he had to accept. And so the name Flip Island was definitely given to the island and it would appear under this name on modern charts.

Secondary names were then discussed and Uncle had no difficulty getting agreement for the name Mount Clifton for the volcano that dominated the island. The conversation on this subject continued. Geographical names led to interesting debates among the children and the results were these: The bay into which the river emptied was called First Sight Bay because that was where the castaways first saw the island; the river with its winding course took on the name of Serpentine River which was justified.

As to the marsh in the north, near where Uncle found Clifton, that was called Safety Marsh, to the cape at the northern end of the island, Senior Cape, and to the one at the southern end of the island, Junior Cape in honor of Marc and Robert, to the lake the name of Lake Ontario so the abandoned family could remember their absent country, to the channel between the islet and the shore the name Harrison Channel in memory of the unfortunate captain of the *Vancouver*, and to the islet the name of Seal Islet. Finally, to the port situated between the beginning of First View Bay and the mouth of the river the name of Deo Gratias, a recognition that God had so evidently protected the abandoned family.

Belle and Jack were a little regretful that their names had been omitted from this geographical list but Mr. Clifton promised to use them with the first discoveries that would be made on the island.

"As for your wonderful mother," he added, "her name will not be forgotten. Uncle and I will build a comfortable home which will be used as our principal residence and this place will be carry the name of the one cherished by everybody. It will be called Elisa House."

This last idea was vividly applauded and the courageous mother received no end of kisses.

The discussion was prolonged into the evening. It came time to go to sleep. Mother and children retired to their beds of hides and moss. Master Jup himself had already gone to his hut.

Before going to sleep, Uncle and Clifton went alone as usual to examine the surroundings around the grotto. When they were alone, Uncle thanked the engineer once more for giving the island his name.

"We now have a real island," he said, "whose existence is legally verified and which can be placed on the maps with pride and note, sir, that we can claim the right to have discovered it."

"My worthy friend," Clifton replied, "it is important to know if Flip Island was inhabited before our arrival on these shores and, I say again, if it has other inhabitants."

"What do you wish to say, sir?" Uncle shouted. "Have you some indication of this?"

"I have one," Clifton replied, lowering his voice, "only one. I have no need to tell you that there is no purpose in causing our small colony any anxiety."

"You are right, sir," Uncle said. "What is it?"

"This. You remember the cock with the horn which we captured and which is now acclimatized to our poultry yard?"

"Perfectly," Uncle replied.

"Well, my friend, I do not believe that his horn, this appendage that our cock carries on its head is a natural one. When this cock was a young chicken someone made a cut in its crest and implanted this false spur at the very base of its crest. After fifteen days this graft took root and is now an integral part of the bird. It is the work of a human hand."

"And how old is this cock?" Uncle asked.

"Barely two years old which proves that in the last two years men, probably white men, were on our island."

⊙

# Chapter XXIV

Uncle followed the engineer's advice and kept the secret of this last conversation but the consequences that Clifton deduced from the presence of the horn on the cock were absolutely logical. Someone was on the island at some time in the last two years, that fact could not be in doubt. Uncle had doubts that they were still here since he had found no trace of human creatures but this question could not be resolved without a complete exploration of the island in the coming year.

The month of October passed with windstorms and equinoctial rain. The boat was sheltered near the surf. The keel was overturned and it would pass the winter at the foot of the cliff. The hut where the wood was cut and stored was filled to capacity. Meat reserves were increased but hunting from time to time could still supply them with fresh game. As to the poultry yard, it prospered and it was already too small. Everyone, including the children, took part in feeding the birds. They now had male and female bustards surrounded by their chicks. These long legged wading fowls belonged to the houbara species, characterized by a sort of cloak around their necks formed of long feathers. These bustards ate grass or berries without distinction. The ducks had multiplied. They were shoveler ducks whose upper jaw is extended on each side by a membranous appendage. They splashed about in an artificial pond. They also noticed a couple of black game cocks with their numerous chicks. They were the Mozambique cocks deriving their name from the black color of their crests, carbuncle and skin, but their flesh is white and very tasty.

It goes without saying that inside the grotto Uncle had made shelves and wardrobes. One corner in particular was reserved for a large quantity of vegetables. The pine cone almonds had been collected in abundance. One could also see a certain quantity of this root belonging to the aralia family found everywhere on the globe.[1] These were the roots of the dimorphantus edulis, aromatic and somewhat bitter but tasty. The Japanese eat it in the winter. Uncle often ate some of it at Yedo and they were excellent.

One of mother's ardent wishes was finally satisfied thanks to Uncle's advice. His experience was always useful.

It was at the beginning of November that Harry Clifton said to his wife:

"Isn't it true, dear friend, that you would be very happy if we could bring you sugar?"

"Without a doubt," Mrs. Clifton replied.

"Well, we can make something similar."

"You found cane sugar?"

"No."

"Sugar beets?"

"I don't know about that, but nature has placed a very common and precious tree on this island. It is the maple."

"And can the maple give us sugar?"

"Yes."

"Who ever heard of such a thing?"

"Uncle."

In fact, Uncle was not mistaken. The maple, one of the most useful members of the acerinea family, is commonly found in the temperate regions, in Europe, in Asia, in North Indies and in North America. Of the sixty species that comprise this family, the most useful is the Canadian maple, also called acer saccharinum, because it yields a sugary substance. It was during one of their excursions to the south, among the hills on this part of the island, that Clifton and Uncle had found numerous groups of these trees.

Winter was the best season for the extraction of the sugar from the acer saccharinum. They decided to use the first days of November to do this. Father, Uncle, Marc and Robert returned to the maple forest leaving Fido and Master Jup to guard Elisa House.

---

1.   Angelica and ivy belong to this family.

In passing near the warren, Uncle made a slight detour to visit the bear pit which was always empty to his great disappointment.

Upon arriving at the forest, Robert, with his usual frivolity, laughed on seeing these so called sugar trees but they paid no attention to his jokes and went to work.

Using his ax, Uncle made deep incisions in about a dozen maple trunks and soon a clear sugary liquid came gushing out. They were barely able to collect it in the vases they brought with them. They could see that harvesting it, if it could be called that, required little work. When the vases were full, Uncle carefully closed them and returned to Elisa House.

But all was not over. From the moment it is collected, the maple liquid takes on a white color and a syrupy consistency but this is still not the kind of crystalline sugar that Mrs. Clifton was asking for. They had to purify it in a sort of refiner which fortunately was very simple. The liquid was placed over a fire which subjected it to a certain evaporation and a foam came to the surface. As soon as the substance began to thicken, Uncle took care to stir it with a wooden spatula which accelerated its evaporation and at the same time prevented it from taking on an acrid taste. After boiling for a few hours, the liquid was transformed into a thick syrup. This syrup was poured into argile molds that Uncle had fashioned into a variety of shapes. The next day the syrup solidified into cakes and tablets. It was sugar with a slight reddish color but it was nearly transparent and had a perfect taste. Mrs. Clifton was delighted and more so Jack and Belle who foresaw sweet desserts and cakes in the future and more so than the children, Master Jup who had become something of a gourmand. It was his only fault but they could pardon him for that.

The colony would no longer lack sugar. First it would be used to make a delightful composition that would change the way they used the fermented coconut juice. Here's how.

Clifton knew quite well that the young shoots of certain conifer trees could be made into an antiscorbutic liqueur used on vessels making long trips. For this purpose they used the shoots from the Canadian firs and the abies nigra that grew on the lower slopes of the central peak. They were advised to collect a considerable quantity. The young shoots were boiled in water on a hot fire and the liquid was sweetened with maple sugar. They left it to ferment and obtained a pleasant and healthy drink which Anglo Americans call spring beer, in other words fir beer.

Before the first frost came on, there was still one important project that had to be completed. It would present no difficulty, it is true. It was to plant little Belle's single grain of wheat which could produce ten ears with eighty grains each, making eight hundred grains in all. Then, at the fourth harvest, and they could perhaps have two harvests a year at this latitude, they would have an average of four hundred billion grains.

They had to protect this grain from all destructive possibilities. It was planted in a terrain sheltered from the sea's winds and Belle was put in charge of protecting it from insects.

The weather became cold and rainy about the end of November. Fortunately the grotto was comfortably arranged. It needed only an interior chimney which they had to put in without delay. This was difficult work. It required many attempts but Uncle Robinson finally made a sort of clay stove It was large enough to be heated by wood and could give out enough heat. There still was the question of removing the smoke to the outside. That was a difficult one. They could not dream of piercing a shaft through to the top of the grotto since the thick granite above it went up to a considerable height. Clifton and Uncle then tried to make a lateral opening in the wall through to the outside of the cliff. This required time and patience. They had no tools. However, using a well sharpened spike that Uncle found in the boat, they succeeded in making a passageway for a long bamboo pipe that had been bored through along its entire length. Another pipe, made of clay, was shaped to go above the stove and in this way the smoke could reach the outside. They then had an almost acceptable chimney. It smoked a little when the southwest winds blew but that presented no difficulty. Uncle was enchanted with his work.

The rainy season arrived at the end of November. They had work inside the grotto. Uncle, who had gathered a certain quantity of osiers, showed the children how to make bread baskets and wicker baskets. Using osiers and clay he himself made large cages in which the hosts of the poultry yard could find a refuge for the winter. In the same way he made Jup's hut more habitable. The latter helped him to carry the necessary materials. During this work, Uncle chatted with his companion, asking questions and giving his own answers naturally. They were two real friends. When the hut was finished, Master Jup was very satisfied but he could not complement his architect with words.

As to the children, they found the place so elegant, they baptized it with the lofty name of Jup Palace.

In the first days of December the weather suddenly became very cold. It became necessary to try on their new clothes. The members of the little colony looked completely different dressed in skins with outside fur.

"We look like Jup," Uncle said with a laugh, "with this difference that we can remove our clothes but he cannot remove his."

The Clifton family looked like a group of Eskimos but that was not important since the cold wind could not get under the warm fur. They all had clothes they could change into and they were able to face the winter weather.

About the middle of December, torrential rains fell. Serpentine River overflowed from the masses of water that flowed from the mountain. Their first encampment was inundated up to the foot of the cliff. The level of the lake rose and Clifton was afraid that it would overflow, causing damage to the plantations and even reaching Elisa House. He realized that they had to build an embankment to hold back the rising waters because all of the lower area between the lake and the shore could become inundated.

Fortunately the rain stopped and the overflow subsided in time. These setbacks were followed by hurricanes and squalls that damaged the forest. They heard the noise of the trees breaking apart but Uncle did not complain about that saying that he would let the storm do its work as woodsman. There would be no need to spare the supply of wood. They could collect it without having to cut down the trees.

It goes without saying that they made a good fire in the chimney of Elisa House. Why economize on the wood? The reserve was inexhaustible. The sparkling fire cheered everyone while the two youngsters chattered about. They worked as a family. They made arrows and baskets, mended the clothes and took care of the food, everyone working at his specialty, following a plan devised by Clifton.

They did not neglect intellectual and moral education. Clifton gave his children daily lessons. He had collected a few pieces of paper that he had on him at the moment he left the *Vancouver* and there he carefully recorded the various events that occurred on this deserted island. The notes were brief but precise. It would allow them to reconstruct the daily history of the abandoned family which was only a true account.

From *L'Île mystérieuse* (*The Mysterious Island*, 1874)

And so the year 1861 came to an end. Clifton and his family had lived on Flip Island for nine months. At first their condition was deplorable but now it was bearable. They had a comfortable grotto well protected by a palisade enclosure, a full poultry yard, an oyster park and an almost completed yard for large animals. They had bows, gunpowder, bread, amadou and clothes. They had no lack of meat, fish or fruit. Could they look forward to the future? Yes, without a doubt.

Nevertheless a serious question was always on Clifton's mind. The incident of the cock with the horn was always a subject of conversation between Clifton and Uncle. They had no doubt that men had already set foot on the island but were these men still here? Evidently no, because they had found no trace of them. Clifton and Uncle had banished all fear in this regard. They no longer thought about it when an unexpected incident occurred that made them change their minds.

It was the 29th of December and Marc had captured a very young hare who was doubtless lost far from its burrow. This animal was killed, roasted and served for dinner. Everyone had a piece and Uncle, who had his share, had one of the legs of the animal.

The worthy sailor ate with appetite, guzzling his food, when suddenly he let out a yell.

"What is it?" Mrs. Clifton asked him vividly.

"Nothing, Madame, nothing, except that I broke a tooth."

It was really true.

"But what was in the hare's flesh?" Clifton asked.

"A stone, sir, a simple little stone," Uncle replied. "It was my luck!"

"Poor Uncle!" Belle said. "One tooth missing."

"Oh, mademoiselle!" Uncle replied. "I still have thirty two. I had one too many."

Everyone laughed and went on with their meal.

But when the meal was over, Uncle took Clifton aside.

"This was the stone I was talking about, sir." he said to him. "Do me the pleasure of telling me what you would call this stone."

"A lead pellet," Clifton shouted.

In fact it was a lead pellet.

⊙

# Where's the End?

As noted in the introduction, when Verne finished the first part of *Shipwrecked Family: Marooned with Uncle Robinson*, he sent it to his publisher, Pierre-Jules Hetzel. It was anticipated to be part of a long, multi-volume book; Verne's serials in his publisher's magazine had sometimes filled two years of issues with a single story. However, Hetzel rejected *Shipwrecked Family*, urging his author to abandon it and start over. Ever willing to follow his editor's guidance, Verne began again, turning the project into the classic *L'Île mystérieuse* (*The Mysterious Island*, 1875).

What would have become of the family in the original version? *The Mysterious Island* offers a strong suggestion, and the reader is urged to turn to that novel, in the authoritative new critical translation published by Wesleyan University Press in 2002. The reader of *Shipwrecked Family* will find facsimiles of some of the characters and incidents. In *The Mysterious Island*, Verne also explains the fate of certain characters from *Les enfants du Capitaine Grant Enfants* (*The Children of Captain Grant*, 1867) and *Vingt Mille Lieues sous les mers* (*Twenty Thousand Leagues Under the Seas*, 1870)—although the timelines of all three novels, set in the 1860s, are mutually incompatible. Verne took the author's liberty of altering the background of his own works even as he treats them as referential, extra-literary sources. This suggests that, having already rewritten *Shipwrecked Family* into *The Mysterious Island*, he was not about to start again to resolve the temporal contradictions with the previous works.

Verne's readers had faced such a situation before. When *De la Terre à la Lune* (*From the Earth to the Moon*, 1865) stranded its protagonists in lunar orbit, he waited four years before writing the sequel, *Autour de la Lune* (*Around the Moon*, 1879). While the two books recount a single journey, and are often spoken of and read together, there are major distinctions. *From the Earth to the Moon* is a largely politicized novel, a satire of militarism and its role in leading mankind to conquer space. *Around the Moon*, while continuing the story, is much different from its whimsical predecessor, providing a "hard" science fiction account of the actual circuit of the moon, and return to Earth, later brought to life by Apollo 8 (and, unintentionally, Apollo 13).

Hence, even when finishing his novels, Verne was not above tricking his readers or offering plot twists at variance with what had gone before. The resolution he might have given *Shipwrecked Family* is anyone's guess, although *The Mysterious Island* provides the best blueprint.

# Appendix

# Verne's Prefaces To
# His Robinsonades

On January 19, 1889, George Munro copyrighted a translation of *Deux Ans de vacances* as *Two Year's Vacation*. By February 16, it had appeared in the Seaside Library pocket edition No. 1157, papercover, 260 pages, illustrated, priced at 20 cents. This American volume contains the preface by Verne, which was omitted from the simultaneous British editions.

> Quite a number of Robinsons have already excited the curiosity of our young readers. Daniel Defoe, in his immortal Robinson Crusoe, has depicted the solitary castaway; Wyss, in his *Swiss Family Robinson*, has represented an interesting family under similar circumstances; Cooper, in *The Crater*, society, with its manifold and diverse elements; and in *The Mysterious Island* I have brought several unfortunate savants face to face with the difficulties of the situation. Then, too, there is a *Robinson of Twelve Years*, a *Robinson Among the Icebergs*, etc., etc. But in spite of the infinite number of stories included in the list of Robinsons it has always seemed to me that to complete it there should be a description of the experience and adventures of a party of children from eight to thirteen years of age, cast upon an island, and struggling for subsistence in the midst of the passions and prejudices naturally aroused by differences of nationality.

On the other hand, in *A Captain at Fifteen* I have undertaken to show what even a brave and intelligent child can accomplish when he is obliged to face the dangers and perplexities of a responsibility beyond his years; but, to make the contents of that book profitable to all, it seems to me it must be complete.

It was for this twofold purpose that the new work now offered to our readers under the title of *Two Years Vacation* was written.

In 1989, Sidney Kravitz translated Verne's preface to *Second Homeland*, as a favor for personal research the editor was undertaking on Verne Robinsonades, and it is published here for the first time.

## Why I Wrote *Second Homeland*

The "Robinsons" were the books of my childhood, and I retained an undying recollection of them. The frequent readings which I made of them could only strengthen this in my mind, even though I could never racapture the impressions of my youth in my later modern readings. There is no doubt that my taste for this kind of adventure instinctively led me toward the path which I would follow one day. This led me to write *The School for Robinsons*, *The Mysterious Island*, and *Two Year's Vacation*, whose heroes are the kin of the heroes of Foe and of Wyss. No one should be surprised that I devoted myself completely to this work of the Extraordinary Journeys.

I can recall from memory the titles of the books which I read so vividly: These were *Le Robinson de douze ans* (*Twelve Year old Robinson*), by Madame Mollar de Beauliev, *Le Robinson des sables du désert* (*Robinson of the sands of the desert*) by Madame de mirval. Also in the same vein were *Le Aventures de Robert Robert* (*The Adventures of Robert Robert*) by Louis Desnoyers who published the *Journal des Enfants* (*Children's Journal*)

From *Seconde patrie* (*Second Homeland*, 1900).

with other such stories that I cannot forget. Then came *Robinson Crusoe*, that masterpiece which is nevertheless only an episode in the long and tedious narrative by Daniel Defoe. Finally, *The Crater* by Fenimore Cooper could only increase my passion for these heroes of the unknown island of the Atlantic or the Pacific.

But the inspired imagination of Daniel Defoe had only created man alone and abandoned on a desert land, able to survive thanks to his intelligence, his ingenuity, his knowledge, thanks likewise to his trust in the ever present Almighty, and inspired at times through prayer.

Now, after a human being isolated under these conditions, why not put there a family, a family thrown on a coast after a shipwreck, a family closely united, a family not despairing of Providence? Yes, such was the work of Wyss, no less lasting than that of Daniel Defoe.

Rudolph Wyss, born in Berne in 1781, died in 1850, was a professor at the University. We have from him several works in addition to *Robinson Suisse* (*The Swiss Family Robinson*) which was published in 1812 in Zurich.

In the following year, the first French translation appeared. It was translated by Madame Isabelle de Bottens, Baroness of Montoliev, born in Lausanne in 1751, died in Bussigny in 1832 who made her debut into literature with a novel in two volumes entitled *Caroline de Lichesfield* (1787).

There is reason to believe that Rudolph Wyss was not the only author of the celebrated novel, but that it was done in collaboration with his son. It is to both, in fact, that Madame de Montoliev dedicated the sequel to this novel, which appeared in 1824 in Paris under this title: *Le Robinson Suisse ou Journal d'un père de famille naufragé avec ses enfants* (*The Swiss Robinson or the Journal of a Father and his Family Shipwrecked With its Children*).

Thus the translator had the idea of continuing the work which she had translated and I was anticipated by her and probably others, and it does not surprise me that several people have thought about doing this.

In fact, this novel was not ended with the arrival of the corvette, the *Licorne*, and this is what Madame de Montoliev previously stated in the preface to her translation:

> Four consecutive editions have proved how much the French public has come to appreciate this writing which has brought happiness to children and in consequence to their parents. But a sequel and a finish is lacking. Everyone wants to know whether this family which interests them, will remain on this island where every young lad would like to go. I have received countless letters on this subject from the children themselves and from my publisher begging me to write a sequel so as to satisfy their curiosity.

It is proper to note here that other translations of Rudolph Wyss' work were made after that of Madame de Montoliev, among others that of Pierre Blachard in 1837. The result is that if Madame de Montoliev is not the only person to translate *The Swiss Family Robinson*, neither is she the only one to produce a sequel, since I have left my mark, under the title *Second Homeland*.

Besides, in 1864, Hetzel's house published a new translation of this story as a result of the collaboration of P.J. Stahl and E. Muller which revised it by giving it a more modern allure in composition and in style. Properly speaking, it is this very edition, also reviewed from the scientific point of view, which is succeeded by *Second Fatherland*, and is offered to the readers of

*Magasin d'Éducation et de Récréation* (*Magazine of Education and Recreation*).

Really, wouldn't it be interesting to continue the recital of Rudolph Wyss, to again find this family in a new set of circumstances, with these four lads so well established: Fritz enterprising and courageous, Ernest a bit egotistical but studious, Jack the mischievous and little Francois, to watch the changes in their character as they come of age after twelve years on this island ?.... After the discovery of Burning Rock, wouldn't the introduction of Jenny Montrose into this little world change their lives?... Doesn't the arrival of M. Wolston and his family on board the *Licorne* and their installation on the island call for a sequel to this story?... Shouldn't there be a complete exploration of this wealthy island since only the northern part is known to them?... Doesn't the departure of Fritz, Francois and Jenny Montrose for Europe call for a story of their adventures until their return to New Switzerland?...

And so I could not resist the desire to continue Wyss' work, to give it a definitive conclusion which, besides, would be done sooner or later.

So then, driven on by my imagination, I plunge into my project, to live side by side with my heroes and it produces a phenomenon: It is that I have come to believe that New Switzerland really exists, that it is an island in the northeast part of the Indian Ocean, that I have seen it on my map, that the Zermatt and Wolston families are not imaginary, that they live in this very prosperous colony which they have made their "Second Homeland!"... And I have but one regret, that my advancing years prevent me from joining them there!...

In conclusion, this is why I believe that it was necessary to continue their story to the end, and that is why I did a sequel to *The Swiss Family Robinson*.

⊙

# Contributors

**Sidney Kravitz** (1926-2009) is indelibly remembered in among Jules Verne aficionados as a devotee of *The Mysterious Island*. In the late 1980s, dismayed by the persistent reprinting of the poor 1874 translation of Verne's novel by W.H.G. Kingston, Kravitz undertook his own translation of Verne's epic. He then freely shared his text with fellow admirers of Verne and the novel, until his selfless effort was finally rewarded as his work formed one of the founding texts in the Wesleyan University Press Early Classics of Science Fiction series. In addition to this 2002 publication, Kravitz also undertook translation of Verne's other castaway story, hitherto unpublished in English, *Shipwrecked Family: Marooned with Uncle Robinson*. Kravitz also wrote many articles in his professional field for mathematics and engineering magazines throughout the world.

**Brian Taves** (Ph.D., University of Southern California) has been an archivist with the Motion Picture/Broadcasting/Recorded Sound Division of the Library of Congress since 1990. He is the author of well over 100 articles, 25 chapters in anthologies, in addition to books on P.G. Wodehouse and Hollywood; on fantasy-adventure writer Talbot Mundy, in addition to editing an original anthology of Mundy's best stories; on the genre of historical adventure movies; and on director Robert Florey. In 2002-2003, Taves was chosen as Kluge Staff Fellow at the Library to write the first book on silent film pioneer Thomas Ince. Taves's writing on Verne has been translated into French, German, and Spanish, and is writing a book on the 300 film and television adaptations of Verne worldwide. Taves is coauthor of *The Jules Verne Encyclopedia* (Scarecrow, 1993), and edited the first English-language publication of Verne's *Adventures of the Rat Family* (Oxford, 1993).

# Acknowledgements

The North American Jules Verne Society thanks Madeline Wagner and the estate of Sidney Kravitz for making this publication possible.

The society also appreciates the efforts of members who have contributed to this volume, including Malcolm Henderson, Dennis Kytasaari and Henry Franke, and such friends as Elvira Berkowitsch, Jean Frodsham, and Pachara Yongvongpaibul.

**Peter Overstreet** modified one of the orginal covers from the first French Hetzel editions of Jules Verne for this book. A professional Illustrator for two decades, he is director of "Legion Fantastique," the world's only Jules Verne re-enactment society.

The Palik series, while spearheaded by the North American Jules Verne Society, represents a cooperative effort among Vernians worldwide, pooling the resources and knowledge of the various organizations in different countries.

We are particularly grateful to **Bernhard Krauth,** chairman of the German Jules-Verne-Club since 2005. A deep sea licensed master working today as a docking pilot in Bremerhaven, Germany, Bernhard has published several articles in relation to Verne in France, the Netherlands and Germany. Intensely interested in the illustrations of the original French editions of Verne's work, he has been deeply involved in a project to digitize all of the illustrations, more than 5,000 in all. The project is for common, non-commercial use, and nearly all of the illustrations in this publication were made possible through his generosity.

# The Palik Series

The last two decades have brought astonishing progress in the study of Jules Verne, with many new translations of Verne stories, even with the discovery of many new texts that had not been known before. Still there remain a number of Verne stories that have been overlooked, and it is this gap which the North American Jules Verne Society seeks to fill in the Palik series.

Through the generosity of our late member, Edward Palik, and the pooling of expertise by a variety of Verne scholars and translators around the world, we will be able to bring to the Anglophone public a series of hitherto unknown Verne tales.

Ed Palik had a special enthusiasm for bringing neglected Verne stories to English-speaking readers, and this will be reflected in the series that bears his name. In this way the society hopes to fulfill the goal that Ed's consideration has made possible. The volumes published will reveal the amazing range of Verne's storytelling, in genres that may astonish those who only know his most famous stories. We hope to allow a better appreciation of the famous writer who has, for more than a century and a half, been the widest-read author of fiction in the world.

CPSIA information can be obtained
at www.ICGtesting.com
Printed in the USA
JSHW010723100123
35525JS00007B/74